I0664069

Surfing Dude

The Richard Jackson Saga, Volume 6

Ed Nelson

Published by Eastern Shore Publishing, 2024.

Table of Contents

Other books by Ed Nelson

The Richard Jackson Saga

In the Richard Jackson World

Stand-Alone Story

Cast in Time Series

Dedication

This is dedicated to my wife Carol for her support and help as my first reader and editor.

Also, the BHS class of 1962 just because.

Professionally edited by Janet E. Rupert

Quotation

That is exactly how it happened, give or take a lie or two.

James Garner as Wyatt Earp, describing the gunfight at the OK Corral in the movie *Sunset*

Copyright © 2021

Chapter 1

We got back last night from England. We stumbled into the waiting limo, which took us to Jackson House. Our bedrooms were ready, to the point that the staff had made up our beds. Not that it would have mattered to me. I crashed for ten straight hours.

Monday, I woke up still tired from the trip. Not sleepy, tired. I hoped there wasn't much planned for today. I went ahead and showered, which helped immensely. I almost felt human when I went to the kitchen to find a cup of coffee.

I found out quickly the world had changed as we now had a cook. I don't think the head chef chased me to the family breakfast room. I didn't even know we had a family breakfast room. Mum and Dad were there with coffee, tea, and newspapers. From their subdued greetings, they weren't in any better shape than I was.

The room was bright and sunny. A buffet along the wall had a full self-serve breakfast in warming dishes. I helped myself to scrambled eggs, bacon, hash browns, wheat toast, orange juice, and coffee.

I think I could get used to this family breakfast room. I wondered what the lunch and dinner rooms would be like. Maybe there was an afternoon snack room and even a midnight snack room! There would be no heavy thinking on the agenda today.

After a while and several cups of coffee, I asked if there was any schedule or plans for the day. Dad told me there weren't any but that there would be a business review tomorrow morning. It would be all of my companies under Jackson Enterprises: Jackson Productions, Jackson Home Products, Jackson Personal Products, and the newest, Jackson Transportation.

"How long will it take?" I asked Dad.

"Plan on it being most of the day. It has been months since there has been an update, and I'm certain you will have to make some decisions."

That didn't sound like a thrilling way to spend the day, but I was interested to see if I was actually making any money. I certainly had been spending it as if I had it.

Mum informed us she would be out with Anna Romanov and Sharon Bronson for most of the day. They had some things to check out, but she didn't go any further than that. I was curious about what they might be up to but knew that Mum had told us all she was going to, at least to me. Dad probably already knew.

I went back to my room and changed into running gear. This would be the first time I could run the trails in the park in the back of the house. I ventured onto the trail by using the man-sized door in the wall near the stables. I found out quickly that the running I had done in England on their flat trails had not kept me in shape for this.

It wasn't like running up a mountain, but it still pulled muscles that hadn't had a workout since Campbell's Hill in Bellefontaine. My run took me past a public parking area. A map was posted, so I spent a few minutes reviewing it. This was a large park, and there were many miles of trails. They joined and separated, but all circled back. If nothing else, I wouldn't get bored by the scenery.

I headed back to the house at lunchtime. I had probably done ten miles and was sweating like one of those horses we didn't have in the stables. Mum would put me out there if I didn't have another shower soon.

Denny and Eddie were out in the backyard when I got home. They were playing lawn darts. Mary came riding through on her bike just as Eddie threw. The dart missed her, but it was close. The kids didn't seem to think it was a big deal, but I saw disaster in the making. There were horseshoe pits near the outer wall. I suggested they throw it next to them. This would be parallel to the wall, so there was less chance of someone running into the line of flight.

The boys saw the sense in that and moved right away. Mary was already gone like a madwoman on another round of the house.

After cleaning up and putting on fresh clothes, I had lunch. It turned out we had a family dining room, which we would use for lunches and dinner. There was also a formal dining room that looked like it would seat over a hundred. I later learned that it would only seat sixty.

At lunch, there was a menu next to each place setting. It had light, medium, and large meals listed. Since I had been running, I was hungry and chose a large meal.

I decided to take a ride in one of my T-Birds. They had brought all our vehicles from Ohio, including the Chris-Craft from Indian Lake. It was on its trailer in the garage area. All the cars were lined up with their keys in the ignition, so it was easy to take off.

At least, I thought it was. The guards at the front gate stopped me, and they wanted to know where I was going, the route I expected to take, and what time I would return. I must have looked like I was going to pitch a fit because the head guard quickly told me that was standing orders for all the family. He even showed them to me in writing. Both Mum and Dad had signed them, so that ended that.

I told them I was going for a ride with no particular route in mind and that I would be back in time for dinner at six. This worked as they opened the gate with no further comments or questions.

I didn't have any plans, so I drove to downtown Beverly Hills to see what was happening. Since it was Monday, but school hadn't started yet, plenty of kids walked past the stores. I didn't see any of the few I knew from Hollywood High, so I just kept driving.

As I drove, I mentally reviewed my summer. It had been full and different. You might say it was action-packed, which it was, but what I remembered most was the girls I had interacted with. There was a girl in Argentina, Dorotea. I thought I would remember how she looked forever, but now all I had was a general impression. It was a good impression, that was for sure, but only an impression.

Then there was Christina. What a gold digger. Her looks took me in. I learned a lesson there. I was so lucky that Mary spilled chocolate on her to reveal her true character. I guess someone up there was looking out for me.

I almost missed a red light and had to jam on the brakes. I realized I could think heavy thoughts or drive, but not both. I headed back home and got ready for dinner. Even Mary was quiet during dinner.

Later that night, I read a book about Gerard Gates, a sailor stranded in Antwerp with no citizenship papers. He found work on a coffin ship, the *Yorikke*. After spending most of my summer on a freighter, what the author wrote was easy to imagine and all too real and horrifying.

Chapter 2

Since Tuesday would be busy, I was up early doing my exercises and then had a run. I only went a couple of miles, figuring I would be ready to clear my head for a good workout this evening. While I liked the money part, sitting in meetings all day wasn't my idea of a fun time.

After my shower, I put on one of my best suits and a tie. If I was going to be a businessman, I should look the part. Heading to breakfast, I passed the kitchen and heard some bad language. Looking in, I saw the cook had cut herself opening a can of Crisco, breaking the strip the key was attached to. It didn't look like a bad cut, and she continued to open the can with a pair of pliers. I went on by; we all had cut ourselves that way, one time or the other.

I hadn't put my jacket on, just had it slung over my shoulder when I entered the breakfast room. I stopped dead because we had company. Sharon Bronson and Anna Romanov were sitting there with Mum and Dad.

Sharon piped up as I stood in the doorway, "If you were older, Rick, I would be chasing you."

Anna chimed in with, "Sharon, I would be giving you a run for your money."

I looked at Mum because I knew she wouldn't let this stand; she would keep my head from swelling. My Mum betrayed me. She winked at me!

Dad didn't help; he took Mum's hand and said, "I'm glad I got this one nailed down early."

In my best British accent, I replied, "Good morning, all. I would say 'ladies' if any were present."

This must have been the right thing to say as they all laughed, taking the awkwardness away from the moment; at least, it was awkward for me.

"May I inquire why we are honored with your delightful presence?" I asked as I joined them at the table after pouring coffee and filling a plate from the buffet.

Mum spoke up, "We are meeting with a lawyer today. Sharon is opening a rehabilitation clinic; Anna and I are co-sponsors. It will be for alcohol abuse."

They went on to tell me that they would fulfill several of their personal goals. It would help Sharon's image and prove to the world that she had owned up to her problems and had changed. Mum and Anna needed a charity to support their public images.

Best of all, it would actually help people. They made it clear this wouldn't be a place where a drunken actor could check in for a week and then declare themselves cured, only to do it all over again.

They were throwing out possible names. Dad put in, "It is a shame Ike's wife Mamie wasn't a drunk. Naming it after a first lady would make the clinic instantly prominent."

He was quickly booed down as this was plain tacky. I wondered what Dad disliked about Eisenhower so much; it carried through on everything involving the President. Yet, at the same time, whenever Ike saw me, he was very cordial.

Sharon asked me why I was all dressed up.

"I have a business meeting to attend today."

"Wow, I never dressed up for my agent."

"Yours was a slimeball, but this is other stuff."

"You have other business besides acting?"

Mum and Anna started laughing.

"Sharon, Rick is the original overachiever. He has invented things, such as the electric hair dryer you use. He invented the adjustable showerhead. Now he has a shipping container company and even his own navy," Mum told her.

I wasn't certain that I wanted all my business shared publicly, but I had a more immediate question.

"My own navy," I choked out.

"Oops, your dad wanted to spring that on you."

Dad spoke up, "We needed a testbed for the cargo containers, and it was easier to buy an old ship that was being retired."

"What sort of ship?"

"You may have heard of it, the *Pride of Liberia*."

"You're kidding!"

"Nope, you're in negotiations to buy the whole shipping line, plus your Mum forgot to mention Narrow Freight, the trucking company."

"You mean Popeye now works for me?"

"I'm sorry, Rick. He has left the *Pride*."

"That's a shame; I would have liked to see the look on his face when he realized that he was now working for me. I would have him chipping paint all day. Nah, not really, he is a good guy, and I would treat him well, but it would have been fun for a minute.

Mum started to cough, but Sharon talked at the same time, distracting me.

"Maybe Rick isn't too young!"

Mum waved a fist at Sharon as she continued to cough. She took a drink of water, which calmed her down. She still continued to glare at Sharon.

Sharon realized maybe she had gone a little too far as she backed down.

"I want to get a better reputation, not be a cradle robber."

I'm not sure how I felt about that. It would be a pretty big cradle to fit me.

This ended the table conversation as the ladies soon left. As they were leaving the room, I heard Anna talk about going shopping after their meeting. They would have a whole limo they could fill with their trophies!

Both ladies quickly agreed, so I knew there were no problems, at least as long as Sharon kept her hands off of me. Mum never said anything, but I had noticed a pattern of bad things happening to people who made my life difficult, from hot chocolate to machine-gun bullets. I was beginning to suspect that my mum was not a person to cross.

Dad and I went out to the courtyard, where a second limo was waiting. I raised one eyebrow at Dad. He was blushing as he muttered about keeping up appearances. Actually, it was fine with me. I was starting to get used to this life.

At Dad's office, we went to the conference room. Roberta Grimes and a young man, maybe thirty years old, were waiting for us. Dad introduced me to Don Pearson.

"Rick. Jackson Personal Products has enough going on that you need a vice president to handle things."

"I thought that all we were doing was licensing the hairdryer?"

"That in itself is enough to just justify hiring Don, but there is something else going on."

"What's that?" I inquired.

"You know the electric curling iron you were going to patent but just missed out on? Well, they want to sell the patent, and it seems like a good fit. My board recommended Don as having the correct background. I asked him to look into the situation and the possibilities for the business today. It will be your decision as it is your business, and Don's decision whether or not to accept the job."

This overview of the situation only took a few seconds. I greeted Roberta as an old friend from Bellefontaine. I asked her how she liked California and Los Angeles in particular. She smiled as she told me she loved it. She had been out here since the first of the summer. I was invited to stop by and see her new office in this building. I could find her there or in the photography studio next door. Hmm, as if that was news.

Don had a firm handshake; my first impression was that he was a good guy. He was just a little shorter than me. He had a good tan, highlighted by his blonde hair and blue eyes. He was dressed in a sports coat with no tie. His Bulova watch showed that he was doing okay in the world. He was married, as evinced by the ring he wore.

I asked about his background. He was a graduate of Stanford University with a degree in business. He had been working with a private equity firm that specialized in companies that had licensing agreements. When I asked him what he was looking for, he told me.

"Money!"

"Good answer; now what does that mean?"

"I am starting a family and want to advance. I am at a good company, but my growth there is limited. A senior partner told me that it would be best if I looked elsewhere."

"How are you getting along with them?"

"Fine, my dad is a senior partner. Mom is the other. They just feel that what they are doing is so specialized that there isn't much room for expansion. They are in their early fifties, so I won't be inheriting the business soon, and then it will be split between five of us."

"Well, I guess your dad will give you a good reference."

"He would hear from Mom if he didn't!"

I think all Mums and Moms are the same.

I asked him what he was looking for in the way of salary. At twenty thousand dollars, it was good, but I had an idea of how to sweeten that pot for him.

"Don, what are your ideas for the business?"

That unleashed it. I quickly found out that business graduates knew how to make charts, graphs, spreadsheets, and projections. He had really done his homework as he proceeded to show me. There were untapped markets around the world for the hairdryer. We had no agreements in place in Australia or most of Europe.

There was even potential growth in South America and South Africa that we had not looked at. Just the licensing fees would have a possibility of ten million a year starting next year with no end in growth in sight until the expiration of my patents. He even had a plan for an R and D Division for replacement products.

This led him to the possibility of the electric curling iron. He didn't think it would be as great as the hairdryer but would be very good, in the five million a year range within the next two years. The patent was for sale because the holders wanted a quick payout and couldn't acquire the capital to start it up. We could have it for one million dollars. I suspected that number was picked out of the air as making them rich, which it would if handled correctly.

That thought stopped me cold. Where was I in my financial life that those with a million dollars were rich, but only if handled correctly? I would have to give that some thought. Was I getting too big for my britches?

Chapter 3

Don's presentation took almost two hours. The time flew by as he worked with us. Dad, Roberta, and I didn't have many questions, but he was thorough in his answers. Roberta confirmed the accuracy of his numbers, well, at least the math. Some of the projections had to be taken on faith, but they seemed conservative to me.

I thought more than one in one hundred people in the US would buy a hairdryer. I wouldn't be surprised if it were as many as one in twenty. That is, if fashions didn't change. Short hair would kill us now; men wearing shoulder-length hair would be a blessing, but that wasn't about to happen.

At the end of the time, I asked if Dad and I could be excused for a minute. In Dad's office, I told Dad I wanted to hire Don but that I would like to get him really bought in.

"How would you do that, Rick?"

"By giving him a share in the Personal Products Division."

"How much are you thinking?"

"I think five percent would be a worthwhile amount."

"It is. Think about this. I was told about a common practice by one of my advisors. It's called vesting. In this case, we could start him out at one percent, and each year he works for us, he gains an additional percent up to five percent if he reaches his profit goals. If he misses a goal, the only penalty is no additional percentages that year."

"That sounds good, Dad; from what I have read, this should be in the form of a contract with protections for us, like firing for cause."

"Exactly. Do you want to proceed? If so, you can make him a verbal offer, with me confirming it as your legal guardian upon his acceptance of the written contract."

"Let's go for it."

"On the electric curling iron, I think it will be a good product for us and certainly a good fit for this division, and I bet we could get it for less than a million."

"You probably could, Rick, but do you want it at that price?"

That stopped me cold. Why would I not want it at a lesser price?

"Just think about it. Is the money that you save that important to you? Consider what you have now and your near-term potential. Then consider what it would mean to the patent holder. It makes them rich in their eyes. If the product is wildly successful later, do you want them to resent you?

"Actually, the projected success will have them second-guessing themselves, but if they get what they ask, they should only complain about themselves. Mind you, I said, 'should,' not will. People can complain about anything. At least this way, the court of public opinion will not be against you."

I realized Dad was right, both about the money and my public image or, as Mum would put it, penny wise, pound foolish.

"Ok, let's offer their full asking price."

Later I realized that this was a turning point in my life. I was becoming a real businessman. Yes, I had made things happen, but this was the first true structured thing I had done.

It was a good thing Don was sitting down when I made the offer. It was all the money he was asking for with a world of possibilities behind it. The composed and assured young businessman who had made the presentation looked a little wobbly for a moment. That didn't stop him from getting a "yes" out quickly.

Dad reconfirmed the offer and asked Roberta to have the corporate counsel join us. Does Dad have corporate counsel? Things had been going on behind my back.

Roberta brought a gentleman into the room. In looks, at least, he was a stereotype of what I thought a corporate attorney should look like. Brown suit, dull tie, shined wingtip shoes. Dad introduced me to Mr. Sam Wingate.

We all sat down, and I waited for Dad to start. It took a moment for me to realize that he was waiting for me. It was my business!

I recapped to Mr. Wingate what the offer was. He was making notes on his long yellow notepad. I thought the longer notepad was cool-looking, as opposed to what we used in school. I would have to get some. He told us that he could have a draft for all parties written up by this time tomorrow. That worked for all of us.

After that, I told Don to go ahead and start negotiations on the electric curling iron and that he was to offer the full asking price. He wanted to know why, as he was certain we could buy it for less. I explained the reasoning, not telling him that Dad had just walked me through it.

I could tell from Don's reaction that he wasn't certain if I was sane, but he was getting while the getting was good. I had no problem with that as I wasn't certain myself. One thing I noticed was that Don was Don while Sam Wingate was Mr. Wingate. The only real difference was that one worked directly for me, and the other didn't. I had to think about that. I wanted to respect those who worked for me.

We all shook hands, and Don practically floated out of the room. One nice thing is he calls me Rick instead of Mr. Jackson. That boded well for our relationship.

I thought we had done a good day's work. It was after eleven, so I could have some fun today. Maybe a trip to the beach?

That is when life caught up with me.

Dad commented, "That ran a little long. We will be pushing it to complete everything today."

"Wasn't that all?" I asked.

"I must have dropped you on your head when you were a baby. How many other business divisions are there?"

"Oh," I said as my day at the beach disappeared.

"Who's next?"

"Transportation."

As Dad was telling me this, Roberta was escorting people into the room. They were all in suits and ties. Two of them looked comfortable and confident. One was scrawny looking, at least he was shorter than the others, and he was pulling at his neck like he wasn't used to a tie.

Dad introduced me to Luke Harding, who told me he was the leading contender to be president of Jackson Transportation, then Todd Goodson, VP of Production from Transportation. Dad went on to tell me they were still looking for a VP of Sales.

I glanced at the last guy, curious about his role; he had a silly grin. It took a moment, then the coin dropped.

"Popeye!" I shouted as I picked the guy up into a hug. I glared at Dad for his little trick, but having Popeye here meant I forgave everything.

"What are you doing here? Not that you aren't more than welcome."

Dad broke in, "Rick, let us step into the hall for a minute."

Dad explained that I needed someone to actually go to the docks and work with the longshoreman's union. He thought Popeye was our man.

"Rick, before we get started, I need to bring you up to speed on some things." Leaning into the conference room, he said, "Roberta, would you get Helen, my secretary, to bring some coffee in, please?"

Does Dad have a secretary?

Dad and I went back to his office.

"Long story short, Rick. The actual waterfront is the biggest obstacle. The unions don't want to lose jobs. Your Mum talked to Lucky. The family contributed to him through our Swiss accounts. That enabled us to make a deal with the major ports. We will fund training with the new equipment and not fight them when they ask for more money to operate the special cranes we will have to have in place. That is where Popeye comes into play. He will be our troubleshooter on the docks."

That made a lot of sense to me when I thought of those bar-hard fists of his.

"We also will be funding the port conversions, at least those in New York, Charleston, Savanah, Houston, and LA here in the US. Hong Kong, Singapore, London, Liverpool, Sydney, and Marseille are among others abroad. We will invest over two hundred million dollars in the next two years."

"Does the family have that much?"

"We do, but you will be funding it."

"I know I don't have that sort of money."

"That's why the United States Government is giving an economic development loan to Jackson Transportation. I think I told you previously that Ike wants to accelerate international trade. He and his advisors feel this is the quickest way to do it. Look at it this way, I know you have been concerned about how being rich will affect you. Now you will be in debt up to your eyeballs. Poor boy, your problems are solved! That is also why my staff has expanded to support other ventures we will be doing with government backing."

Somehow this didn't make me feel any better.

We returned to the conference room. The proposed president, Luke Harding, started a presentation on his vision for how the business would be for the next five years. It was ambitious. The one thing that bothered me was that he only spoke to Dad.

At one point, I tried to ask a question. He almost sneered at me as he said, "Son, we don't have time for interruptions. Let the adults get down to business."

Chapter 4

I went all cold inside. Normally when I was mad, I felt like I was seeing red. I had never had this feeling before. I wasn't angry with this man; I wasn't anything with this man; and I couldn't have cared less if he lived or died.

"Mr. Harding, thank you for your time. I will not need your services."

Harding gaped at me like a hooked fish. He looked at Dad for help. Dad didn't say anything to him.

"You can't decide not to hire me. Jack, you are the president. Tell this kid to butt out and let us get to work."

I spoke up, "Mr. Harding, Dad is the president since I'm too young to sign contracts, but make no mistakes about it. This is my company, and it is my money that is funding this operation. We will pay your expenses for attending this meeting now. Good day."

I hoped we wouldn't have to call security. I wondered if we had security on site.

A very red-faced Harding left the room.

Popeye winked at me. Somehow this told me I had done the right thing.

I turned to Mr. Goodson. "I'm sorry about that. I hope that won't prevent you from considering an offer."

"Actually, I will now consider an offer. I wasn't going to work for that ass."

Dad hadn't said a word during the entire exchange. When I looked over at him, he had a smile on his face.

"Rick, I had a brief meeting with Harding earlier. I wasn't impressed with his attitude either. You are better off without him."

I looked over to Popeye, "Why are you wearing a suit and tie?"

"Harding told me I had to."

"Lose the tie, never again for me."

"Thanks, Boss."

"Dad told me what you will be doing for us. Why did you leave the *Pride*?"

"She is in for a major refit for handling the containers. Besides, my girlfriend wants me to get a job ashore."

"Girlfriend?"

"Yeah, her name is Sybil."

"Aunt Sybil? My Aunt Sybil?"

"Yep," Popeye replied with a huge smile.

"That's great."

"Where are you going to live?"

Dad broke in, "That's one of the things that we will have to work out. We need Jackson Transportation to be located where travel is easy. Popeye will have to be traveling the world for the next few years."

"Popeye, what do you think?"

"Well, Sybil wants to travel with me, so it really doesn't matter to me."

"Okay, you can work it out."

I then turned to Mr. Goodson.

"Have we scared you away yet?"

He just shook his head slightly and said, "Not yet."

I had a feeling we were close.

Mr. Goodson, tell me about your background. He continued to fill me in on his background in producing trailers pulled by semi-trucks. That sounded like a good fit to me.

"Has anyone talked to you about salary?"

"Harding filled me in on what he thought I should get. It wasn't enough for me to take the job."

I looked over at Dad and asked, "Same deal as Personal Products?"

He just nodded yes.

"Okay, we are going to have a production division as a separate company under Jackson Transportation." I then proceeded to explain the salary and percentage ownership that would vest over time. To say he leaped at the offer would be putting it mildly.

I told him that Mr. Wingate, Dad's corporate attorney, would be presenting him with a contract, but in the meantime, we shook hands on the deal. After that, it dawned on me to ask.

"Where will we be producing the containers?"

"There's a factory for sale outside of Pittsburg, near my home. It is set up to build semi-trailers so that it would be perfect for us."

"You have any idea what they are asking?"

"No, but I will find out."

"Okay, it looks to me like I need to find a president for Jackson Transportation quickly. I'm certainly not qualified to run this business."

Todd chuckled, "From here, you don't seem to be doing too badly."

"Thanks. I will try to say 'hi' tomorrow when you sign your contract."

At that, Todd saw that we were done with him, and after he stood to leave, we had handshakes all around.

This just left Popeye, Dad, and me.

I turned to Dad, "It seems to be the piece of the puzzle we are missing is someone to head up Jackson Transportation to run our ocean freight and truck line."

I turned to Popeye, who I noticed had slipped his tie off and unbuttoned the top buttons on his shirt. He looked more like the man I knew.

"Popeye, do you think Captain Grumby would be interested in the ocean freight position?"

"Nah, he already has bought a boat, the *Minnow*. I saw it out in Hawaii. It's a neat little craft. I think he will do well, though the guy he brought on as his first mate seemed goofy as hell to me."

"Let's talk about your pay."

"Okay, but I've not much experience with this negotiation stuff. The union always set the rates."

"Let's keep it simple; the same deal as Todd, but it is part ownership of Jackson Transportation."

"You sure, Rick? That's a lot of money."

"Besides the fact you are almost family now, you took a young green kid at sea and treated him right. I will never be able to tell you how much that helped me."

That was the first time I had ever seen Popeye blush. If he had been chewing tobacco, he would have swallowed it.

"Thanks, Rick, you were worth working with."

I turned to Dad.

"Do you know what happened to the guy who ran Narrow Freight?"

"He's still there. He works for us now."

"Do you think he is up to the job?"

"Well, Narrow ran out of money because the owners took all of it out of the company. He didn't seem to be part of that."

"Do you think it is worth trying him out?"

"Well, he actually is doing the job right now. As we expand and he proves he is up to it, we could then give him the part-ownership deal. He is already making the base salary. You will have to get him down to Argentina to talk to Howell Freight to make certain they are on the same page."

"That works for me, now the ocean-going part."

Dad thought for a moment, "The Scottish Lines is our partner in this; they seem to know what they are doing. Why don't you let them take the lead? The owners made some noise about what death duties were going to do the owners. Maybe you could buy them out if the management does a decent job."

"That takes care of that in the short term, but it is really critical for us. Popeye, have you met them?"

"The owners, no, management, yes. I think they will do a good job."

"Dad, could you talk to them for me?"

He smirked as he said, "I have people for that."

Roberta, who had been sitting quietly at the other end of the long conference table, spoke up.

"I could check their books out for you, or at least, I have people who could do it."

What's this? I have people? I need people. I have people, Dad, Roberta, Popeye, and many others now.

"Okay, but it just dawned on me that someday accounting will have to come inside."

Dad looked embarrassed.

"Rick, that process has already started. Roberta, as our outside accountant, has helped set it up. She will do our independent audits. After lunch, I will take you down the block and show you the Jackson Enterprise building."

"I have a building?"

"Things have been moving quickly. Actually, I own the building and am renting it to you."

People, a building, a truck line, my own navy—this had been some morning.

A thought entered my head.

"Popeye, where are you staying?"

"With Sybil, at Jackson House."

"My aunt is here?"

"Her flight should be getting in soon. I should head for the airport."

Popeye stood to go; we shook hands again all around.

"Jack, thanks again for arranging a limo for this trip. This LA traffic is horrid."

"No sweat, I would hate to face Peg if you guys got lost."

"Yeah, she was always a holy terror, why I remember...."

Dad shut him down. I wondered what he remembered.

Chapter 5

After they left, I told Dad I felt so far in my head that it was mind-numbing. He told me not to worry, that he understood. I had to be in on the operations' foundation, but the people we hired would actually run it. I just had to be comfortable with the top people since I would be relying on them. Roberta agreed. Dad pulled out an organization chart and went over it with me.

It boiled down to that I would be listed as the CEO of Jackson Enterprises, Dad the president since I was not of legal age to sign contracts. When you took it down to basics, I would be a figurehead for operations but the power when it came to the direction of the companies. While all this was being discussed, lunch was brought in.

We had no sooner finished up than Mark Downing, my partner in Detroit Faucet, joined us. Mark was a sight for sore eyes, and I felt like I could understand what was going on in this business segment, Jackson Home Products.

After we caught up on our personal lives and he made certain to call me Sir Richard, which earned him a slug on the shoulder, we had a financial review. Things were looking good. Sales were up. Profit margins were rising. Mark wanted to expand and had a financial plan to back it up. It looked good to me, but I asked Roberta if she had had a chance to review it. She had, and the numbers were sound.

At that, I sort of sat there and waited for the next step. Finally, Mark asked me if it was okay to proceed. That woke me up. I'm a part owner, and he needed my agreement to proceed.

Trying to look like I had a clue, which I didn't really, I asked him where we would obtain the required eight million dollars in financing.

Mark told me, "Roberta found a bank in Switzerland that would loan us the money at less than market rates."

Hmm, I wonder who owns a bank in Switzerland. I made a point of not looking at Dad.

Mark then brought up another subject.

"Anna Romanov's line is doing wonders for our sales. She has a new partner and would like to open a new line for the smart young set. She has the over-thirty market locked, but no one has upscale products for the younger market segment. She would like to bring Sharon Bronson in to be the face of those products."

I took a moment to think.

"Anna actually has her own company; we just sell the product to her so she can do whatever she wants. Saying that, I think it is a great idea."

Mark blushed before he told me.

"So that you know, Anna brought Sharon to Detroit for a tour. Later Sharon and I got together for dinner."

"What's that got to do with the price of tea in China?"

"Uh, I guess nothing, but I just wanted you to know."

"Is there any chance that this might go somewhere?"

"It's too early to tell, but I sure hope so."

"Hope what?" asked Sharon Bronson as she and Anna entered the room.

I thought Mark had blushed earlier. I bailed him out.

"We were discussing the price of tea in China, and Mark thinks it is looking good, very good."

That remark got me some weird looks. Roberta was quietly choking at the end of the table. She looked at Sharon and shook her head no. Mark might hope he can catch Sharon; I don't think he has a chance of getting away.

Boy. Popeye and my aunt; Mark and Sharon. Wonder if I will have any romantic interest today.

We then discussed Anna's plans. She didn't have to but felt it was best to keep us current with her plans. Mark and I assured her that they made sense to us. I think we would both be out of our minds to disagree with the lady, so it was all moot.

One of Anna's concerns was that she had to bring out new ideas to keep at the design front of things. She wanted to know if we had any thoughts. As she asked that, the jingle from the Spearmint ads with twins, "double your fun," was running through my mind.

"How about having two shower heads in a shower, one each for front and back?"

"That's a good thought, Rick."

Roberta Grimes brought up, "It would be nice to have a shower head on a flexible hose, but I hate those red rubber things they use."

Mark came back with, "In the plant, we have metal armor around the hose so that it won't get burnt or cut. You could chrome that up and make it look nice."

Just like that, Anna's product line was freshened. She promised all of us a nice gift for the ideas.

The last business item of the long day was Jackson Entertainment. *Bandits of Sherwood* was doing well at the box office, and with my points in the movie, lots of money was being made. Until the first payout, we would not really know how much, but it would probably be several million. Payouts in the movie business were a funny thing. First, the studio would want to be paid for its services. Their accountants were famous for the games they could play.

I thought I would get a fair shake because of my relationship with the studio management, but I still asked Roberta to really go over the numbers they presented. Since I had points in the movie, I had access to the raw data on the books, and she could spot any overcharges quickly.

Speaking of movies, I do have one coming up. Shooting will start in January, but they want the cast together early to start the ball rolling. I have been given three different titles so I have no idea what it will be. Titles changed all the time, so it was no big deal. I just thought of it as the *Surfing Movie with Hot Girls*. Now that was something I could get excited about!

Then there was the mail. I have three major mail sources: business mail delivered to this office, fan mail to the studio, and personal mail at home. There was only one business letter that had been set aside for me. My staff was handling the rest. I would really have to meet this mysterious staff.

The letter was a request from the American Shipping Association to give a presentation at their annual meeting on the future of containerized shipping. It took me almost a heartbeat to decide this wasn't for me. I had to wonder about a group that would want the opinion of a fifteen, almost sixteen-year-old kid on their industry.

"Dad, do you know if these people know how old I am?"

"Good question Rick. I will try to find out. In the meantime, you probably want to take a pass on this."

"You got that right."

"Rick, have you thought further about what you would like to do with your life?"

"Not really. I'm still interested in space but haven't really defined how I could be involved."

"You do know that right now. You have enough money that you would never have to work in your life if you don't go crazy about it. Also, what benefit will you receive from further education? You normally go to school to prepare yourself for the work world."

"I would go crazy not doing anything, and I believe you need a full education to be able to live a full life."

"I had to bring it up, but I'm so glad to hear your answer. Just think how your Mum would make our lives a living hell if you decided anything different."

I didn't even want to think of what Mum would do. Suddenly, I couldn't wait to get my tenth grade started.

"When I'm at the studio tomorrow, I will check on how my tenth grade can be handled. I would still like to get it done by the New Year."

"Sounds like a plan. This has been a busy day. Let's head out."

I looked at my watch; it was 6:00. So much for a day at the beach.

Later at dinner, I decided to have a little fun with Mum.

"Mum, after the business review today, I realized that I could quit all work today and that I really don't even have to graduate from high school."

Some jokes don't work.

Afterward, Mary looked at me and shook her head.

"Stupid boy."

I couldn't disagree. Who knew that Mum could out-swear Popeye?

I retreated to my room to read for the rest of the evening. Denny and Eddie wanted to play pool, but I had some thinking to do. Not about my education. That was a given, but what did I want to do with my life?

After going in circles for several hours, I gave up. All I knew was that making money was good, that I enjoyed acting, and that I was interested in obtaining an engineering degree. I would acquire skills such as becoming a licensed pilot along the way. I wondered if I should take some real acting lessons.

So far, I have played Rick Jackson with a small range of emotions. Should I try to expand? There were also the skills that most actors tried to acquire, such as dancing. I had the fighting skills under control and could ride a horse. There was still high-speed driving, jumping off buildings in a single bound, and all that other Superman stuff.

My biggest worry was whether I would ever have a normal girlfriend-boyfriend relationship. I wanted more of what I had seen in Argentina, not what I had experienced in England.

Chapter 6

I remembered that I hadn't checked for mail. Our mail at home was put in a basket in the library for us to pick up. Even Mary had hers from her friends in Ohio. Actually, all the other kids got more mail at home than I did. I received thousands of fan letters, but they were all opened at the studio, and it was rare that I even saw one of those.

In my basket was a small stack of letters. Some of them had been lying there since the beginning of summer. They were from Judy King, Cheryl Hawthorne, the BSA, the White House, and my studio.

I opened Judy's first as it was the oldest. I had met her at a golf tournament in Ohio and had seen her several times. We were fond of each other but never seemed to be at the right time or place for each other. The last I heard, she had a boyfriend.

She started with the usual and told me how her school life was going. Friendship and social great, but learning was boring. Then she got to the meat of the letter. She told me she currently didn't have a boyfriend. Her last one was too foreign for her. He had Roman hands and Russian fingers. I felt an urge to break those fingers. She went on to tell me that she missed our short time together and asked if I was ever in Columbus to look her up. Hmm, maybe I would have to buy a company or open a plant in Columbus.

The second letter was from Cheryl, who had gone to school in Bellefontaine with me and whom I had considered my girlfriend. Her dad had received an Air Force promotion to brigadier general, and they were transferred to Washington DC, ending that relationship. He may have received another star since then.

Cheryl said she had been thinking of me for a while. Earlier in the summer, she and her parents had been at a Schaefer's Canal House restaurant on the Delaware Canal. A ship had gone through, and she swore she saw me standing on the flying wing. Her dad had teased her about her cowboy, but she really did wonder how I was doing and if I would please write.

Would I write? It had been me on that ship.

The next letter was from the Boy Scouts of America. I would be receiving another award for heroism for knocking down that IRA gunman who was going to shoot Queen Elizabeth. The presentation would be in the Rose Garden at the White House on Friday, October 9th, 1959. There was an RSVP enclosed.

That explained the next letter, which was an invitation for Mum, Dad, and me to have dinner with the president and first lady on the evening of Thursday, October 8th. There was also an RSVP enclosed with this letter.

I set the RSVP cards aside to discuss them with my parents. Besides, I had a thought I wanted to bounce off them.

The last letter was from the studio. Earlier on the plane ride home, as I was falling asleep, I had been thinking I didn't have a movie commitment. Actually, I did. Sharon Bronson and I were going to do a California surfing movie. The letter was very timely. They wanted me to be at the studio tomorrow morning at nine to talk about the movie and my role.

I went downstairs to talk to Mum and Dad about the RSVP to the BSA and White House. They had already retired to their evening suite, so I decided I would catch them at breakfast.

I went down to watch my brothers play pool but could not get into playing, so I returned to my room and soon had my lights off for the night.

I was up early, as usual, to get in my morning run and exercises. After cleaning up, I went down for breakfast. Both Mum and Dad were at the table, so I brought up the White House invitation. They both agreed we three should go. I asked if it would be okay to see if Cheryl Hawthorne and her parents could join us. They didn't see why not. They knew Cheryl and I had been close to each other in Bellefontaine.

Of course, I didn't bring up that I wanted her dad to see the cowboy having dinner with the president. I don't think they would have approved of my motive.

I at once returned to my room and penned a reply with my request back to the White House. I also did one for the BSA. I dropped them off in the outgoing mail basket on my way out to the studio.

Of course, I had to choose the wrong car. I had two identical T-Birds. Well, almost identical. One had a studio sticker, and the other didn't. When I got to the studio, a new guard was on duty, and you would have thought I was trying to get into Fort Knox or something. After getting that straight, I was fifteen minutes late for my meeting.

There was a pretty large group there. Our director and producer were people that I had not met before. The director, Mr. Levine, seemed okay, but the producer Tom Jensen came across as a little weird.

I wondered if he was on drugs. I had heard of drugs, and they told us how marijuana would drive us crazy in our seventh-grade health class while we watched the movie *Reefer Madness*, but I had never met anyone on drugs before. I was going to watch him carefully. I would be ready for him if he tried to hurt anyone.

Of course, Sharon was there, and she gave me a cheerful wave over to the seat she had apparently been saving next to her.

Mr. Levine didn't mess around. He started with, "Now that Mr. Jackson has graced us with his presence, we can get started."

It didn't come across as mean, but I also felt like it was Mr. Hurley getting ready to issue a detention. They can't do that on a movie set, can they?

"We are going to be shooting the outdoor scenes in Hawaii starting in January. You will be called in for some blocking shots individually and maybe sound checks, but most of the work will start in January. The studio will contact you in the next month with your travel arrangements."

Mr. Levine continued explaining that Hawaii had been chosen because of better weather and better surfing.

"Rick, you and Fred Madison will be taking surfing lessons in the meantime. We have arranged for that down at Huntington Beach. You and Fred stay behind, and we will discuss the particulars."

I looked around to see who Fred Madison was. He looked about sixteen, but I bet he was older. He looked like the guy next door: good-looking but also with a little goofiness about him. I bet he would be my sidekick in the movie for a little comedy relief. Can't have the star looking stupid, you know!

Sharon, who would be my opposite, was sitting next to a girl who looked about Fred's age. That is, she looked sixteen but was probably older. She would be Sharon's girlfriend and foil for Fred. Hmm, I wondered who the rich bully would be.

Oh, that guy over there. He looked more like a twenty-something, well-built, and could pose as a snob easily. Later as I got to know Phil Sampson, I would realize he was the nicest guy you could meet and never a snob, but he sure could act like one!

Of course, this was all guessing on my part, but I hadn't seen any depth in the plots of the various movies I had worked in.

"It is too early to hand out scripts as the writers haven't finished. They are having some plot issues."

Maybe there was some hope for this movie after all.

Mr. Levine then asked if there were any questions.

I asked, "What about our schooling?"

"Well, Rick, you are the only one still in school, so we will discuss that later."

At least my guess on ages wasn't too far off.

Mr. Levine droned on a bit about how excited he was to make this movie. Looking around, I realized that most of the cast and others present felt the same way I did. This was a B-movie if we did it right and a joke if we didn't. It could be a stepping stone to better things, but it was a job, a job every one of us liked, but still a job.

When Mr. Levine finally wound down, he asked Tom Jensen if he had anything to say. He shook his head no; his mouth was full. He had been eating potato chips the whole time he was here. I wondered what could make him so hungry.

All but Fred and I were dismissed. Our session wasn't awfully long. We were told the address of a surf shop in Huntington Beach. It had just opened, and Mr. Levine knew the owner, so he was trying to give them a leg up. The name was Katin Surf Shop.

We will be going for lessons starting Monday, for three weeks or more, depending on our progress. Fred didn't think it would be hard for him as he had been surfing since he was eight years old. I would have some catching up to do.

Fred knew where it was. I agreed to drive, so he gave me directions to his apartment. It was close to my old one, so finding it wouldn't be a problem. As expected, I agreed to pick him up at six on Monday. I guess the waves were better early in the morning. He called it the Dawn Patrol.

I think I would enjoy being with Fred. He had a ready smile but wasn't a smart mouth.

The meeting didn't take long, and Fred headed out. That left Mr. Levine and me to discuss school. It was easy. I was to stop by the studio school on Monday afternoon and set up a schedule. He asked me what year I was in. When I told him about the tenth grade, he shook his head.

"Looking at you, Rick, I would have thought you were in college. You have definitely rounded the corner from puberty. As a matter of fact, you have no signs of childhood on your face. If you keep this look, you can play young adult parts for many a year."

Well, I could see what his interests were. I thanked him and left.

I wandered out to the back lot before I left and said hi to the guys in the stunt area. They all bowed to me and called me Sir Richard. That started an impromptu brawl. It's my fault that Don Palmer ended up in a water trough. He wasn't paying attention, and it cost him. It was his fault for not looking. That is my story, and I am sticking to it!

Of course, that didn't get me far with Mr. Monroe, who walked up. I tried to explain how it was Mr. Palmer's fault, but he didn't buy it. I would have been more worried if he hadn't given a small laugh every time he looked at Don. As for Don, he didn't seem upset, which gave me concern. I remembered his comments about not getting into a fight while angry and that revenge was a dish best served cold.

In the end, Mr. Monroe welcomed me back and asked me to stop by his office next week when I had some free time. This left me with Mr. Palmer, who was now taking a ribbing from his friends. I knew this was going to hurt sometime in the near future.

I told him I would be back on Monday for my school schedule and would like to arrange more lessons in unarmed combat. He told me he was looking forward to it. Yeah, it was going to hurt.

After that, I drove back home. I went to the library, found an old friend, and read in the afternoon. I wondered if there would be a woman in my life with red-bronze-auburn hair and gold-flecked, tawny eyes.

For some reason, I just didn't have much energy. I read for the rest of the afternoon. I had dinner with the family and then watched some TV with them. I have no idea what was on later. I went to bed early.

Chapter 7

I felt rested when I woke up. After my warmups, I took off on what was going to become my morning routine through the state park next door. It felt good to be running. I still had to get in shape for running up and down hills, but it wouldn't take long.

After my morning ritual, I joined the family for breakfast. Everyone was there, and the talk was of school. Mary and the boys would be going to Tucker Academy, a private school in Hollywood.

Apparently, they had a very good reputation. It was a day school only, for kindergarten through 12th grade. As a co-ed school, there would be socialization. Security, a major concern, was addressed with a brick-fenced-in campus-like setting with tight entrance control. The average class size was fifteen students, with a maximum of twenty.

I made the mistake of saying it sounded rather good. Mum was all over that, asking me if I wanted to go there.

A quick "No," and I was out of there with only half my breakfast eaten.

I immediately revised my beach plans for the day. Instead, I grabbed a sports coat and headed to the studio to complete my Hollywood day wear.

I drove the T-Bird with a studio sticker, so I was waved through the gate, even with the new guard. They seldom lasted because it was actually considered a stepping stone to getting into the movie business. Once at the gate and meeting people, a career of some sort would start. It was seldom in front of the camera, but it would be a much better-paying job.

I had thought about bringing the other Bird so I could get a sticker, but after thinking about it, I remembered how people would treat me with a stickered car. Maybe I would be better off having an anonymous car. Who would ever think any T-Bird would be considered anonymous?

I was taking a chance that I would be able to talk to someone at the school. Mum had scared me with the idea of sitting in a classroom.

I was in luck. Miss Sperry was in, doing some paperwork.

"Rick, so good to see you. I heard you were back and was hoping you would be stopping in to arrange classes."

"I am so ready!" I exclaimed.

I guess I gave myself away with the emotion I showed.

"How's that, Rick? Most kids hate the start of school."

Kid?

I hadn't thought of myself that way for a while, but she wasn't wrong. I proceeded to tell her about Tucker and Mum's comments. She laughed and then told me.

"I think she was having you on. She called yesterday, and we had a long talk about this year."

Hmm, this revenge would be served cold.

She offered me a cup of coffee and asked about my summer vacation. Of course, she, like the rest of the world, knew of my knighthood but wanted a rundown of the whole trip.

She was shaking her head about getting chased out of Argentina. I may not have been as forthcoming as I could on all of the details. Africa, I told pretty straight—well, nothing about diamonds. She heard about everything but a certain blonde or a Spanish beauty in England. There are just some things that don't need to be public.

Maybe I wasn't as good of an actor as I thought.

"Rick, I would like to hear the whole story when you are older."

"Why don't you think it was the whole story?"

"You blush beautifully. I suspect it was girls in England and Argentina but something different in Africa."

"Okay, I will be fifty in 1994. Try me then." After a laugh, she let me off the hook.

We got into a serious discussion about tenth grade. There would be the required History, Math, Science, and English. She had the California textbooks set aside for me. There would be no class lectures as long as I had the work in on time. She or Mr. Dawson would be available for any questions.

It turns out that Mum had bought a home library with a complete set of Encyclopedias, both Americana and Britannica. There were several dictionaries, one large enough that it required a pedestal stand. I suspect she just liked the look. I hadn't noticed any of those at home, so she probably had them set aside to surprise us. That gave me an idea for my own surprise.

Miss Sperry had my lesson packet made up for the year. They had really been confident that I would be back. They had due dates on them that would allow me to take a normal tenth-grade school year. I intended to have them finished by the New Year. When I expressed that to her, she shrugged like that was expected.

I would have to come in for a mid-term and final exam but no other tests. On the other hand, my assignments would be graded strictly, so I had better pay attention. I promised I would, but all of a sudden, I did feel like a kid making a promise to the teacher. Since I was sitting, I didn't scuff my shoes when I told her I would do all my work.

I made as graceful an exit as I could, not very well, carrying my large box of books and papers. What happened to debonair Sir Richard Jackson, about to be trained in spy stuff? Maybe I still was a kid. Certainly, my confidence went down the drain when facing a teacher.

On the way out to the parking lot, I kept an eye out for a certain unarmed combat teacher who may still be damp. It would be best to give him time to dry out.

After putting everything in the T-Bird trunk, I went back to the main office. I was hoping to get everything taken care of with one trip. Again, I was in luck. Mr. Monroe was in and available. Of course, the ladies at the front desk had to announce Sir Richard was here. Mr. Monroe didn't help as he came out of his office and bowed.

My cold revenge list was getting long.

After the fun and games, it turned out he basically just wanted to say, "Hi."

He did bring me up to date on how the studio workload re-organization was working out.

"Rick, it is paying dividends already. We are saving money, and we are only halfway there. There is no way that we will ever be able to repay you for your ideas and leadership."

"You already have by letting me lead. I learned so much about business from working with your staff. It was amazing. I think we could call this a win all the way around."

"I am glad you feel that way, but I still think we came out ahead. Unless you are doing some things I haven't heard about."

"Are you aware of Jackson Transportation?"

"No."

I then explained to him about my ideas over the summer and what was being done."

"Rick, let me get this straight, you now own your own truck line and your own navy?"

"I don't think of it as my own navy, but yes. Do you think I should wear an admiral's uniform?"

"That may be over the top. You are really talking serious money here, millions."

"My accountants tell me it will be many of them."

I didn't want to use the B-word as that was so unbelievable.

"Do you still intend to continue your movie career?"

"I don't know about a full career, but what else do I have to do? Frankly, I am a figurehead for the business; there is a team in place to run the actual organizations."

"Slow down, Rick, organizations?"

"Well, there is the holding company Jackson Enterprises which owns Jackson Productions, Jackson Home Products, Jackson Personal Products, and the newest, Jackson Transportation."

I then went on to explain about each division.

"Maybe I had better see if I can get Nina back from Switzerland. You must be the most eligible bachelor in America, if not the world."

"Uh, Mr. Monroe, I won't be sixteen till next month. Let's not rush into anything."

"Rick, I keep forgetting how young you are. You come across as so poised and mature."

Keeping my thoughts to myself, I wondered what he would have thought of me in front of Miss Sperry.

It was getting towards lunch, and he invited me to the commissary. It was the usual zoo of strange costumes. There was one really weird group. They were all dressed in black pajamas. I asked about them. Apparently, they were Japanese ninjas. I had read about them somewhere but never gave much thought to what they would look like.

"Someone is making a movie about them?"

"We think they will be a strong niche like Westerns. They will be all action."

"I don't see it. People will just laugh at men in pajamas."

"Our marketing people tell us differently, but time will tell."

Another thing kept happening; people kept coming up to Mr. Monroe to ask questions. The questions didn't seem important; every time, it resulted in an introduction to me.

After the third person, I finally realized that people didn't really have questions. They just wanted to meet me! I didn't get it, but I was polite to everyone. I had learned that early on in the business world. Only be rude when it is necessary, not just because you feel like it.

The sixth person who approached us was Mr. Palmer. He didn't want an introduction as he knew me very well. He was there to let Mr. Monroe know that he would only hurt me, not break me.

The funny thing is that it made me feel better than all the others. I wisely waited him out before shaking Mr. Monroe's hand and leaving for the day.

I drove directly back to Jackson House. Mum was just coming out of some meetings in her study. I told her that I had picked up my schoolbooks. Also, to make it easier for us kids, I ordered dictionaries, a thesaurus, and several sets of encyclopedias for the library.

It was fun to watch her face. Well, this revenge was not as cold as it could be, but watching her start to stutter was still fun. It didn't last long as her eyes narrowed. Probably my grin gave it away.

"Richard Edward Jackson, you will pay!"

"Oops, I didn't mean to get the full name reaction."

I beat feet out of the house. I spent the rest of the afternoon walking and running around the trails. It gave me time to think and kept me away from Mum.

I spent the evening playing pool with Denny. He was getting to be a shark. I couldn't touch him. I was missing long straight-in shots, and he was walking the cue ball around others to sink shots that I wouldn't have considered.

Chapter 8

After my morning workout, I cleaned up and spent the rest of the morning sorting out all the classwork that I would have to do before Christmas. It looked like a huge stack when it was all together but not so bad when sorted by subject. I then subdivided it into the midterm and final. It looked doable.

I decided to work on each course daily rather than have a math day, English day, etc. I still stuck to my plan of working on all the problems at the end of each chapter or writing the essays. It gave me firm control of the material. If I was going to spend my time on this stuff, I might as well learn it for real rather than just to pass a test.

It took me three hours to finish the first set, but I felt the project was very doable. Maybe I could take my final before Christmas and be ready to start eleventh grade on the first of next year.

After lunch, I drove down to Huntington Beach to check the area out. The Katin Surf shop was easy to find. It sat by itself just north of town. It was across the Pacific Coast Highway from the water but had a really good view. The beach was huge, and I wondered if they would someday build houses on the beachside of the road.

I went inside. It was a laid-back place. There was a couch and chairs up front, and some old guy all dressed in blue was talking to someone named Corky about his boat, the *Southern Seas*. A lady with the reddest hair I had ever seen asked if she could help me.

I explained that I would be starting lessons on Monday for a part in a movie. She wanted to know all about it as surfing hadn't made it to the big screen yet. I ended up spending several hours there, and the old guy measured me for surfing shorts. They were made from canvas so tough I think it would stop bullets. It would stand up to the abrasion from sand and water; at least, that is what Corky Carroll told me.

Nancy let me know he was one of the best surfers, so listen to any tips he would give me.

I went home and helped Dad straighten up things in the sub-basement. We had built extra bedrooms down there, so we had a real retreat if needed. When it was first mentioned, I thought that was extreme. Now I had seen more of the world and was getting a better understanding of the money now in our life, it made more sense.

Saturday, I performed my daily workout and then really hit the schoolbooks. I ended up doing two complete sets of lessons in the morning and another after lunch. These lessons were not set up as one school day, one lesson. They were more like one lesson, one week, not quite one for one but close.

I was brain-dead by three o'clock, so I drove down to a local driving range with my golf clubs. I banged away for an hour. I needed the practice after a long layoff.

When I returned home, I had a message waiting. Fred Madison wanted me to call. When I got ahold of him, he asked what I was doing tonight. I told him I had no plans. He asked if I wanted to go cruising. That sounded good to me. We agreed we would catch a burger somewhere along the way. Mum and Dad were fine with it, especially after I told them I had no plans to stay out later than eleven o'clock.

On my way out, Dad asked if I had bail money! I wanted to know why he asked.

He laughed and said, "Well, you have been known to have interesting things happen around you."

It so happened I had several hundred on me, but I wasn't about to let him know that. It would be admitting that I had the same concerns as he did. There must be a teenage rule against that. If not, there should be.

Fred didn't know about my T-Birds, so he was excited to drive around with the top down. We went to West Hollywood and drove up and down Sunset Strip. We had offers to drag for pinks. I declined every time because it was obvious the cars were all set up for dragging, and I would have lost my car.

Girls were everywhere. I was ready to stop at the first ones who waved, but Fred convinced me to check out all of the mile and half drive before we committed. I was glad we did. Each group seemed prettier than the last.

After two rounds, two girls stood out, a blonde and a brunette. Fred wanted the blonde, which was okay with me. We pulled over and asked if they wanted to join us for a burger at the drive-in a block down the way. They piled in; the blonde, whose name was Jane, got in the back with Fred. The brunette, who was Betsy, stayed upfront with me.

They wanted to know all about us. When Fred told them he was an actor, they squealed and wanted all the details. It became clear that they wanted a studio introduction. When I was asked what I did, I told them, not a lot, because I was still in high school. That cooled Betsy down. When we stopped at the drive-in, she climbed in back with Fred and Jane.

That's how the evening went, the girls sitting in the back, hugging, and kissing Fred. I was glad to tell them I had to be home by eleven. I dropped them off at Fred's place and didn't want to know what happened next. I could have told them I was an actor also, but something about it set off alarm bells.

When I got home, no one was up. I made it by eleven but would get no credit for it.

At breakfast the next morning after my regular workout, Mum let me know that I had got in at 10:47. It seems we have guards at the gate who log us in and out. That doesn't seem fair. They don't even have to wait up to keep track of when I get home.

I was smart enough not to say that out loud.

No one had any plans for the day. The busy week on top of the vacation had caught up with everyone. My brothers would be starting school tomorrow, so they were dreading that. Mary was excited as this was her beginning. She was looking forward to meeting girls her age. That would be good for Mary. I didn't see how a bunch of five-year-olds could be a problem. It is not as though they would be underfoot here at home.

I spent most of the day getting ahead on my schoolwork. I managed to knock out four units today and still go to the driving range to slaughter some golf balls. My long shots were still long, but I needed a lot of work on my short irons. I could hit a ten-foot circle but not put them in a fruit basket. That was the nice thing about this range, for a fee you could try about anything.

After working in a sand trap, I would need to take a shower when I got home. I must have had a ton of sand in my hair. I never got around to practicing putting, and that is what I needed most.

It was starting to get dark when I got home. I skipped the shower. I found I didn't have as much sand as I thought. At dinner, everyone was quiet, so we broke up early. I double-checked my schoolwork, but my heart wasn't in it. I finally gave up and watched TV until eleven and called it a day.

Today, Labor Day is the last day of vacation for the boys. At breakfast, they were in a mixed mood. Normally they would complain about the end of the vacation, but at the same time, they would be happy to see friends again and catch up on events. This year it was the moaning about the end of vacation and unspoken dread about starting a new school.

Mary was different. She was starting school for the first time and was looking forward to making a bunch of new friends that she could invite over to play. She was just chatting away, but no one seemed to listen to her. The boys were in their private misery. Dad was futilely trying to read his newspaper, and Mum and Mrs. Hernandez were discussing a menu for some upcoming dinner.

I tried to settle the adrenaline-charged child down a little by telling her that she may not make new friends as fast as she hoped. That went nowhere quickly.

"I have a magic weapon that will bring all the girls around."

"What's that, Squirt?"

"You are silly. When they learn that my big brother is Sir Richard, the movie star and singer, and American Hero, they will want to come, just to meet you."

Have you ever felt someone walking over your grave? I just had those sorts of chills down my back.

"Don't you think I'm a little old for them?"

"Stupid boy, of course, you are. Some of them will have older sisters just the right age."

Maybe if I took off now, I could catch a tramp steamer on its way to Shanghai.

"Well, don't be upset if things don't work out."

"Don't worry, Rick, Mum and I will see that you get a nice pretty girl. We will chase the bad ones away."

Mary had a funny look on her face. I turned my head just in time to see that she was getting a Mum look. You don't want to get a Mum to look, at least not in our house. That went a little further in confirming some suspicions I had about events in England. Hmm, wonder how you get to McMurdo Sound?

Chapter 9

I finished breakfast and went to clean up. I had eased up on my running today, just enough to warm me up but not to tire me. I was thinking surfing lessons might do that.

After cleaning up, I put swimming trunks on under my clothes. I wasn't certain that my surfing trunks would be ready. Are they called trunks? Anyway, after checking out with the guards, I headed over to pick up Fred.

He was ready, but he looked worn out. As we headed to Huntington Beach, I asked him how Saturday night ended up.

"It ended up last night. They stayed Saturday and most of the day yesterday. I went out to pick up dinner and came back to a mess. They cleaned out my TV, radio, record player, albums, and most of my good clothes. The only thing they didn't find was my hidden money. I keep that in the freezer wrapped as broccoli."

"Sorry to hear that. I guess that is the danger of picking up strange women and bringing them home."

"Yeah, be glad you didn't end up with one. I need to get checked out at a clinic; I may have picked up something."

I pictured them going through security at Jackson House, then running into Mum. I don't think we would have been robbed. I would have gotten an earful but not robbed.

"Something about them didn't ring right," I said.

I got to listen to him the rest of the way to the beach, but I guess I would have been bummed out if it had happened to me.

We parked in front of Katin's and went in. Our instructor Corky Carroll wasn't there yet, so we sat down to wait. Nancy had my surfing shorts waiting, so I went to the back room and put them on. I knew surfing trunks didn't sound right.

I was sitting on the couch when three guys strolled in. One came right over to me.

"Get up, Dude, that's my spot."

Nancy broke in, "Murf, that is not your spot. I'm getting tired of your rudeness. You are banned from the shop."

This Murf guy turned to Nancy as though he was going to give her a hard time. I stood up. I guessed Murf was a bit of a bully type, He turned back to me when he felt me move. I had a good six inches and forty pounds on him. He looked at me while Nancy was telling him to get out. I did the one eyebrow-raised trick, but it didn't seem to faze him.

This Murf laughed at me and said, "You may be a big guy, but I bet you have never done any serious fighting in your life."

I thought about two dead men on a bank floor in Colorado, arrows penetrating Russian agents, drawing down on cattle rustlers.

"I've had my share."

One of his buddies must have recognized me because he whispered to the guy. I heard, "Sir Richard."

Murf sneered, "So with your fancy name and titles, you would get the police on me after I whipped your butt. This place is a dump, anyway. I'm on to bigger and better things."

With that, he and his accomplices left.

"Rick, I'm sorry about that, but Murf thinks he owns the Surf. He's a jerk and will end up in a bad situation if he doesn't change his ways."

"No worries, Nancy."

Corky walked in, and that changed the subject. He helped Fred and me select a board that would fit us. I ended up with a ten-foot longboard of the new material polyurethane. It was called a pig board. Why I have no idea. At least it didn't weigh a ton like the wooden boards I had used before.

Since I knew how to get into a wave, stand up on the board, and steer it, most of my first day's instructions were refreshing rather than learning. Corky told me that all I needed now was to catch and ride several thousand waves, and I would be a surfer.

He forgot to mention the part about chasing the board down if I lost it or getting dragged across the sand. My skin was raw by late morning. I was glad to take a beach shower and head home. Fred was in a little better shape, but not much. Our lessons with Corky were on Monday, Wednesday, and Friday for the next three months.

After dropping Fred off, I headed home for another shower, hot this time. I then had lunch and went to my schoolwork. I was writing an essay when Mary came into the library. She didn't interrupt me. She just stood there.

"What's up, Mary?"

"Do you think the kids at my new school will like me?"

Wow, not the same kid as at breakfast.

"Why wouldn't they? You're nice and don't try to hurt other people's feelings. You are cute, so what's not to like?"

"I don't know. They don't know me, so they may not like me."

"Hmm, you are going to be in kindergarten?"

"Yes."

"So, it's your first year of school?"

"Yes, it is. You know that."

"So, if it's your first year, it must be all the other kids, also."

"I suppose so."

"What do you think all those other kids are doing right now? Tomorrow, they have to meet a bunch of new kids, and they don't know if they will be liked."

"Oh."

"I bet they are afraid no one will say hello to them. That would be terrible. I know I would feel bad if no one said hi to me on my first day of school."

Mary nodded wisely, "That would be sad. I better say hi to them so they will feel good about school and not be scared."

"That sounds like a good plan. Now, do you think people will like someone who helps them not be scared?"

"Yep."

"So, there's your plan, be nice, say hi, and you will have friends."

The sad Mary that had been standing there was the normal cheerful, happy Mary once again. As she turned to tear off on some mysterious Mary mission, I realized Mum had been standing there.

She turned to walk away but gave me a parting, "Well done."

I worked for another hour when I realized that I was stiffening up from the strange exercise I had done earlier. I went for a run and ended up doing my normal five miles for the day. Another shower, how many was that for the day, and I went back to the books until dinner.

At dinner, we were informed that there would be a charity event at the house on Sunday, September 20th. It would be a sit-down dinner for thirty couples. The children were to attend the gathering but not the dinner or events afterward. We would eat our dinner in the family dining room. I was glad to be counted as one of the children. That helped a little when we were informed that we would be in tuxedos.

On that high note, I retired to my room and read about gray leathers, which sounded more attractive than a penguin suit.

I was up a little earlier than normal, half an hour, so I could do my morning exercises and run while still being cleaned up and dressed for the day as I joined the rest of the family for breakfast.

Mary was bubbling over about school. She couldn't wait to get there and say hi to all the scared little girls. She was going to help them, and they would be her friends. She couldn't wait!

Eddie asked her about what she was going on about, so she explained Ricky's way of making friends. She just knew it would work. You could see the wheels turning in Eddie's head, so maybe he would give it a try. Denny, who was a high and mighty junior high student, paid no mind.

Dad asked me about my plans for the day. Was I going surfing?

"I don't think so, Dad. I now understand what I need to do. There is no plan for me to be a world-class surfer. They just don't want me to look stupid on a surfboard. Three times a week for the next three months should get me there easily. I have the basics down, so now it is repetition and learning to read the waves."

Denny, a typical junior high student, asked, "How do you read waves? Are they in English?"

I treated it as a serious question.

"I know the theory but not the actual practice. There are three main types of waves, reef break, point break, and beach break. They are waves breaking just like they sound. Breaking over a reef like at Pipeline, breaking over a point of land like Rincon, or breaking over a plain beach like Ehukai Beach in Hawaii.

A reef is the best quality for a showy ride because the waves break hard and fast. The point break wave is a long smooth ride. The beach break is short, steep, and powerful. They give the longest tube ride, so I suspect that is what they will shoot in Hawaii.

"What's a tube ride?"

"It is the showiest surfing move. You start at the peak of a wave and try to get ahead of the wave by going over the leading edge, the lip. The idea is to surf down the front wall of the wave and be under the falling lip, you move across the wall as the wave falls, so it looks like you are in a tube. If you get too far ahead of the wave and get to the bottom of the trough, the wave will fall on you and wipe you out.

"These make the most dramatic camera shots, so I think that is what we will be doing. Other things that affect how a wave moves are the wind and tide. So, while I know the words, I don't know the reality of doing it.

"Huntington Beach is a classic beach break and has more consistent waves than anywhere else in California, so that is why we are practicing there."

"What's a wipeout?"

I think the little bugger knew about a wipeout and was just trying to cause trouble.

"That's where the wave tips you over, and you then have to retrieve your board and start all over."

I wasn't about to say, oh yeah, it could also brain me with a ten-foot board, and I could drown. I didn't think Mum and Dad needed to hear that.

Dad spoke up, "There is a rare chance that the board could flip around and hit Rick in the head, leading to worse problems, but overall, it is safer than driving on the freeway.'

"Jack, should Rick be driving if the freeway is that unsafe?"

This was spinning out of control quickly.

"Peg, that is a good point."

That's when I realized that my parents had had me. I shook my head and stood up from the table.

"What I am going to do today is see about flying lessons, so I don't have to drive on those dangerous freeways."

Mary asked, "Rick will you fly me to school so I don't have to be on those dangerous freeways."

"Sure, thing, Squirt."

"Thanks."

Mum and Dad were looking at each other with a what have we started look?

"Have a good first day of school, guys and doll. I am out of here."

Now that was time well spent!

Chapter 10

I looked in the Yellow Pages and found the nearest airport with flight instructions was Santa Monica Airport. I drove to the offices of a company advertised in the phone book, but they were out of business. I stopped at a restaurant, The Hump, to get a cup of coffee and to borrow their Yellow Pages.

While the waitress was bringing my coffee, I heard two people talking about the airport. The residents didn't want the airport around them because of the noise at night and the danger of crashes. They had all sorts of requests in front of the city council. If they had their way, the airport would be closed and made into parkland. Not even the industry would satisfy them.

They hadn't allowed the runway to be lengthened in 1958, driving Douglas away and losing forty-four thousand jobs to Long Beach. Whatever makes them happy, I guess. I realized that this area would be more trouble than it was worth to get flying lessons.

Ontario, California, had a small airfield. It was further than I had planned on driving. It was close to Cucamonga of Jack Benny fame. The area was planted in grapes which I don't think would be concerned about aircraft noise.

It took me an hour to get there, but it was worth the trip. It didn't look like I thought it would. I expected a small dusty airport with a short runway, several hangers, and a broken-down-looking office building with a windsock on a pole on top of the roof. There would be no control tower.

It was quite different from what I imagined. It was Ontario International Airport with commercial service daily to Las Vegas by Western Airlines and Bonanza Airlines. There were two, what looked like to me, long runways. Later I was to learn the east/west runway was 6,200 feet and the northeast/southwest runway 4700 feet. There was a nice control tower, plus a small terminal building, about a dozen small hangers, and several office buildings.

When I pulled onto the airport grounds, I saw a sign pointing to flight lessons, so I must be in the right place. I followed several arrows to a small building with a sign, Flying Lessons.

Inside was a small office with a desk that was overflowing with paperwork. Behind the desk was a wizened-looking man dressed in jeans and a plaid shirt, wearing a funny-looking leather jacket with a patch. The patch had a tiger with wings. It was too hot for a jacket. It must have been over one hundred outside. There was no air conditioning, only a fan blowing back and forth.

"Kin I help you?" he asked.

"I would like to see about taking flying lessons."

"I can't take on anyone working for their lessons. I need the cash up front."

"That's okay. I will pay cash upfront. That said, I don't know what I have to do to learn to fly and get a license."

"You know how much it will cost? It could run into the hundreds of dollars."

Rather than play twenty questions, I pulled a wad of money out of my pants pocket.

"How much?"

"Two hundred dollars."

I counted it out and handed it to him.

"Let me get you a receipt."

"How about a handshake instead?"

"I like your style, kid. I'm Bill McGarry."

He extended a hand and gave a firm shake.

"Rick Jackson."

"Nice to meet you, Rick. I was sitting here wondering how I would pay my rent this month. You have saved me."

That stopped me for a moment. Rent this month? What if he had no more students? Would he go out of business and leave me high and dry? Maybe this handshake wasn't such a good idea.

"Uh, glad I saved you. What about next month?"

"All I had to do was get through the next ten days. After that, I have a contract kick in with Bonanza Airlines to start a new batch of pilots that will keep me going for another two years."

"Good, you had me scared for a moment."

"Sorry about that. Now my method of teaching isn't the same as others. I believe in learning as you are flying. You will be soloing and flying your friends in no time."

"How old do you have to be?"

"No problem there, only seventeen."

"I will be sixteen in October."

"No kidding! I would have pegged you at twenty or so. Well, that slows things down, but we can get your flight lessons out of the way and get you soloing. Why aren't you in school?"

"I'm on a study program with the studio I work for."

"So, you're that Rick Jackson. My daughter will want to meet you."

I knew better to ask him how old she was and if she was good-looking.

"Now, what do I have to do to start."

"Read a bunch of stuff."

At that, he opened a filing cabinet. From his desk, I expected a mess. It had neatly labeled folders. The surprise at the neatness must have shown on my face as he said, "Daughter."

The thick folder he gave me contained forms I needed to fill out and study material. Some of them made sense, such as the *Pilots Handbook of Aeronautical Knowledge* and *the Airplane Flying Handbook*. But what was the *Weight-Shift Control Flying Handbook* all about?

"Now, when can you come out to start your lessons? We can have you ready to solo in fifty or sixty hours of classroom and flying instruction.

"I can do Tuesday and Thursday afternoons, plus a Saturday or Sunday afternoon if needed."

"Let's start with Tuesday and Thursday, four-hour sessions. Each session will be a combination of classroom and flying. We can't do four hours today, but I would like to get you up into the air."

"Works for me. Let's go."

And that is what we did.

He took me up in a Cessna 172, a fairly new aircraft that looked like it had been flown a lot, at least from the worn upholstery. This was a different experience than I had as a passenger in a larger aircraft. I could tell we were flying.

Mr. McGarry let me take the controls and do some simple turns and ups and downs. He talked me through everything. He took over as we landed, but he talked me through each step even then.

There was no question I was going to be a pilot!

I was still bubbling over at dinner. I gave the family a quick update on my day and the small adventure. Mary wanted to know if I could fly her to school tomorrow. I had to tell her I couldn't fly passengers until I was 17.

"But Rick, I will be old and out of school by then!"

"Well, you may still be in college. How was your day? Did you meet any new friends?"

Hopefully, that would distract her.

"Yes! Your idea worked. There are six of us, and the teachers have already given our group a name. They call us the Brat Pack."

I hoped I would never meet them.

Eddie joined in, "I tried it and met three other guys who seem nice."

I looked at Denny. "Did you meet any guys that way?"

He looked down a little and said, "I didn't try it with any guys, but I did get two cute girl's phone numbers."

Dad snorted, and Mum shook her head. I think I saw another gray hair sprout but didn't mention it.

The boys had some homework, and Mary had some sort of a project that involved popsicle sticks and glue. Mum helped with that.

I dove into my new aviation material, and that was how a peaceful day at the Jackson's house ended.

Wednesday was clear and bright, in other words, normal. My run was fun. I tried a new route. It went into an area with even steeper ravines than the main path. I was running on a particularly steep bit of trail. Since I was going uphill, I naturally slowed down.

Slowing down is probably what allowed me to hear a weak "help."

Not certain that I heard anything, I stopped. It came again.

"Help me, please."

Looking down into the ravine, I saw a person at the bottom. I worked my way down a fifty-foot embankment to the person. At the bottom, holding her ankle, was an attractive young lady. She was dressed in shorts and a t-shirt, so it was obvious that she had been out running.

She was bleeding from a lot of surface cuts. None of them looked serious, but overall, there was a lot of blood.

"Help me, please. I can't stand on this ankle. It might be broken."

"Let's see if we can walk you out here by moving down the ravine. There is no way you could get up this hillside."

We tried, but she couldn't use that leg, even with me supporting her. I picked her up in my arms and started carrying her. Fortunately, she wasn't that heavy, maybe one hundred and five pounds. I had lifted enough so I could estimate her weight, not that it mattered. I was getting her to safety.

She put her arms around my neck.

"My name is Veronica Beckham, but I prefer Ronnie. What is yours?"

"Rick," I puffed out.

She may not be heavy, and I may be strong, but this was tough territory.

Luckily, the sides of the ravine dropped quickly. About a hundred yards down, the sides were shallow enough that I could carry her out of it. A couple came running up the trail as we came back onto the path. They looked to be in their early thirties and very fit.

They stopped as they came up to us, so I explained the problem. They quickly offered their help. As we were walking, they introduced themselves as Tom and Sharon Simpson. They had a car at the nearest trailhead and would drive Ronnie to the emergency room.

Tom even helped carry Ronnie. She may be little, but it adds up!

I was hoping there would be a payphone near their car, but no luck.

I helped get Ronnie into their car, and after that, I excused myself.

"Ronnie, you are in good hands here. I have an appointment, so I have to take off. Are you okay with that?"

"Certainly, Rick. Thank you for your help."

I turned around and took off. Just as I was getting into the woods, I heard.

"I didn't even get his full name!"

Oh well, good deed for the day done.

Chapter 11

Dad asked me how my run went at breakfast, and I told him fine. No sense in opening up a discussion on my actions this morning. It was no big deal.

Dad reminded me that I hadn't talked to Susan Wallace, my publicist, or John Baxter, my entertainment agent, in a while.

The first thing I did after breakfast was call and make appointments with both of them. Then I had to hustle to pick up Fred and get to the beach.

Fred was getting excited about going to Hawaii for the movie, especially the surfing part. He had a good point. It might be fun to shoot the pier at Huntington and Malibu, plus walking the nose at Rincon, but Hawaii sounded so cool.

At that moment, if we could grab our boards and a Woody car, we would have been ready to go for it, though the Woody would sink about five feet offshore. Maybe we could paddle it out past Santa Catalina with a guitar. Yes, we were being silly.

From there, we speculated about surfing in Peru, Australia, and South Africa. We had heard talk about all those places.

It was, as usual, a nice day at the beach. I caught a couple of good waves and a lot of rays. I am lucky in that I don't burn easily. I just got darker and darker all the time.

Mum had told me we had a lot of Irish in us. Family legend was that Spanish sailors washed ashore from the Spanish Armada, giving birth to the Black Irish, and that I was a descendant of them. My black hair supported that theory. Whether or not it was true, I had no idea. It sounded good, though.

Dad contended that there was some Shawnee Indian in the family mix. My cheekbones were higher than normal, so maybe that was it. I wondered which story would impress the girls the most. Maybe I could claim a combination?

After surfing, I asked Fred if he wanted to come to the house to play pool. This time he said yes, and out of nowhere, he told me that penicillin was a wonder drug. Too much information!

Fred had never been to Jackson House, so he was really surprised when we had to stop at the guardhouse, and I signed him in. Then he saw the house. To say he was shocked was an understatement.

"Rick, your family lives in this castle?"

"It's not a castle, though if you want to be technical, it was modeled on Kohl's house near San Francisco, which in turn was modeled on a palace in England."

"Oh, excuse me. I'm not up on the differences between a palace and a castle."

"One is fortified, and the other isn't."

"Oh. I should have guessed a knight would live somewhere like this."

"Don't make too big a deal about it. My mum doesn't want us to forget our roots."

About that time, a limo pulled in. Mary was being brought home from her half-day of kindergarten.

"Yeah, I can see you are sticking to your roots."

Since he said it with a laugh and a smile, it was okay.

I took him through the formal front door. Hey, I was proud of our house and wanted to show it off.

Dad wasn't home, but Mum was in the library with Anna, Sharon, and several other ladies. I tried to sneak us by, but she spotted me. I had to take Fred in and do the introductions all around. They were talking about Sharon's new charity project.

I didn't catch the ladies' names, but I did remember one was a Douglas and the other two Knight and Brown. I wondered what their husbands did. They would have to be heavy hitters to be in this group.

Mrs. Douglas seemed to be interested in meeting me. She told me that her husband Donald had mentioned me when he heard she was coming to Jackson House. I had no idea who he could be, so I made a few polite noises and ran for it. They were talking about dinner plans, not something a fifteen, almost sixteen-year-old wanted to be near.

I had to tell Fred what was going on.

His only question was, "Who is Viscountess Jackson?"

"Oh, that is Mum."

He surrendered at that point and quit talking about my roots. Maybe I should show him our invitation to the White House.

I showed Fred my room which resulted in a lot of wows. A trip up the elevator to the top of the tower was nifty. He asked why I was going to the beach. I could catch all the rays up here that I needed. Even without a suit if I wanted. I don't think so.

We then took the elevator to the basement and played pool for several hours. His playing was just a little better than mine, so we had fun. Mrs. Hernandez sent a maid down with a plate full of snacks and several Cokes, so we were in hog heaven.

Fred had to kid me about not forgetting our roots. I took it in good stride because he was right but not being mean about it. I told him that if he worked hard, he too could live this lifestyle. Oh, yes, and have a ton of luck.

I took him home before dinner. The meal itself was quiet, other than Mary telling us about her new friends. She had invited a group over on Saturday, so I thought I would try to make myself scarce. The boys answered the questions with the words okay and boring, so all was good with them.

When I retired to my room for the night, I sat on the sofa and read a short story that was listed in my English homework. I thought the story was completely overrated. I would have fired Nippers and

Turkey for their bickering and thrown the other guy out instead of letting him live there.

This was one story where I elected to write as short of an essay as I could in response to the questions in the text. They didn't have drugs for depression in those days. I did check on electro-shock therapy, but it wasn't available then. Anyway, I found the story depressing, with no point in it even being written.

My morning run was not as eventful as yesterday, which was a good thing. My weight workout had plateaued, which was fine by me. I didn't need a spotter as I wasn't trying to up weights or bulk up. I was more concerned about keeping my core strength up and having a toned look without looking like a muscle-bound weightlifter.

I had seen guys down at the beach in Venice who looked deformed to me, as they had bulked up so much.

At breakfast, Dad asked me about my plans for the day. I told him I had flying lessons in the afternoon but that my morning was free. He suggested that I use the morning to visit my office staff since I had never been there.

That seemed like a good idea, and I kicked myself for not thinking of it on my own. What sort of businessman was I that I didn't even show interest in those working for me?

I hit the books hard half the morning. First, it was schoolwork, then flying ground school. Since I didn't know what was expected on the first day, I surveyed all of the coursework I had been given. At least now, I had an idea of what I needed to learn.

Today I started to study the material, starting with the aeronautical knowledge book. It was well-written but very dry. Since I owned these books, I underlined items and wrote in the margins.

I had never done that before. In public school, it was death to write in your book, so I had never tried it before. That even carried over to all the books I had bought to study at home. The world is changing! Whoever thought I could write in books.

Next thing you know, I would be allowed to throw away my soda bottles and not return them. Dream on.

Chapter 12

I was immersed in my work, and Mum came in and reminded me that I had mentioned going to my office and that I had an appointment with Susan Wallace for lunch. It was at a small sidewalk café next to my office.

I put on a blue sports coat over my polo shirt and was good to go. I didn't want to be too high and mighty during my first visit, but I wanted a professional look. For California, this was professional.

There weren't any parking spots along the street in front of Dad's building, so I drove around the back to see if there was parking there. There was plenty of parking but what caught my eye was the spot with the sign, *Reserved for Richard Jackson.*

I usually wasn't impressed by most things that were indications that I wasn't your normal teenager. For some reason, seeing my name on a parking sign made me feel special. I felt special until I went to open the back door and found it locked. There was no bell to ring and no window in the door, so I had to walk around to the front public entrance. Yep, I'm special.

In the front lobby, there was a sign indicating the offices of Jackson Enterprises were on the second floor. Ignoring the elevator, I took two steps at a time.

The second-floor foyer was the waiting room for my offices. There was a desk with a receptionist. I noticed a young man was sitting in a chair reading a book. From the cover, I could tell it was by E.M. Forrester. My kind of guy!

Anyway, the receptionist, a middle-aged woman, said, "Good morning, sir."

I started to introduce myself, but she had gotten up and opened the door to the offices for me.

As I was going into the office, I heard the young man ask, "Who is that?"

"A visitor," was the terse reply.

Once I was inside the office, I had no idea where to turn. Another young man introduced himself as my accountant and immediately resolved my confusion. He took me around the office and introduced me to the half dozen people who comprised my business staff; it was so many, so quick, that I had the names and titles confused.

Still, I spent my time going around with them and getting an update on what each was doing. Without really understanding everything they were telling me, I made positive sounds of appreciation. I finally realized they were keeping a running summary for me of each division's status, including its finances.

Each person had their own office. They were a mixed bag of men and women of different ages.

I had a question for my accountant but had forgotten his name and was now too embarrassed to tell him that I had forgotten it. Someone called him Jim, so I went with that. He looked to be in his early thirties, so it didn't bother me to call him by his first name. I asked Jim if there was anywhere I could talk to everyone at once.

He promptly had everyone go into the conference room. I asked if the receptionist could come in. While she was joining us, someone asked if I wanted any coffee. I liked this group already.

Once we were all settled with coffee, tea, or soft drinks in hand, I started.

"As you know, my name is Richard Jackson. Please call me Richard, Rick, or even Ricky. The next one who calls me Sir Richard will have to put a quarter in the coffee fund jar I noticed in the break area."

This brought out some smiles, so I must have been on the right track.

"As a matter of fact, why is there a coffee fund jar in the first place? That should be charged to petty cash. That is to include all the drinks, not just coffee."

Now I had a room full of smiles. Since I saw Jim making a note, I figured it would happen.

"Now, in the first few minutes of my visit, I realized that I should have been here sooner and more often. My question to the group is, how often should I come in?"

They looked at each other, and a few small conversations broke out. I let it go on for a few minutes. Finally, a forty-year-old woman spoke up for the group.

"If you could stop by once a week for an hour, we will be able to update you on each division."

"Which day will be best?"

"Friday afternoon."

"That's it then. I will be here at one o'clock every Friday if I am in town for a business update. We will have to figure out how to handle it starting the first of the year, as I will be in Hawaii on a film shoot. Is there anything else?"

The woman whose name I now remembered was Janet, said shyly, "Could I get your autograph for my daughter?"

"Certainly."

That gave me a thought. I asked our receptionist to call the studio and have them send over a stack of unsigned photos. I planned to sign them and pass them out to any who desired them.

That led to another thought. I turned to Jim, who was the default office manager.

"Jim, we need to have our first Christmas party. Will you get a planning group together?"

"I will be glad to. Will it be just for the office workers, or are spouses included?"

"Make it for the whole family. There are only a few of us, so I think we can afford it."

"How about a budget?"

Leave it to the accountant to think of that.

"Start at five hundred dollars and see what you can come up with."

From the look on his face, I think my budget was about ten times what he thought it should be. From that, I decided to hold my thoughts on a Christmas bonus until later. Maybe until I found out if my companies were making any money.

From the easy atmosphere, I felt like my first visit to my office had been a success. I did remember to ask Jim about a key to the back door.

"Oh, that is on your keyring in your office."

"My office?"

Instead of answering, he took me to a corner office that looked out the front of the building. It was the biggest office I had ever been in, and that included the studio offices. I had a massive wooden desk. There were several chairs in front of it. A sofa and several chairs are set up around a coffee table in one corner.

Opposite it was a conference table that had eight chairs around it. There was a wet bar set up with a hot plate for a coffee pot, with the littlest refrigerator I had ever seen. There was even some artwork on the walls, but I didn't take a good look at it.

Some of it was pretty bright and impressionistic; I didn't know how I felt about that. They were signed by some guy who called himself a Pollock, which didn't seem cool.

A door at one side of the room opened to a private restroom which even had a shower. I realized I could live in this room if I slept on the sofa.

"Who did all this?"

"Your mother, and two friends. Someone said that they were Anna Romanov and Sharon Bronson, but I don't see how that could be."

"Trust me, it was them. My mum and they are in business together and thick as thieves."

"You mean those famous ladies were in here! The office is going to die when I tell them. They missed a chance of a lifetime to get Miss Romanov's autograph, and the younger set will feel the same way about Miss Bronson."

And I thought I talked a little too formally at times.

I offered, "Maybe we can invite them to our Christmas party."

Changing the subject since I was afraid Jim might have a stroke.

"Who is that young man sitting in the lobby? He appears to be settled in."

"He's a reporter for some paper. When the office first opened, we had many requests for interviews, and many reporters camped out in the lobby. It has dwindled to him."

On an impulse, I told Jim to bring him in. Jim introduced me to Dennis Lawson, a freelancer. His goal in life was to get a story and sell it to a newspaper or magazine. A really hot story would get sold to the AP or UP. From his looks, he had not been at it very long.

"Dennis, I understand you are the last man standing as far as waiting in my office lobby."

"I hope you will give me an interview, so it pays off. Frankly, I am running short on time and money."

"How's that?"

"I guess it is really about money. I'm about broke. I've tried to get a job with a paper or magazine but don't have the ins, so I haven't connected. I decided to try freelancing, but I will have to look for another trade if I don't sell a story soon."

"I have some time, and I have to face this sooner or later. Go ahead and ask your questions."

That may have been a mistake because, after several hours, I think he knew more about me than I did. He kept his questions about my business interests, but he wanted to know how each of them developed.

He was aware of my patent on the movable shower head but not that I was a part owner in Detroit Faucet. He quickly realized that DF was the manufacturer of the Anna Romanov collection. I didn't mention Sharon Bronson going in with Anna as they had not announced it yet.

He was aware of the hairdryer and the fact it was licensed out. I did tell him about our expansion plans for the overseas market.

Of course, the big deal was the container business. He learned about Narrow Freight, our connection with Howell in Argentina, and The Scottish Line. I briefly explained the various ports we would be working with.

He asked very few questions about my movie career. I got the impression he thought it was a hobby. He knew enough about me that I could tell he had done a lot of homework. There were no questions about singing, which was probably for the best.

We finished up just before noon, which worked out well as I had a lunch meeting with Susan Wallace. He had a steno pad full of notes. Dennis asked if he could send his rough draft to me for review to ensure that he had no major mistakes.

"You're willing to let me see it before it's printed?"

"It is in my best interest to have you pleased with the story. Not that I see anything negative, but the happier you are, the more likely I will get access in the future. Since you currently are my only access, I need you a lot more than you need me."

"I will be happy to review it. This could be the start of a good deal for both of us."

I was thinking about my other newspaper and magazine connections when I said that.

Susan arrived at our agreed-upon restaurant at the same time I did. We did the European kissy-face thing like most other people in Hollywood. I had to laugh at myself, a kid from Bellefontaine doing kissy face.

After we were seated in the restaurant, we took a few minutes to catch up on our personal lives. She was happy with the way things were going. I was low maintenance for her, especially compared to the scumbag she represented before. At one point, she told me she almost felt guilty about taking my money.

"Oh, will you work for free?"

"Not that guilty," she said with a laugh.

After we ordered our food, she asked, "Rick, do you have anything I could pass on to your media contacts?"

"Not much," as I brought her up to date on my latest movie.

"What about your knighthood?"

"Well, there is an official investiture in April. I'm planning to be in London for that. I am getting an award from the Boy Scouts at the White House for that. That reminds me, my parents and I are having dinner with Ike the night before."

She drew herself up straight in her chair.

"Nothing happening? I forget you are a teenager and don't live in the real world. Did it ever occur to you that your fans may be interested in that sort of detail?"

"Uh, no."

She just shook her head.

"What else are you up to?"

"Well, I had an interview with a freelance business writer this morning."

She didn't say anything; her look reminded me of Mum. Is this in the women's handbook?

I repeated the highlights of the interview.

"Let me get this straight, Rick. I knew you had invented the hairdryer and had an interest in a faucet company. Now I find out you own a trucking line, an ocean-going ship, and hold the patents of something that may revolutionize ocean freight."

"Yes."

Thinking quickly, I tried to distract her with some new information to dig myself out of my hole. Yes, I saw that I was in a hole. I told her about being a Shellback and the other sailor honors for crossing the equator and prime meridian.

As her face got redder and redder, I realized that I had better shut up.

Have you ever heard the term, when you realize you are in a hole, stop digging? Well, I had to stop digging.

It got to her. Finally, she started laughing.

"Rick, you are incredible. This is a gold mine of publicity. I will share this with each of our contacts. This all will keep you in the entertainment news and, from the sound of it, the business news for months. Is there anything else I need to know?

"Don't think so. I am on track to complete tenth grade by the New Year. Oh, and I start flying lessons this afternoon."

I don't know why she started throwing the untouched rolls at me from the breadbasket on the table. Luckily, she wasn't that good of a shot. What I thought was funny was the flashbulbs that started going off. It turns out half the paparazzi in Hollywood were there. I could see the headlines about my agent and me having a falling out.

At that point, I left money for our uneaten meals, and we bailed out of there. We both found the whole thing totally off the wall funny, so we parted on a good note. She suggested that I pass the business article by her before giving it an okay. That sounded good to me, so I agreed.

Chapter 13

From lunch, I headed out to the Ontario Airport for my first real lesson. As I was pulling up to Mr. McGarry's office, a little British sports car was pulling out.

It was an older model MG. It was cool looking. I think it was a 1948 MG-TD but wasn't sure. When I was younger, I thought about one but found out they had problems. Not only that, the one time I had sat in one, the foot pedals were so small. I could cover all three with one foot. It was in racing green with those neat wire-spoke wheels.

In a glance, I took that in, but what caught my attention was the young lady driving. She didn't look much older than me, and what a looker with dark black hair. She gave me a jaunty wave as she accelerated out of the lot. I would like to find out her name and what she does.

McGarry was waiting for me in his office. His first comment was, "You just missed my daughter. She wanted to meet you but had to get back to school."

"That's too bad. Where does she go to school?"

"Stanford. She's a junior."

"Why did she want to meet me?"

"She thought it would be nifty keen to meet Sir Richard Jackson of movie fame. Her words, not mine."

"Well, I'm sure we will meet someday."

Dang, she is so good-looking! When will I meet someone local my age?

"If she got to know me, she wouldn't be as impressed."

"Yeah, the young girls always go for the good-looking, famous rich guys. Tough to be you."

"You might be surprised. I can't seem to meet any girls my age."

"I hear you; I remember being young and wondering if I would ever meet the girl before I died."

"Before you died?"

"Never mind, let's get started on your lesson. Where are you on your reading?"

I explained that I had looked over everything and had a good start on one of the manuals.

"Good, let's get into the air and talk about that."

Getting into the air didn't go as quickly as I thought it would. He had the crazy idea that we had to ensure we had fuel in the tanks, no water in the fuel, oil in the sump, tires not flat, and the wings hadn't fallen off. He had a preflight checklist that we used to make certain that everything was okay.

When we got inside, he had me make certain the rudder would turn, and the ailerons worked. As we checked each item, it clicked with me that if you messed these up, you couldn't get out and walk home.

When we finally did take off, he had me work the radios with the control tower and check our headings. We flew around the valley and talked about what I had studied. He had me steer the plane between questions, changing altitude and direction many times.

Pretty soon, I would answer a question, and he would say take it up one thousand feet, slow climb, turn left forty-five degrees, and I was able to do it without breaking out in a sweat.

He even let me try a touch-and-go. It went well. At least I didn't break anything though I did bounce it back into the air several times. He called it a day and reminded me same time next Tuesday.

I drove home on the road but was mentally flying. I loved it.

Dinner was normal; that is, a continuous conversation, mostly about the kids' day at school. The boys were slowly fitting in. From what Mary was telling us, I think we would be calling her Queen Mary soon. She already had her court of ladies in waiting.

Well, at least a...what do you call a group of five-year-old girls anyway? There must be a special name like a pod of whales or murder of crows, a sound of shrieks, maybe a gaggle of giggles? No, a gaggle is geese. What about a tantrum of girls? Yeah, I like that, a tantrum.

Anyway, Mary was excited about all her new friends. Again, note to self, avoid groups of little girls.

I spent the evening studying. So far, my schoolwork was not held up by having to ask questions. The books in the library were more than sufficient. As usual, I spent more time sidetracked on the books referenced in the textbooks. It seems like nothing is ever simple like it is presented in school. Heroic people did crummy things, and crummy people did heroic things. This applied to nations as well as people.

The lesson I was learning was that humans could be trusted as long as it is in their self-interest. Just when I thought that was a hard and fast rule, I would hear machine-gun bullets hammering against the landing craft door. Why can't things be cut and dried?

By the time I had finished my studies, I was ready to call it a night.

Breakfast was the usual madhouse as kids needed to be pushed out the door with all their books and homework in hand. At least Mum didn't have to put anyone in a snowsuit anymore. I hated those, and when older, the eight-buckle arctic black rubber boots we wore.

The morning had become routine: pick up Fred and surf till lunchtime. I must say I enjoyed surfing, but when you have to do it on a schedule, it becomes a chore. I think the worst part was listening to the guys talk about Saturday and Sunday surfing when the girls showed up. Surf bunnies, they called them surf bunnies. They were in school during the week. Most of the guys were over twenty-one, so they were flirting with jailbait. Not smart, in my opinion.

Since my life wasn't surfing, I passed on surfing on the weekend. Somehow it didn't seem worth the effort even to meet new girls.

I had lunch with my movie agent, Mr. John Baxter. We met at the Brown Derby at eleven-thirty, which was our usual meeting spot. I had asked for an earlier meeting as I had to be at my office at one o'clock.

Once settled, we made inquiries about the health of our family members. He had the latest batch of pictures of his granddaughter to share. I joked that he might be representing the little beauty one day. He was horrified at the thought.

"Rick, I wouldn't want my little girl to be associated with most of the people in this industry, present company excepted, of course."

I didn't get it because I first thought of Mr. Wayne, Anna Romanov, and Sharon Bronson. Then I remembered Paul Grant and that agent of Sharon's.

"I get it, but there are a lot of good people involved."

"I know. I'm just a cynical old man."

"Maybe cynicism is acquired by a lifetime of experience."

That comment made me think of my lessons from last night. I would have to think about that.

"Are there any offers that look good right now?"

"There is nothing that screams Oscar. The way I look at it, Rick, you are in a good position right now. If you continue to take summers off, the next time you could start a movie will be in the fall of next year. Why don't we wait and see what develops between now and next summer? I hesitate to ask, but are you okay with money right now?"

I almost spit my Coke through my nose at that question.

"Yeah, I'm okay."

"Why the reaction?"

I did the fair thing and brought him up to speed on Jackson Enterprises.

Mr. Baxter got a concerned look on his face.

"Will you be continuing your acting career?"

"For the time being, yes; I enjoy it, and I can't do much else until I finish high school and start college. I suspect I will have to quit acting then."

"Serious question then, you have been in B-movies until now. Do you want to aim higher?"

"I have never given it any thought. Do we have any control over that?"

"Depends how bad you want it."

"What do you mean?"

"If necessary, you could finance your own movie. The problem would be in finding the right vehicle."

"No, I don't want it that bad. Do keep your eye out for the 'right vehicle,' and we will see what develops. I have to think of a serious business image for the future."

"An A-list actor would have a more serious image than a B-lister."

"Well yeah, but I think of this more as a kid having fun rather than a career."

"Well, Rick, I must say, working with you is different than anyone else I have ever worked with."

About then, Mr. Cobb came over.

"Rick, we haven't seen you for a while. By the way, congratulations on your knighthood."

"Thank you, Mr. Cobb. It still seems strange to be called Sir Richard."

A loud British voice from the next table spoke out.

"It certainly cheapened the knighthood."

I turned quickly and saw that it was the rather boorish Richard Burton. He may be a good, notice I didn't say great, Shakespearian actor, but in his personal life, he had little charm from what I had seen of him at the studio. Considering the source, I ignored him. Well, for a moment.

I spoke out, "Yes, the knighthood has been degraded. Next thing you know, Burton will receive one."

Things got quiet in the restaurant, but Mr. Cobb changed the subject.

"Frank Sinatra was in last night and asked for you. I told him you hadn't been in for a while. He asked that I pass a message to you; he is ready for another duet."

What is this world coming to, Richard Burton, an actor, and I'm considered a singer? I think Mr. Baxter had earned his cynicism. In the meantime, Burton had apparently decided that he didn't want a scene, as he left the restaurant with his party. I noticed that Elizabeth Taylor was with him. I wondered what that was about.

Chapter 14

From the restaurant, I went to my office. I had promised to be there every Friday at one o'clock. I was fifteen minutes late, which was not my usual style, but the traffic was horrible.

Since we met yesterday, there was not much news, but we ironed out a format for presenting the information I needed. One nice thing was the studio had sent a messenger over with the publicity photos, so I had an autograph session. We decided that next week there would be a photography session and that we would have a catered open house for friends and family of the office staff.

I felt very strongly that I needed to win these people over. They worked for me, but I wanted a loyal crew. Thinking of that, I asked Jim Williamson, my accountant, for a minute in my office.

"Jim, are we paying everyone fairly?"

"More than fair."

"Good, that is the way I want it. What about benefits?"

"We are at the top of the industry."

"Well, keep it that way. If it seems to be out of line, let me know, but we want to be considered the place to work. There will be a lot of dollars flowing through this office in the future, and I don't want anyone to think we aren't sharing properly. As a matter of fact, do we have a bonus plan?"

"No."

"Work one up and present it to me next week. The open house is next week, not the week after."

With a grin, Jim said, "I will be glad to. Do you know how high you are willing to go?"

"Hmm, make it so that each person can increase their salary by fifty percent. Have a portion of it a group effort and the rest individual. While we are at it, our attitude will be getting the work done correctly, not being on time or hours spent."

Jim thought for a moment. "Can we be flexible on working hours?"

"I don't see why not."

"For some of the staff and their families, it would be better to come in early. For others staying late is best."

"That will work better than you think. Remember we are an international company. I can see the day coming when we will need twenty-four-hour coverage in several languages."

"At least it won't be boring around here."

"I hope not. Now I feel a golf course calling me."

From there, I drove out to Calabasas, where I found that I could tee off in half an hour by myself with John Jacobs as my caddie. What luck.

My luck stopped there. While hitting long was good, my putts were bad. You might just call them raunchy. John was cool; he suggested that I spend more time on the putting green next time out. I couldn't disagree with that.

Afterward, I went home, showered, had dinner, and hit the books until bedtime. Where are the girls?

I extended my morning run as I was getting back into shape. After a hearty breakfast, I was kicking around trying to decide if I wanted to do schoolwork or take the day off. It didn't take much convincing to take the day off.

Now I want to make something clear. I love my sister.

Mary was growing up. She was still very much a kid, but you could see the person she was going to be emerging. Mostly this was a good thing, but the thoughts of sororicide crossed my mind more than once. Nevermore than this morning. I had forgotten that she was having friends over.

I took the elevator up to the tower, thinking I would enjoy the view for a while. Instead, when I exited the elevator, I got an eyeful of half a dozen five-year-olds lying on lawn furniture. They were all lying on their stomachs, but all were topless! I tried to back away without being noticed, but one girl saw me and screamed. That set them all off.

I ran back into the elevator. Have you ever noticed how slowly those doors can close?

Thinking hard on the way down, I decided to be proactive in self-defense. I hunted up Mum immediately.

"Mum, I just had an awful moment."

I then went on to describe what I had interrupted. She told me she would look into it. I would have taken her more seriously if she hadn't been smiling.

I decided that studying my ground school lessons was a good way to spend the rest of the morning. After lunch, I hit the schoolbooks.

Later at dinner, Mary told me she was sorry about startling me. Mum was going to buy a sign that they could put at the elevator door on the first floor to warn people not to go up.

I looked at Mum and asked, "You are going to let them do it?"

"Oh, they have to stop. The sign will be for me."

I looked at Dad, but he was struggling not to laugh, so he was no help.

"That is too much information, Mum!"

Mary just sat there and smirked.

After dinner, I went back to the schoolbooks. Where are the girls?

Sunday, I did something rare for me—nothing. Well, after my workout, I went to the beach and had a long walk. I stopped for lunch at the old hotel in Malibu. I drove around the area, thinking how nice it would be to have a beach house in this area. I didn't want to be on the sand. I wanted to overlook the Pacific. I drove around the area, learning about it. Maybe someday I could have a house here.

That night I read about Robert Leffingwell being nominated for secretary of state so tensions might be eased with the Soviet Union and the ensuing problems. It had to be a work of fiction. There is no way that politics is like that.

Monday, I awoke bright and ready to go. I flew through my exercises. While running, I thought about how I had not practiced archery since I got home and that I needed to start my next-level training in unarmed combat.

That was going to hurt, but it had to be done. Maybe I was a little hasty in throwing my instructor in the horse trough. Maybe troughs were meant to be my exclusive domain.

After breakfast, I picked up Fred and we headed out to the beach. When we got to Katin's, where we always met Corky to begin the day, there was our producer Mr. Tom Jensen.

"Rick, I'm just checking up to see how things are going. Corky here tells me that you have the basic surfing skills needed for the movie, so that is going fine. Now that I see you, we have another problem. You are getting tanned too dark for your movie character. Remember, he is not a professional surfer, just a guy on holiday."

"I just naturally tan dark."

"No problem. Since you have the skills, just back down to one day a week. That will keep the tan you have but not get any darker."

This was okay with me because, frankly, surfing three days a week was becoming a chore rather than fun. However, the look on Corky's face gave me pause.

"What's wrong, Corky?"

"It's not your problem, but I was counting on the money to be able to go on the world champion tour this year."

I shook my head about this and said nothing more. As Corky and Fred started toward the beach, I told them I would catch up in a minute.

When they were out of hearing, I told Mr. Jensen that I wanted to do something for Corky as he had really helped me get better at surfing.

"What do you have in mind, Rick?"

"Some sort of sponsorship on the world tour."

He thought for a minute.

"Do you have any idea of how much money is needed?"

"From what Corky said, the better part is five thousand dollars. Most of that is airfare for Hawaii, Australia, Peru, and South Africa."

Mr. Jensen said, "The movie itself could sponsor part of it, but not all. He will be in the credits as it is. If he did well in the championship, it might help the box office."

At that time, Mrs. Katin said, "The shop could help with a thousand dollars."

I added, "I will chip in two thousand but want to keep my part silent."

"Okay, the movie can do two thousand. The Katins and I will work out the details with Corky."

I called Jim Williamson, my accountant, told him what was going on, and instructed him to cut a check for two thousand dollars to Katins, who would add it to their sponsorship money.

Mr. Katin asked me why I wanted to do it quietly. I told him that I had enough publicity in the world and would like to do a good deed without it being a big deal.

I then spent the rest of the morning out on the ocean. Now that I didn't have to do it three times a week, I enjoyed myself.

After dropping Fred off, I headed to a doctor's office for my flight physical. I need to get that in and several other forms for my student certificate.

The less said about the physical indignities of that visit, the better.

I went on home for lunch and walked into a madhouse. Mrs. Hernandez told me that Mum had left in a hurry to go to the Tucker Academy. Apparently, Eddie had been hurt. Mum left word that when I got home, I was to stay there until she returned.

Dad called from a hospital to let us know that everything was okay. From a hospital! How could things be okay? Mrs. Hernandez had picked up the phone, so I was hearing only one end of the conversation.

After she hung up, she told me that Eddie had a broken arm from a fight at school. It was a greenstick fracture so it would be in a cast, but he would be okay. She had no details of the fight.

Now Denny being in a fight was something I could picture. Eddie just didn't fit that image.

I tried to do something productive, like studying, but I couldn't concentrate. I couldn't even read for pleasure, so I ended up going for a long run.

My parents arrived in the late afternoon with Eddie and Denny in tow. I have never seen them so mad-looking.

The story came out quickly. Two boys had told Eddie that he had to give them his money. He said no. They knocked him down and jumped on his arm, breaking it. There had been no witnesses so it was his word against theirs.

A meeting had been scheduled at school with the kids and their parents for tomorrow morning. In the meantime, the headmaster had suspended both Eddie and Denny, so there would be no more trouble. The other two kids were to be allowed to attend classes.

I asked about Mary, and that is when I learned that the kindergarten was run separately from Tucker Academy. It was on the school grounds but was owned by several retired teachers who had reached an agreement to rent an unused building from the school.

The building was separate from the main campus, fenced away from it, and even had its own driveway entrance. Mum had gone so far as to call the kindergarten about any relatives of those boys who might attend the school. There were none.

Of course, we all showed our concern to Eddie. He tried to take it in stride, but you could tell it bothered him to no end. He told us how all the kids knew about the bullies, but no one could do anything because their parents were important people.

You can guess how that went down with Mum and Dad.

Before dinner, the entire household staff stopped by to check on Eddie. Even the guards from the front gate came in one at a time. While they offered to "see" to the boys, the family agreed that might not be the best answer.

After dinner, the family was able to settle down. I spent the rest of the evening studying.

Chapter 15

On Tuesday, my parents and Eddie went to the school. Denny and I played pool. He still was able to kick my butt every time. We both wondered about what would happen at school. It was Eddie's word against theirs. We both figured Mum would overwhelm everyone there.

Around eleven o'clock, they returned from Tucker Academy. From the looks on their faces, it wasn't good.

I have never heard the word bloody used so many times in my life. When Dad finally got Mum settled down, the story came out.

When they arrived at the academy, they were taken to a conference room where four boys and four sets of parents were waiting: the two boys and two witnesses.

"But didn't Eddie say there weren't any witnesses?"

"He did, and I believe him."

"Did you tell them they were lying?"

"It wouldn't have done any good. Eddie did say they weren't there, but the headmaster discounted it. He was brown-nosing the parents. They are a local judge, the county sheriff, the prosecutor, and the editor of a small paper in the Valley."

"What happened?"

"Eddie and Denny have both been kicked out of the academy."

"I ought to kick all their butts!"

"How do you think that would play out on the national stage? Someone your size is beating up on twelve-year-olds. The sheriff would arrest you; the prosecutor brings charges; the judge finds you guilty, and the newspaper cries to the world what a beast you are."

"Then what are we going to do?"

It never occurred to me that we would let it go as a family.

Mary broke in with a suggestion that I use my bow and arrow on them. Everyone agreed that probably wasn't a good idea, though Eddie did smile at the thought.

Dad spoke up, "Mum and I have some thoughts, but we want to talk them through. We will discuss it at dinner."

The only ones who didn't seem upset were Denny and Eddie. They were out of school.

I went for my flying lesson; it went great. Putting my concerns for Eddie aside, I was more determined than ever to gain my license. I even began questioning Mr. McGarry about what sort of an airplane I should own.

That took him back for a moment. Then he realized that I could probably afford it. He quizzed me on what I would like to do with it. That puzzled me until he asked, how many passengers, long trips, short trips, fast trips, acrobatics?

"Oh, I hadn't given it thought. I just want to be able to fly my own plane. I did promise my sister I would fly her to school when I could, but they don't have a runaway at her kindergarten."

He shook his head when he heard that.

I only bounced the plane once when I tried to land it, so I was getting better.

At dinner, my parents presented their plans.

Dad told us, "Since we can't fight city hall, we will change city hall. I made some phone calls today. All three of the elected officials are up for re-election this year. There are one Republican and two Democrats. They will be opposed in their primaries and if needed, in the general."

I asked, "How will you handle them with them being from different parties."

"That part has already been started. One of our lawyers on staff is a Democrat. Another is a Republican. We have been using them to gain influence in local politics. They attend central committee meetings and are both going to run for a seat on the respective committees. That has already been in the works. It is how most big businesses keep their feet in both political camps."

"As far as the newspaper goes, it has a small competitor that is for sale. We are going to buy it and run the other one out of business."

"What about the boys' schooling?"

"They are being homeschooled until we can get them back into Tucker after the first of the year."

"Will the academy take them back? From the sounds of that, the headmaster likes the other people too much."

"The new headmaster will be fine. Tucker Academy seems to be an old family business that has not kept its finances in order. The last of the Tuckers, Miss Doris Tucker, would love to sell the place and retire in peace.

"Her only stipulation is that the property must remain a school and not be developed. If she allowed development, the place would have sold long ago. It appears a foundation, Academics for Tomorrow, is about to make an offer."

Since the foundation is being supported by a holding company belonging to Mum, I think we will have a say in the new headmaster.

I had pictured in my mind what had happened to the Russians. I realized that might have been overkill, literally. Remind me never to really get Mum and Dad mad at me.

That night I read about young J. Pierrepoint Finch, a window washer who joined a huge corporation by starting in the mailroom and became chairman of the board two weeks later. I thought it was absolutely impossible until I thought of my situation.

I was up early as usual in the morning and did all my exercises. At breakfast, I told Mum and Dad that since I didn't have to go to the beach, I would stop by the studio. I hadn't advanced at all in my unarmed combat since I had returned, plus I hadn't touched my bow and arrows, sword, or longstaff since I had been back.

They agreed that would be a good use of my time. Mum had some questions about my schoolwork, but I was ahead of my schedule there, so she had no concerns.

The guard at the studio gate was another new one, but I had the T-Bird with the parking sticker, so he waved me through.

I stopped by the schoolhouse and dropped off my accumulated work. Miss Sperry took a quick look at it and declared me to be on target. She would look at it in detail and let me know of any issues.

My next stop was the stunt yard. I ran into Dick Wyman there, and we spent a while catching up. Mr. Dawson and Mr. Palmer joined us, so we went to the canteen for a cup of coffee. I was quizzed on my plans for my various fighting skills.

After half an hour's discussion, it was decided that I would spend Wednesday and Friday mornings at the studio brushing up on my skills and trying to advance in unarmed combat. Somehow in the conversation, we started referring to it as UA.

From there, we began a sword workout. Boy, was I rusty, but at the same time, the flow started to come back. Mr. Dawson asked me if I would be willing to be an extra in a sword-fighting scene in a movie that was currently underway.

Of course, I said yes. It was going to be later today so that took care of the lunch plans.

By lunchtime, between sword fighting, exchanging staff blows, and being thrown around the landscape, I was ready for a break. As usual, the studio canteen was a menagerie.

There were Revolutionary War sailors, World War II submariners, prohibition gangsters, and FBI agents. At least, I thought they were FBI agents from the suits and snap-brim hats. What topped it all were actors dressed like refugees from something by Homer. One big guy looked like he had been cleaning out the Aegean stables.

Lunch was pleasant as Dick Wyman, Mr. Palmer, and Mr. Dawson all joined me. They were all encouraging about my skills. Yes, they were rusty, but I hadn't lost them yet. Mr. Palmer thought I would be at the brown belt level soon. In reality, he didn't award belts.

His attitude was all about practicality. No belts, no fancy uniforms, no controlling of attitude. His world revolved around using unarmed force to kill or disable an opponent. He looked at emerging schools such as karate and tai-chi as hobbies. To him, these skills plus weapons such as rifles were tools of the trade, no more, no less.

To him, a bow before a fight allowed your enemy an advantage. You either reacted instinctively to an attack or decided to attack and did it without signaling intentions.

That said, he placed emphasis that you didn't want to lose your temper as you would be giving up an advantage. He had nothing against being mad, just against giving up advantages.

Mr. Dawson had similar feelings but tempered them with caution.

"The real killing with sword and staff hasn't occurred for a long time, so what you are being taught may not be the best. Tricks of the trade will have disappeared along the way. I'm still trying to teach you the real thing the best I can."

Dick Wyman's words of wisdom were, "You really need to learn how to use guns, pistols, rifles and never forget the good old shotgun for close-in work. These will trump what you are being taught."

Neither of my other two instructors disagreed. I wasn't bad with a pistol, which I knew from my appearance with John Wayne and after-hours shooting. I had the feeling that not only rifles and shotguns would be different, but that shooting at people would be different from targets.

They all agreed with me and thought I should take some classes. I agreed but wondered where I would find the time.

Mr. Dawson and I went to the studio office after lunch to have me sign the paperwork for my work as an extra. I would be paid the extra day rate and receive no credit for the movie. My face might not even be on screen, only a body swinging a sword.

Makeup was simple. Used to spending an hour or more, I was surprised at the five minutes I was given to change clothes, then the ten minutes to apply face makeup. This definitely wasn't star treatment.

It turned out I was one of fifty people in an all-out melee, the movie's grand finale. When the movie was finally released in 1961, my face was on the screen for all of three seconds. Of course, my fan club did pick up on those three seconds.

We finished up around four o'clock, so I headed home.

At dinner, there was talk of what was being done about Denny and Eddie's schooling. Miss Sperry was going to homeschool them at our house. It couldn't be at the studio because of California regulations governing studio schools. It appears you had to be a child actor in a movie to be eligible. Who would have thought?

Mary made certain that she would be allowed to go to kindergarten. She made the point that her friends might be lonely and scared without her. We all agreed that wouldn't be good and that she should continue going to class.

Dad mentioned that negotiations had been opened with the small newspaper *Simi Valley News* and Miss Tucker about the academy.

There would be a meeting with the lawyers who were active in their respective parties about good candidates to support in the primaries.

Eddie was quiet during dinner. You could tell his arm was bothering him. We had signed his cast, but that wasn't the same as his friends signing it. He had talked to two guys on the phone, but they weren't allowed to visit. I guess Eddie had cooties. When I told him that, it got me a wan smile.

Mary kissed him on the cheek and told him that his cooties didn't bother her.

Eddie ruined the moment when he wiped his cheek off and said, "Yuck, girl cooties."

Mary just giggled.

After dinner, I spent the evening at schoolwork.

Chapter 16

The next morning got off to a good start. My running on the hillsides had finally brought me back into condition. Running on the flats all summer hadn't been kind to me. Also, I hadn't been as diligent with my weights as I should have been.

As I ran, I reviewed where I was at with my various goals. Physically, I was exactly where I wanted to be. Business seemed to be going well, but that was due to other people knowing what they were doing. I may have had the original ideas, but I had no illusion that I was the one making things happen right now. It looked like a good ride, so I had better hang on.

Movie-wise, my career was in good shape. However, I did take Mr. Baxter's words to heart about where I wanted to take it. Like everything else, if I were going to do it, I needed to do it right, so how could I become an A-lister?

School was on track. As a matter of fact, I was a little ahead of the curve on my schoolwork. Flying lessons were going great. I couldn't wait until Mr. McGarry said I was ready to solo.

I needed to become proficient at using long guns somewhere along the line. I think my pistol work was okay, but then I had never been compared to someone who knew what they were doing.

Then there was ballroom dancing. Yes, there were several dances like the tango that I was good at, but I had never done most of the common dances. At least to be able to perform at the level required in a movie.

I think we could forget about a singing career. I doubt if anyone would be interested in signing me up to sing again.

These were the immediate items. What were my long-term goals? I realized that the events of my life had pushed me in good directions, but in what direction did I want to go?

All these thoughts went through my mind as I ran. I had been running through the miles-long park, just following the path ahead of me. By the time I realized that I had been running for a while, none of the areas of the park looked familiar.

Now the simple thing would have been to turn around and head back. What's the fun in that? Instead, I took the next fork in the trail that veered to the right. This should take me towards the highway and one of the many entrances to the park trail. I could then look at the map board and figure out where I was.

My plan worked to a point. I got to the road and saw the map board. Some jerk had torn the map off!

Now I had two choices, follow the road downhill towards my house, or follow the trail and hope it went back that way.

I was getting tired enough that I chose the road. It was a sure thing. After running downhill for several miles, there was another entryway, and its map was intact. I was still almost ten miles from my house. Well, I wanted a good run.

Looking at the map, I saw the trail now ran parallel to the road. I chose to get back on the trail as it would go easier on my legs. As I got closer to home, I started to see other runners.

The gate to the back of our house was in sight when I noticed an orange flash running through the woods. It was some sort of animal, but it was big. It disappeared so quickly I had no idea what it was. I wasn't even certain that I had seen anything.

I showered and went in for breakfast. Since I had run so far, everyone else was finishing up. I filled a plate from the sideboard and joined the family.

The boys were excited about something in the paper. I looked over at the headline to see what had them excited.

Uh-oh, a Bengal tiger had escaped from a small local zoo. Was that what I saw? Then I started to wonder. Had I shut the back gate and locked it? To be safe, I went out to check.

I could see the gate was closed, but I could see that a ten-foot fence didn't mean a lot to a Bengal tiger as it was rummaging in our garbage can.

I returned to the kitchen door and saw Mrs. Hernandez talking to the cook.

"Mrs. Hernandez, will you please find me the largest piece of meat you can?"

"Why?"

"I want to feed the tiger in our backyard. That should keep him there while you call the sheriff."

"Funny, Rick."

"I took her by the arm, led her to the back door, and pointed out the window."

"She let out a shriek that got the tiger's attention. It wandered over to check out things."

In the meantime, the cook, whose name I didn't know, handed me a ten-pound roast from the refrigerator.

"You can explain to Peg what you did with the roast."

I cracked the door open and tossed the roast to the tiger. It didn't hesitate at all. It nailed that roast in midair and settled in for a small feast.

In the meantime, Mrs. Hernandez had come about and had the sheriff's office on the phone.

Looking back at the tiger, I saw that the roast couldn't even be classified as a small feast as it was almost done with its meal.

I asked the cook for more meat.

She handed me a package of T-bone steaks. This was getting expensive fast.

I threw those out the door. If we kept this up, the tiger would be ready to move in with us.

Mrs. Hernandez had now summoned my parents, who the kids accompanied.

Of course, Denny and Eddie thought it was cool, and Mary wanted to keep the big kitty.

By now, the tiger had scarfed down the meat. It must have been content because it stretched out for a nap.

Dad had left the room and returned with a rifle that I had never seen before. At first, I thought it was a double-barreled shotgun.

Dad told me it was a .470 Nitro Express rifle by Holland and Holland. It was made for big-game hunting in Africa. You literally could kill an elephant with it.

Of course, this immediately upset Mary. Dad was quick to assure her that he would only use it if the tiger tried to come into the house.

"But what if it is only looking for more to eat?"

"I think its favorite food is little girls."

"Oh, then shoot the bugger!"

"Mary! Watch your language."

"Mum says it."

"That doesn't mean you can."

We were saved by a deputy sheriff arriving.

He took one look out the door and was pulling his service revolver. I don't know how he thought that might help.

Dad spoke up, "Son, that thing would just make him mad. Why don't we wait for a vet with a tranquilizer gun?"

"This one killed its keeper to escape. It has to be put down."

"Peg, take Mary to the front of the house."

When they had left, Dad asked the deputy if he wanted to use his rifle or if he should do the deed. After a moment's thought, the deputy decided it would be better if he pulled the trigger.

The tiger was still taking its nap, so the deputy took the time to call his office and reconfirm that the tiger needed to be taken down. It was. He had his facts straight.

The deputy opened the kitchen door and took careful aim at the tiger. When he pulled the trigger, a chain of events started. He missed! From twenty feet, he missed.

Secondly, the kick of the rifle was more than the deputy was expecting. He went down on his butt, and the rifle broke free from his grasp. I grabbed it in midair.

As I turned to look at the tiger, I saw more tiger than I ever wanted to see. It was now ten feet from me and getting ready to leap. Later, I flashed back to the bank robbery in Colorado as I reacted the same way. I held the rifle and fired. I was luckier than the deputy as I blew its head off. I mean it. The tiger's head was a ruin.

My holding onto the rifle was no better than the deputy's as I was also knocked on my butt, and it went flying. This time it was caught by Dad.

I've had adrenaline rushes before, but nothing like this.

The deputy and I, whose name I learned is George Burrill, both sat in chairs for a while shaking. Everyone there was excited. Denny ran to his room, brought his camera back, and took pictures of the tiger. All the others were talking a mile a minute.

I'll never forget Dad saying to Mum, "Now what do you think of boys and their toys?"

It was the only time I could remember Mum being at a loss for words. Apparently, she had given him some grief over buying that rifle.

With a start, I remembered something I had to do. I dialed Susan Wallace on the kitchen phone. Luckily, she caught it on the first ring in her office. I updated her on the events of the morning.

She told me she would have a reporter and photographer from the *LA Times* there as soon as possible.

Deputy Burrill called his office and let them know the tiger was down. He didn't give any details.

After he hung up, he told me the sheriff was on his way.

Dad called the front gate and let them know people would be arriving from the sheriff's department and the *LA Times*. "Let them in and escort them to the kitchen."

The first to arrive was the sheriff and another man. From the way Mum and Dad stood straight and looked at them, I figured out exactly which sheriff this was.

The sheriff was as surprised as they were.

"I didn't know you were those Jacksons."

The way he said it, it was their fault for not letting him know they were rich and famous.

The other guy had a camera with him and was taking pictures of the tiger.

The deputy was explaining events to the sheriff. The guy with the camera was now taking notes and started his own questions. He wanted it clear that I shot the tiger, not the deputy.

From Mum's glare, it didn't take a lot of guesswork to deduct that this was the newspaper guy. A look at Eddie confirmed it. The little guy sure could shoot daggers with his eyes.

The sheriff and newspaper guy didn't stay long. The sheriff told the deputy to contact the zoo that the tiger had escaped from to come to pick it up. They would know how to dispose of it.

During the next hour, things settled down. Cook provided coffee, sodas, and cookies as we sat around and rehashed events. From the deputy's perspective, he had missed with a strange weapon, losing it in the process. I had snatched it out of the air calmly and killed the tiger.

From my perspective, I got lucky in catching the rifle and took a desperation shot, which hit through no skill of my own.

From the looks on the faces of those present, they liked the deputy's version better.

We learned more about the rifle. It was made for big-game hunting in Africa. Dad had bought it on impulse at a charity auction he and Mum had attended. He had no use for it. He just thought it was neat. At least, he didn't have a use for it at the time he bought it. It was now going to be hung on the library wall in pride.

The reporter from the *Times* and a photographer showed up next. We had our stories down pat for him. You could tell he liked the deputy's version better than mine.

Of course, they had to stage the picture of me with the tiger, like I had been on a big-game hunt. They had to roll the tiger over, so the ruined side of his head didn't show.

Four people from the zoo arrived in cars and a truck. They were brought around back. While the tiger was being loaded into the truck, it took three zookeepers, the deputy, me, and the photographer to lift the beast. The only way we could do it was to place the tiger on a tarp and lift the edges of the tarp.

I was told they could come in as high as nine hundred pounds, but this was a lightweight at eight hundred and twenty-five. I would hate to meet a big one!

A faulty counterweight on a door had not let the door come down, so the tiger wasn't in a separate area when its keeper entered the area. It had mauled the keeper. It had even eaten some of the poor guy's arm.

The *LA Times* reporter was practically drooling over these events.

While we were doing this, Dad had been talking to the zoo director. At the end of their conversation, they shook hands. I wondered what deal had been struck.

Dad was busy. Next, he was having a long talk with Deputy Burrill. Dad handed him a business card when they were finishing up, and again they shook hands.

The rest of the day was unsettled, to say the least. After everyone had left, I was tired. I was never tired this early in the day. I told

Mum that, and she laughed at me. "How far did you run? How much excitement have you had? Go take a nap."

Now, I had not been sent for a nap for a long time, but with no argument, I went and slept for two hours.

Chapter 17

I spent the afternoon doing high school work. I was so immersed that I was able to get the morning events off my mind. After dinner, I spent some time with the kids watching Mr. Magoo. It was one of his theater cartoons. Eddie was excited that this week's *TV Guide* reported that there was going to be a regular cartoon on TV called the *Mr. Magoo Show*.

Dad stopped in and was surprised that they would allow Mr. Magoo on TV since he was so mean and nasty. That caused some discussion, as we thought he was just an addled old man. Dad watched for a few minutes and agreed that the character had changed from when he was younger.

I spent the evening with my flight manuals. When it was time for bed, I was out like a light.

My run on Thursday was nothing like Wednesday's, both in distance and ending.

When I joined the family for breakfast, I could tell something was happening.

Rather than saying anything, Dad handed me two newspapers, our local paper and the *LA Times*. The headline of the local section of the *LA Times* was, "Sir Rick saves his family from a man-eating tiger." The local paper's front-page headline was, "Jackson murders rare tiger."

The LA story was correct, well, correct as it could be. They took Deputy Burrill's version of the event rather than mine. The local rag had me murdering a poor defenseless tiger that had strayed into my backyard. In the last paragraph, there was a line about a zookeeper being reported as injured in the tiger's escape.

While the paper didn't outright lie, they twisted the facts to make me a villain. That really made me glad that I had called Susan right away. I was now a believer in what she had been telling me.'

To say that Mum and Dad weren't happy would be an understatement. There was also no question where Mary had learned the word bugger. I just hoped Mary didn't know what it meant.

I said, "The Russian option is looking better to me."

Denny asked, "What's the Russian option?"

"Not an option at this time," replied Dad.

From the look on Mum's face, I'm not sure she agreed.

The conversation went nowhere after that. Denny cornered me in the hall and asked about the Russian option.

"Violence, Denny, full-on violence, and that's all I'm going to say."

Fortunately, he let it go at that.

I thought it would do me good to get out of the house, so I drove over to the studio. I was quickly surrounded by the entire stunt crew in the stunt area. I could see that I hadn't thought things through.

They all wanted to know about the tiger and me. They had seen both the *LA Times* and the local rag, so they wanted to know the real story. It took some time, but we finally had the story told and rehashed. Several of the guys had been on actual tiger hunts and told me that I had no idea how lucky I was to be alive.

I had no problem agreeing with that.

The next couple of hours were spent with a sword and bow. Mr. Palmer felt it was too soon after the tiger event to go hand-to-hand. He said that adrenaline could kick up several days after an event and have unfortunate consequences.

I had lunch with the guys and then headed out for my flying lessons.

The lesson went fine. I was feeling more comfortable all the time. I did the pre-flight walk-around, then taxied the plane to the take-off position, got permission from the control tower, and took off.

I flew in lazy circles for a while, then, with the tower's permission, did some touch and goes. I was feeling pretty smug about the whole thing when Mr. McGarry reached over and turned the engine off.

Yeah, Mr. Palmer was right about adrenaline spikes. My blood pressure must have gone off the chart.

Then my brain kicked in, and I restarted the motor.

The whole incident hadn't lasted more than seconds, so the plane had only lost a little altitude. I told Mr. McGarry it might be best if we landed.

He raised an eyebrow but took over the stick and brought us in.

Once we were on the ground, I told him that he apparently didn't read the newspaper. From the look on his face, he hadn't.

When I explained what happened yesterday, he broke out into a grin.

"All that, and you still reacted correctly, son. You are going to be a good pilot. I knew guys who were stone-cold killers in the air during the war but put them through something like an advancing tiger, and they would have been useless for a week."

We then went back into the office, and he spent the next hour grilling me on my studies. Then he had me take a written test.

"Now get back in the plane, take off, circle the field once, and land."

I didn't think about it. I did another walk around to make certain something hadn't fallen off and got back in the plane. I buckled up and was waiting for him to join me.

He didn't. He just rotated his arm to tell me to go! And so, I soloed.

There is no way to describe my feelings after taxiing back to the school. I thought jumping from a plane would cause a high. I know getting attacked by a tiger was, but the grin on my face was so wide it's a wonder my grin didn't meet in the back of my neck, making my head fall right off.

As I got ready to leave, he presented me with a certificate that he had made up in advance, celebrating my first solo flight.

I couldn't get home fast enough to share this with my family.

It certainly was a more cheerful dinner than last night. Dad told us Operation Green Stick was underway. Since Eddie had a greenstick fracture, that had become the family code name for our revenge. We were under no illusions. This was revenge, pure, plain, and simple.

There was Green Stick School, the purchase of Tucker Academy, Green Stick elections to rid us of the politicians, and Green Stick newspaper, the purchase of a competing paper, and putting the local rag out of business.

After dinner, I tore into my flight books with a renewed interest.

Friday started with a good run through a slight misting rain. It was actually pleasant. It wasn't one of those man, oh man, it pours. After breakfast, I decided to spend the morning at flight school and then go to my every Friday business update meeting.

I had just settled in with my ground-school books when Mary burst into my room. The open door was probably the only reason it remained on its hinges. Recently, she had become a high-energy kid. She wouldn't walk if she could run. She wouldn't run if she could ride her bike at breakneck speeds. I shuddered to think if she could drive.

"Rick, Mum wants you to come to reception. You have a visitor at the gatehouse."

I stood up to go, but she held up her hand for me to wait. She picked up my phone and dialed security at the front gate.

"Scott, this is Mary. What can you tell me about our recent arrival?" I could only hear her side of the conversation.

"Oh, what is that?

"Okay, what else?

"Why do you say that?

"Oh, okay, thanks.

Mary turned to me.

"The man arrived in a car with a federal government license plate, but it is a pool car, so that is no help. He has a Virginia driver's license. Scott says he doesn't carry himself uptight like an FBI agent, so he is probably a spook. Since it is a Virginia license, there is a good chance he is CIA."

"Squirt, where and why did you learn to do this, and how do you know the names of the guards at the front gate?"

"Mummy says that, if possible, you should know about new people coming into your life. You must know and be kind to your guards. They might save your life at the cost of their own."

I wondered what sort of girl Mum was raising.

A glance in the mirror told me I was fairly presentable, so I headed downstairs to the front room we called the reception.

When I entered, there was Mum with a tall gentleman dressed in a suit and tie. His hat was on the table next to him. While I didn't have that much experience with the FBI, he didn't give off that aura. As a matter of fact, looking at him, he was very bland. Must be a spook!

Mum settled it quickly when she introduced me to Mr. Rip Robertson. He introduced himself in a soft Texas accent. While he held out his hand politely, I had the impression that he didn't care about meeting me, one way or the other.

That impression was confirmed when he told me, "I have to train you to notice and be able to evade a tail. I don't know why I was picked, but I want to get this done as soon as possible so that I can get back to my real work."

He wasn't facing Mum when he made this statement, so he didn't see her lips tighten.

Robertson said, "This will take every day next week, four hours a day. We will go from eight in the morning till noon. Be ready Monday."

Mum's look had now turned to stone but quickly changed to a smile as he turned to her.

"Lady Jackson, I don't know what strings were pulled, but I will do the job and move on."

"I'm certain you will do a good job."

He nodded to her and, ignoring me, left. It was obvious he had never heard Mum talk before. It was not a compliment when she told him he would do a good job. It was an order.

After he left, she told me to be ready on Monday and that she had a few phone calls to make.

I went back to my books, but it took a while for me to be able to concentrate. Spy stuff! I thought I would call the studio and tell them I wouldn't be at the beach on Monday.

Chapter 18

After lunch, I drove down to my office. This time I had a key to the back door, so it was easy to get in.

There was a small crowd waiting. They had taken me up on my offer to have a meet and greet with their family and friends. Jim Williamson had talked to the studio, and they had a stack of pictures for me to sign and had sent a photographer along.

It was a little awkward getting started. Despite many public appearances, I wasn't used to walking into a room full of strangers and meeting them. Jim helped a lot. He took me by the arm and introduced me to each worker. They, in turn, introduced me to their friends and family.

We had half a dozen employees who had brought around four people each. This made for a group of thirty people. It took about half an hour for the introductions. While this was going on, a dessert tray and a selection of soda pop, coffee, and tea were unveiled.

This gave people something to do as I met each group. The story about the tiger in the paper was an easy topic of conversation for all, that and what was my next movie. That made it a lot easier for me. I found quickly that people wanted to talk but didn't want to get personal with me. I was fine with that.

After working my way around the room, I sat at a desk with the pictures ready to autograph.

Not that I really noticed, but several cute girls looked the right age in the crowd. Actually, there were four of them, three brunettes and one blonde. I would describe them as all as attractive and having good shapes. Not that I noticed.

Three of the girls were standing in line together. They talked to each other but spent a lot of time looking my way and flipping their hair. When their turn came, each of them gushed at me. They were so thrilled to meet me. I was more handsome in person than on the screen.

In their own ways, the girls let me know they were available for dates. Each of them, in their own way, totally put me off. I was polite and signed the pictures as they requested but did not take any of the offers extended.

While I was signing, I noticed a cup of coffee had appeared on the table, so I took a sip. Whoever did it knew I liked my coffee black. It was a small cup, more like a teacup rather than the large mugs I used, so it went quickly. When it was empty, a small hand replaced it with another full cup.

I glanced up; it was the fourth girl. She gave me a shy smile and turned away.

After the signing, which took almost an hour because not only were there requests from those present, but they also wanted others made out for family and friends who weren't there.

Next was the photography session. This was done with family groups and individuals. It took another hour. I didn't know Sam Nielsen, the photographer, had been sent over, but he seemed to have his act together. He had a screen set up for us to stand in front of and lighting set up. It reminded me of how prom pictures were done.

He had a notebook, and as each shot was taken, he would write down the name of the person at the office who would receive the pictures; once developed, they would be returned to the office to be handed out. After that, distribution to individuals was the responsibility of the office worker.

When the three babbling nitwits, as I thought of them, had their pictures taken, I had to actually move their hands to prevent highly inappropriate pictures from being taken. The studio photographer saw what was going on, stopped the action, and staged their shots.

Afterward, I thanked him for his help. He told me that it was a common problem with sessions like this. The last thing the studio wanted was salacious pictures to get out, at least ones they wouldn't profit from. That bit of cynicism made me laugh.

As he was starting to put his equipment away, I saw the young lady who had been pouring my coffee standing in a corner by herself. I realized that she had not had her picture taken with me.

I asked the photographer to wait.

I walked over to her and apologized first for not getting her name. She looked me in the eye and told me, "Emily Weeks." As she did this, she held out her hand and gave me a firm handshake. Why had I thought this girl was shy?

"Emily, you haven't had a picture with me. Would you like one?"

"Not really, no disrespect, but I'm not a fan. Not that I dislike you, I just haven't paid attention to your work, so I don't see the point in one."

"Well, I certainly won't try to force one on you. May I ask, what does interest you?"

"Right now, I am studying for my pilot's license. I'm almost ready to start flying."

I think I'm in love. That started the conversation. I quickly found out that Emily was in the tenth grade and sixteen years old. She went to Santa Ana High, which is south of LA near Disneyland. She played the clarinet in the school marching band.

Her aunt had invited her along, and she came as it got her out of school for the day, not that she cared about meeting me. After she said that, she blushed.

"That didn't come out right, Rick."

"That's okay. I understand what you were saying."

We then discussed our flying lessons, preferences in planes, and why. She was happy right now with a high-wing, single-engine, while I was leaning towards a low-wing with twin engines. We both agreed that tricycle landing gear was better than a taildragger.

We had been talking for about fifteen minutes when I remembered that there were other people here I should be talking to. Before I left her, I got her home phone number. She told me that her parents would let her take calls up to nine o'clock on school nights.

As I was leaving her, she changed her mind about an autographed picture. She wanted it to show her friends that she had met me. I signed it to a fellow pilot.

I rejoined Jim and finished making the rounds and talking to people. Jim commented.

"That is a cute young lady you were talking to."

"Yeah, that is Emily Weeks. Her aunt Alice works here."

"I know who she is, Rick. I think our employee relations will be good there from the time you spent with her."

I blushed red.

I muttered, "Doing my job."

He let me off the hook with that. I did make a point of talking to Alice Thompson. She was a little reserved with me but was polite. The event wound down. Jim thought it was a great success with my employees. He did give me a five-minute rundown on the financial end of things. Our burn rate of cash was not faster than our income. From that, I took it that we were making money.

I thanked him for all his efforts. I realized that he was acting more as the office manager than just an accountant. I made a mental note to discuss giving him a promotion. I needed to talk it over with Dad.

After returning home, I dug into my flight manuals with renewed vigor. I needed to get my license.

I changed the pace after dinner and did some schoolwork. I was on track to finish the tenth grade by the New Year. I didn't want to lose my momentum.

Later in bed, I read about the murder of a fetologist and was pleased with how Baley and Olivaw solved it.

I had no plans or commitments for Saturday, so I planned on a lazy day. I started out with an easy five-mile run and did all my exercises. After a shower and breakfast, I decided I should touch up my tan, so I headed to the elevator to go to the tower.

When I got to the elevator, the sign was out, so I decided to go to the public basement and shoot pool. When I went into the room, there were five little girls with hula hoops. My plans for the day changed once again, and I took a drive down to the pier at Santa Monica. I tried not to picture Mum up on the tower. Now Anna and Sharon were a different story.

I kicked around at the pier but couldn't get interested in anything, so I went back home. In my room, I noticed a note on my dresser. It was Emily Week's phone number which I had dropped there when I emptied my pockets.

On a whim, I called her home. After identifying myself with her mother, I was allowed to speak to Emily. We told each other how much we enjoyed our meeting. She commented that it would be nice to see me again.

Now I am as dense as any other teenage boy, but some signals can't be missed.

"Emily, would you like to go out next Friday?"

I won't say squeal, but there was excitement in her, "Yes!"

She immediately calmed down and let me know that she was only allowed on a car date on a double date and that her curfew on weekends was eleven o'clock.

That works for me. Do you know another couple we could double date with? I asked her that because the only person I knew to ask would be Sharon Bronson. First of all, it would be too childish for Sharon, and second, Emily's parents would have kittens.

Fortunately, Emily's best friend would be able to go. We agreed on a dinner date and movie, dinner being a hamburger place, and then a movie. I told her it would be my treat for everyone.

Later that night, I thought to tell Mum and Dad that I had a date next Friday. Now I had been living in California on my own, was in business, and basically used to living my own life, so I didn't think it would be a big deal.

Before the questions ended, I was glad Mum hadn't gotten out the rubber hoses, which I was certain she had hidden somewhere.

They weren't upset or anything. This was just a new departure for me, and they wanted to know as much as they could. Out of nowhere, Mary announced she could always drink hot chocolate.

That answered that question. Mum did have the grace to look away for a moment. I winked at Mary, who giggled.

Then I was back to my studies, as Dad said, "No rest for the wicked."

Chapter 19

Monday, after my run and exercises, I contacted the studio to let them know that I would be missing in action from the beach. I also pointed out that I would work at home to keep my tan. I also asked them to pass a message to the stunt yard that I had a change of plans but should be in next week.

I was dressed and waiting at the front entrance for Mr. Robertson, who was punctual. We went to downtown LA, and he proceeded to teach me how to spot a tail. The biggest trick was to look behind you without it being noticeable that you were looking. This meant using every reflective surface possible and being unobtrusive when turning around.

This was combined with looking at who was behind you and remembering them for second looks. This part was the hardest for me. I hadn't realized how little I really looked at my surroundings. He called this situational awareness. While training me, he was rather focused and a little short-tempered as he dropped into instructor mode.

I couldn't believe how mentally tired I was when he dropped me off at Jackson House.

His parting words were, "There will be a real tail tomorrow, so you must pay attention. Though I think teaching you is a waste of my time."

That statement certainly made me feel better. I must be wasting this man's time for him to have such an attitude.

After lunch, I went up to the tower, and thankfully there were no signs posted, so I sunbathed for an hour to keep toned up. I then drove to the studio to see if anything was happening. I was no sooner in the stunt area than I was drafted into being an extra in a movie. They needed someone my height to be a Roman soldier. It was that, or a shorter guy stands on a box, which they could do, but part of the scene was marching the prisoner along, and it would take a while to set up.

Last week I spent five minutes getting into costume and ten minutes in makeup. It was almost no time to get dressed and take five minutes in makeup. The scene took all of ten minutes to shoot. I asked why they were a person short. The director's assistant pointed to a corner where a drunk was sleeping it off.

"He was celebrating his career in movies. This was his first and now the last opportunity."

After the scene, I was heading back to costume to disrobe when an office boy found me.

"Mr. Monroe heard you were here. He wants you in his office right now."

"Give me a minute to change."

"He told me right now, so change later."

We headed over to Mr. Monroe's office. His secretary Donna told me to go right in.

As I went past her, I heard, "I always like a man in uniform."

I looked back to see a smirk.

When I entered the office, Mr. Monroe looked up. From the startled look on his face, you could tell he had not been expecting me to be in costume.

"Aren't we paying you enough, Rick?"

"Yes, sir. I mean you are paying me enough. They were short an extra, so I filled in. As a matter of fact, I didn't even sign the paperwork to get the standard day rate."

"Do that before you leave, or you will never see the money. You know how those studios are. Why didn't you change before you came over?"

"The guy you sent wouldn't let me take the time."

He shook his head at that.

"I asked him to ask you to stop by before you left. These young kids get so wrapped up in things and don't listen."

"You realize that young kid is probably ten years older than I am?"

"He may be older in years, but that's it. I need to hire more mature people. Anyway, I asked you to stop by because the team would like to invite you to their next presentation a week from Friday at three in the afternoon. They have fully implemented the core team concept you helped them develop.

"I know you really developed it and then led them to discover the concept themselves. You know I can never repay you for that. They have blossomed as a team. It is all coming together. I can tell you this. We now have recovered from the financial losses caused by having to sell our theaters. It has put us ahead of the competition.

"Not that the competition are dummies, Rick. You may have single-handedly saved the movie industry or at least given us a business model that works."

"I will be there at the meeting, but I'm not sure I did that much. Yes, as a member of the team, I brought forward the extra-board concept from the railroad. Someone else developed it a long time ago. That and facilitated the team into coming up with a solution."

"Yes, but you did it, not someone else. Now on to more important matters, Nina says hello. She is having a wonderful time at school in Switzerland but does miss you."

"Tell her I said 'hi' back."

"I will. I think it is fair to tell you that she is dating a boy she met there."

"I understand. I wouldn't expect anything different. We were just doing some high school fun dates. Neither of us thought it was going anywhere serious."

'Are you seeing anyone, Rick?"

"I have a first date with a girl this Friday. Other than that, no."

"Well, enjoy yourself."

"I suspect I will see you later."

After returning home, it was back to the books, both school and flight.

I was nervous Tuesday morning when we started our walk through downtown LA. It took an hour, but I finally described a man who I thought was tailing me. Mr. Robertson shook his head. The next guy I was to identify as a tail took me until lunchtime to spot. It turned out it was the same man who had a reversible jacket.

Mr. Robertson was really encouraging.

"I was beginning to wonder if you would ever spot him. Don't take this up as a living because I don't think you would live very long."

Boy was that good for my ego. I became determined to do better tomorrow.

I went home for lunch. Mum was there and quizzed me on my morning. I told her about Robertson's comments. She didn't say anything, but I could tell she wasn't pleased. The question was, was it with Robertson or with me? Rather than fret about it, I asked her directly.

"Mum, am I too slow at picking this up?"

"No, Rick, you aren't. The fact that you were able to figure them out at all on your first outing is good. Mr. Robertson appears to think it is below him to teach you. Let's see how this plays out."

Flight lessons after the morning were wonderful. Mr. McGarry took me through my paces in the air while quizzing me the whole time. He kept asking what I would do if various inflight emergencies occurred. At one point, he spun the plane, and I had to recover. We lived.

As we flew, he had me talk about each move out loud as I told him what I was doing and why. This included letting him know that I was aware of my surroundings, especially all aircraft in our area. I didn't realize how many private planes were flying around us until I had to keep track of them. I figured that my neck size would grow. I had read that it happened to the surviving pilots in the Battle of Britain.

One thing for certain, when I bought my own airplane, I would see about radar. I voiced that thought to Mr. McGarry, a bad idea. He went to great lengths to explain how technology was a help, not a crutch, and that Murphy's Law was alive and well. When I needed that radar the most, it would fail. Get used to looking around.

Just before dinner, I received a phone call from Susan Wallace. Jack Paar had heard of the tiger incident and wanted me to appear on the *Tonight Show*. I explained how busy I was and that the weekend was the only time I had free. She told me she would check on something and call me back.

Within fifteen minutes, she called with a proposal. I would fly to New York Saturday afternoon, tape a segment Sunday morning, and then fly home.

This seemed like a lot of work, but Susan convinced me I shouldn't pass up the chance to be on the *Tonight Show*. It certainly would give me more exposure. When I told Mum and Dad the plan, they thought it would work.

It was interesting; I could decide to fly across the continent and back, and they didn't care. Announce I was going on a date with a girl my age, and they were all over it!

I went to bed a little early and slept all night. I think the thought of the coming weekend made me tired.

Chapter 20

Wednesday was more of the same. It took me almost two hours this time to spot my tail. I asked what I was doing wrong.

"Your tail put on and took off his jacket three times, so you never noticed him. You can quit anytime, you know."

I just loved the encouragement and support I was getting.

After lunch, I went for another long run. I could tell I was getting frustrated and needed to clear my head. Even after running, I was still frustrated, so I did sit-ups, push-ups, and pull-ups until I couldn't do anymore. My arms were like rubber. I hadn't kept count, but I think I may have set some personal bests.

After another shower, I hit the books. I was still slightly ahead of schedule on the lesson plan I had been given. I got kind of lucky in a history chapter. It was on the Ohio Valley American Indians. I did that work in no time.

I spent several hours typing up the essays I had for English. One thing is for certain. I would never be a writer. I would rather be out doing things than sitting at a typewriter. I had read about the future of computers in *Popular Mechanics*. They predicted I would be using them to do my homework.

I could picture that happening with the advent of the transistor, but not for a long time. That kid I pulled out of the water at the Santa Monica pier would be lucky to see it in his lifetime.

I bulled my way through that work and then got on to my newest delight, flying.

The flying textbooks were so interesting that they had to summon me for dinner. The more I studied the theory of flight and its mechanics, the more I enjoyed it. But that all paled with the thought of being up in the sky.

At bedtime, I read about an ex-vacuum cleaner salesman named Wormold. He should have stayed selling vacuum cleaners. He did know his Shakespeare. Actually, I doubt if I would have done as well as he did.

Thursday was a nightmare; it was eleven-thirty until I realized that my "tail" was in front of me.

Robertson wasn't kind in his remarks. I know he didn't want this assignment, but he must never have heard of grin and bear it.

After lunch, I went over to the studio for the afternoon. I spent time at the archery butts and talked one of the stuntmen into some swordplay. At least, I thought it was a stuntman. I should have guessed he was too old for that.

We started slowly, so I made the mistake of taunting him. The next thing you know, my sword was in the dust, and he was at my throat. I was smart enough to keep my mouth shut after that. He was kind enough to give me some tips and even walked me slowly through some moves.

After showing me, he would take me through them at quarter speed, then half-speed, then full-on.

Man, for an old guy, he had reflexes. Every time I thought I had his measure, he would disarm me. I should have been embarrassed, but it was so much fun I didn't bother. We gathered an audience along the way. As people walked by, they would stop. By the time it was done, there was a crowd of twenty or so.

After an hour, he came to a halt and told me he had an appointment. We shook hands, but he didn't give his name. I didn't push it. Anyone that good with a sword could do what he wanted, at least as far as I was concerned.

Dick Wyman was there. He came over, shaking his head.

He started with, "Rick, you're a lucky SOB."

"How come?"

"You just crossed swords with the greatest swordsman in the movies! Didn't you know?"

"No, I didn't. I thought he was a stuntman; then realized that he was too old, and then I was too busy fighting for my life!"

"Well, you just crossed swords with the greatest swordsman in Hollywood and maybe the world."

"There is no question he is great; I didn't have a prayer. My reach is greater; I'm faster, and he made me look like a chump."

"Not a chump Rick, more like a student, mind you, a good student, but one never-the-less."

On the way home, I thought about how I would present it to my parents. I decided on nonchalantly. It played out exactly as I wanted. At dinner, I was asked about my day.

I filled them in on the disaster of the morning. Then I told them I went to the studio for some swordplay. I wound up fighting some old guy. He was fairly good.

I have never seen Dad sputter before.

"You fought with whom I think you did?"

"Probably; for an old guy, he sure is good."

I guess that was over the top because Mum gave me a head slap. It didn't really hurt, but it did get my attention. I had seen her do that to a friend of Eddie's when he mouthed off a little. I don't think Mark will forget that very soon. But I was surprised when she did it to me. Matter of fact, I don't think I will forget it soon.

When we were finished eating, Mary handed each of us boys a written invitation to a tea party starting in one hour. She had hand-printed them on Mum's best stationery. A glance at Mum and I knew that she was in on this; otherwise, Mary would be hearing about the use of her paper.

The invitation was for tea. It stated formal dress, RSVP, and signed your Loving Sister Mary.

Denny was about to kick up a row, but a glance from Dad stopped that. Instead, we all filed to our rooms to get dressed. I put on my best London suit and vest, figuring I might as well go all out.

Both Denny and Eddie did us proud, wearing suits and ties. From the neatness of the tie, I'm certain they had help from one of the parents.

The tea was to be held in the reception, so I made my way there on time. Mary was there, along with Mum and Dad. All were dressed to the nines. We had just sat down, and a maid brought in tea. Another had a plate of dessert cookies and cakes. This was a real tea.

Mary thanked all of us for coming. Now we boys aren't totally dense, so we were on our best behavior. I asked Mary what the occasion was for.

She replied, "This is a practice for when I have my friends over for tea. I want to be able to do it right. I had to obtain Mum's permission, arrange a menu with the cook, and write the invitations. This was more work than I thought."

"So, we are your guinea pigs?"

"Yes, I wouldn't want to practice on my friends. Boys don't care if things go wrong."

"So, I won't be invited to tea anymore?"

Mary got a pensive look on her face.

"Rick, I don't want you to feel bad, but you are really too old to be having tea with five and six-year-olds."

"I think you are right. Maybe we could go out to dinner when you are older."

"Yes, I would like that. I can't go to any of the good places yet because it would be past my bedtime."

"Okay, Squirt, when you are all grown up, maybe ten?"

"Oh, I would think by the time I'm eight."

Eddie had to jump in and spoil this conversation.

"Rick, girls have cooties. You don't want to go out with her."

Dad can do a head slap as well as Mum.

"I would be delighted to take the beautiful Mary out to dinner when she is older."

After that, we spent time talking about how good the desserts were. Since there weren't any left, they must have been good. I wouldn't know as I only had three cookies and two slices of cake.

Later, when I returned to my room, I placed Mary's invitation to tea with other items I wished to keep.

Friday was the worst day of all. I never spotted my tail. When I asked, he laughed.

"There wasn't any. I wanted to show you what it would be like most of the time when you thought you were being tailed."

He went in with me when we returned to Jackson House. Mum was waiting in the reception room.

"Lady Jackson, I have finished my assignment. He has only shown a modest aptitude for spotting a tail. I didn't bother to teach him evasion as he won't be able to evade what he can't see. "

"Thank you, Mr. Robertson, for your valuable time."

"You're welcome."

I started to hold out my hand and thank him, but he abruptly turned and left.

"What a rude man," I exclaimed.

"I agree. That makes what is going to happen next most pleasurable."

"What's that?"

"Next week, I will teach you evasion and refine your ability to spot a tail. I suppose I should have done that in the first place. I will certainly be working later with the other children."

"How will that affect Mr. Robertson?"

"In a little while, he will be calling his office to report his task as complete. He will find he is going to spend the next six weeks teaching other agents how to tail. Their target will be you. He shall have to follow while you lead them all on a merry chase."

Note to self, do not irritate Mum.

Chapter 21

I spent an hour in the office catching up on business. Well, five minutes on business and the rest rehashing last week's open house. The business part was good. Our first full shipment of cargo containers was on its way to Argentina to be picked up by Howell Freight.

I promptly arrived at Emily's home in Santa Anna at 6:30 on Friday night. I had dressed in California casual sports coat, polo shirt, and slacks. The convertible top was down, so I felt pretty sharp when I pulled into their driveway.

I was mentally ready to meet her parents and undergo that awkward introduction. It was as bad as I thought it would be. Bob and Sharon Weeks came across as easy-going people. I suspect that is because Emily had two older sisters in college, and they had rounded the edges off her parents. That was until Emily told me she had to change her sweater.

That gave her father an opportunity to lead me to the kitchen to talk. Why was I nervous all of a sudden? That was quickly dispelled when her dad winked at me and whispered.

"Rick, this is something I have always threatened to do, but I think you are enough of a good sport for it to work."

At that, we sat down at the kitchen table, and he unfolded a cloth where a 45 Colt semi-automatic lay disassembled.

He continued to whisper. "The girls will kill me for this, but I always said I would talk to Emily's boyfriend while cleaning a weapon."

I laughed lightly. Did it have a hint of nerves in it? You bet it did. Mr. Weeks, no longer Bob to me, continued, "Our rules are pretty simple. Emily is allowed out until eleven o'clock on Friday and Saturday nights, with no dates during the week. Sunday afternoons end at dinner time. No phone calls after eight o'clock in the evening.

You must always tell us where you are going and call if there is a change of plans. Oh yes, always with another couple until Emily is seventeen. She will turn sixteen in two months. Any problem with these rules?"

"No, sir."

"Good, now I just saw Emily and her mom peek through the doorway, so she is ready. When she asks, tell her I wanted to know your intentions."

Keeping an eye on the weapon he had just reassembled, I nodded yes. Thankfully, the magazine wasn't loaded.

Her next-door neighbor Jill Thompson and her boyfriend Bill Spurgeon had joined Emily in the living room. We couldn't get out of the house fast enough to a chorus of drive carefully, don't be late, and call if there is trouble.

Emily had a conniption over her dad's actions. I first relayed to her what I had been told to say. After that, in fear for my life from her dad, I told her about the actual conversation. It calmed her down a little. I don't think I wanted to be her father tomorrow morning. As a matter of fact, I wondered how the conversation was going home. Some ideas, while sounding funny, were better to think of than put into practice.

I don't think I will tell Mum about his having a weapon.

As far as dates went, it was uneventful. Not that I was an expert on dates, not having had many. We first went to a drive-in and had pizza in the car. This was an excuse for us to talk and get to know each other. Of course, they all seemed well-versed on my life. I didn't know it was so exciting.

I made certain to ask questions about their lives. They didn't understand that their supposedly normal boring lives were only something I had seen from the outside. I had had a little taste of it in Bellefontaine, and it sounded wonderful.

I found out that none of them were in what was considered the in-crowd at school. Emily played the clarinet in the marching band, while Jill played the sax.

Bill's claim to fame was an active membership in the local historical society. He loved to research the early settlers of the area. This seemed weird to me at first until I remembered Chief Blackhoof and how fascinating his story was.

As we were eating our pizza in the car with the top down, I noticed that a lot of kids were making a point of slowing down and saying, "Hi," to Emily or Jill. A few guys even talked to Bill at what seemed to be the urging of the girls in the car with them.

As the other cars pulled away, I could only hear snatches of the conversation. Words like a movie star, Knight, tiger, see in her. You could tell from their smiles that Emily and Jill heard most of it and were happy young ladies. It seems a few slights and scores over the years were being settled tonight.

Bill wanted to know all about the tiger incident. I gave them the short version; well, there really wasn't a long version. When I told them I was flying to New York on Saturday night to tape an appearance on the *Tonight Show*, they quieted down. I had intimidated them without trying.

I changed to the conversation about flying lessons and how I thought it was cool that Emily was learning to fly. The fact that I had just soloed was impressive but more in the realm of what was real to them. They thought twenty hours before soloing was a little long but acceptable. You could tell they felt Emily was superior on that issue.

Now Bill and Jill had never flown, and Emily hadn't soloed yet, but I wasn't going to bring that up. You could just feel their need to be ahead in something. I could understand that and took it all in stride.

After dinner, we debated going to a drive-in movie or the youth center. Bill was all for the drive-in. Jill followed Emily's lead in the youth center. I had the feeling that Emily wasn't ready to neck with me. That may have been presumptuous to think that, but since nobody knew what was playing at the drive-in, I don't think I was wrong.

I followed the girls' lead. I wasn't looking for a make-out session. I wanted some normal friends. Now don't get me wrong, I am all for making out.

After eating, we did something I had never heard of before. We went to a shopping mall. I was told this was the coming thing in shopping. The Fashion Square Mall opened last year. It was built onto Bullock's department store. It was interesting walking around the stores and looking in the windows. After a while, Neiman Marcus, The Broadway, Harris & Frank, Desmond's, and J.J. Candies looked the same to me.

I wanted to go into the candy store, but they dragged me into the tearoom at Bullock's. We had PB&J sandwiches. They were awesome!

The real reason for going there was quickly apparent. There were kids from everywhere. This was the cool place to be on Friday night. The rec center was history; this is where it was at. I think I was introduced to the student bodies of at least three or four high schools. Emily and Jill were taking full advantage of my fame.

Bill and I just went with the flow. He was a cool guy.

A few of the girls we met tried to be extra friendly, but Emily had her territory well-guarded. I thought it was cute of her. First, she was my date, so I wouldn't be rude and pay attention to other girls. Secondly, she was the cutest one I had met.

A couple of flashy blondes were cheerleader types that thought they were hot stuff. Flashy was the thing that turned me off. When I thought of Mum, Anna, and Sharon, who were the best-looking women I knew, they all were classy looking, not flash. Emily was that same type of understated good looks. Like Audrey Hepburn.

After a while, we guys let the girls know enough was enough. We decided to cruise down South Bristol Street between McFadden and Warner. Traffic was slow, so we were able to talk to kids in the cars in the next lane. Of course, I had the usual offer to race for pinks but wasn't dumb enough to do it.

While we cruised, we listened to the radio about the "British Kept a-Coming," "12th Street and Vine," "A Purple Hat," and "Something Told a Tale on You."

Around ten-thirty, we headed back to Emily's house. I enjoyed the company, but the evening wasn't really that much fun. I hoped that future dates would be better. I guess that answered a question. I was thinking of future dates.

After dropping off Bill and Jill, we headed back to Emily's. After seeing the kiss Jill laid on Bill, I couldn't wait to get to Emily's front door.

It wasn't to be. Her very harassed-looking Dad met us at the front door. I wasn't even given an opportunity to try for a good night kiss.

"Rick, I owe you an apology for my actions earlier this evening."

I had to think for a moment.

"You mean the gun-cleaning stunt?"

"Yes, I was way out of line. Sharon has really let me know about it. Your parents took it in a better spirit than she did."

"My parents?"

"Sharon made me call them and apologize. Your mother asked if the weapon was locked and loaded. I told her it was disassembled and not loaded. After that, she asked what the big deal was. Your dad loved the idea and can't wait for your little sister to start dating. Anyway, I'm sorry I did that."

"Uh, that's okay. I took it in the spirit you intended."

I thought, I could have taken you apart three times before you could reassemble it and load it.

Since I was in the house, I got involved in the debriefing for where we went, who we saw, and all the other details. How Emily could remember who wore what I'll never know.

Mr. Weeks and I bowed out quickly and retired to the kitchen. Over a Coke, he told me he was sorry that his wife got upset, not sorry that he did it. We both agreed that it was a good time-honored tradition and should be continued. After that, we had a serious conversation about my coming year.

He was all for Emily getting her pilot's license. It was a family tradition starting with her grandmother, who was the first woman to win the Bendix trophy. We discussed how my lessons were going. He thought that Mr. McGarry had waited too long for me to solo. Many pilots would be doing it in ten hours, not twenty.

He asked what McGarry's credentials were. I didn't know and told him the only thing that seemed different was his flight jacket.

When I described the Chinese lettering and tiger with wings, he told me, "Listen to him very carefully. If he wanted you to take twenty hours, that was right."

Before I could ask what was so important about a tiger with wings, the ladies joined us. Emily was allowed to walk me to my car. There I got that good night kiss. It wasn't as hot and steamy as Bill and Jill, but nice. We must have lingered too long because the porch lights started flashing.

With a giggle, Emily headed in, and I drove home.

Chapter 22

At breakfast in the morning, I was quizzed about my evening. I hadn't had as many questions about hitchhiking across America or sailing the Atlantic. My standard answers of fine and good didn't cut it. Mum led the interrogation, but I could tell Dad was paying attention behind his paper.

They both chuckled as I told them about Mr. Weeks cleaning his weapon while telling me their dating rules for Emily. Dad added that when Mary started dating, he would be cleaning his Holland & Holland. From the look Mum gave him, I wouldn't bet on it.

After breakfast, I decided to go for a swim.

Last week I was running from girls with hula hoops. This week, I was swimming in the outside pool. As I climbed out of the water, a flashbulb went off in my face. Mary had taken a picture with a big old camera like the reporters in 1930s movies carried.

"What are you doing, Squirt?"

"I'm a papa rats' eye. Since you are famous, I'm going to sell your picture for a whole bunch of money."

There is no way this could have a good ending!

"Who are you going to sell it to?"

"My friend Tara's dad has a magazine and told us he would buy our pictures."

"Where's Tara?"

With that question, Mary got a funny look on her face.

"I don't think I should tell you."

"I will find out, and then what?"

"She is hiding in your bedroom."

"We need to talk to Mum."

We stopped by my bedroom. Tara was huddled down beside my dresser. She told me she was hoping for a picture of my buns. Her dad paid top dollar for buns.

Sororicide was sounding better and better.

This time Mum was frowning when she heard the story. Tara was taken home by our driver rather than waiting for hers. I doubted if we would see much of her in the future. Mary knew she was in hot water, so she sat there trying to look innocent and cute. There is no question about the cuteness. Innocence is another question.

After some thought, Mum said, "I am going to check something out. In the meantime, Mary, ask Denny if he will develop your film. You will pay out of your allowance if he wants to charge for it."

Denny was a sport and didn't charge Mary. After my initial shock, I decided she hadn't done anything wrong. Why shouldn't she make some money off me, the papa rats' eyes were. I loved the way she said that.

Okay, I love my sister. I will kill her some other day or push her into the swimming pool, whichever comes first.

Later in the afternoon, Mum summoned Mary and me for a meeting. With Mum was Susan Wallace. Susan gave me a nice hello and Mary a hug. She said to Mary, "I hear you want to be a papa rats' eye.

Mary cautiously answered, "Tara told me her father would pay for good pictures of Rick. The fewer clothes, the better."

"How much, honey?"

"Fifty dollars for his buns and less for anything else, no frontals because he can't print those."

"Mary, after your mother called, I made some phone calls. Most of the tabloids would pay five hundred dollars for a picture of Rick's buns."

Five hundred dollars! I wonder if I could take a picture using a mirror!

"That rat," Mary exclaimed.

"That is how that industry works. You can never trust them. Now let's talk about what you could do. I talked to one of the tabloid people that Rick leaks stories to. They would buy pictures from you of Rick and any other star and would like you to write a little story along with it."

Mary had perked up when she heard about pictures being bought but looked downfallen when Susan finished.

"What's wrong, Mary?"

"I've just learned to print. I can't write! Not only that, but I can't spell yet."

"Oh, that's a problem. What if I helped you?"

I looked over at Mum. From her expression, I could see the fix was in. This had been the plan since we walked into the room.

"Would you?"

Mary was sharp enough that she looked over to Mum to see how this would go.

"I would be glad to," said Susan. "I will come up with the words, and you can print them out, and they will never know the difference."

Mary suddenly looked canny.

"How much would I get paid for this?"

"One hundred dollars a story, but no pictures of buns, just swimming pool type stuff."

Thus, a monster was born. Well, not a monster, but I had to live with pictures being taken at unexpected times for the next several weeks. It tapered off as it became a chore for Mary, but she always got pictures. She liked the money, so she never slacked off on her deadline.

Mary was excused from the room, and Mum and Susan filled me in on what was really going on.

"We want to stick a thumb in Tara's dad's eye by having someone else get pictures. At the same time, we get to write the story that will go with the picture, thus favorable publicity. There will be one story a month."

"Mary will not be named, and the tabloid will call her an unnamed source. From her printing and the wording, it will be apparent that it is coming from inside the house from a child. It won't take long for the world to figure out Mary is the mystery papa rats eye."

I think Mary had just renamed an entire industry.

"We will not confirm or deny."

"Could I publicly muse if it is legal to shoot little sisters?"

"No, but a threat to take your own collection of pictures to share with her first boyfriend might be appropriate."

"Works for me, Mum. What about Mary having a hundred dollars a month? That seems like a lot for a girl her age."

"She will be saving sixty dollars a month; she will also lose her allowance since she has her own income now. Some of the savings will go toward taxes. That will still leave her with an allowance that is doubled."

I hadn't thought of that. Twelve hundred dollars a year was a lot of money.

Mum continued, "Then Denny will start charging her for developing her film. Hmm, I wonder if we could cut his allowance also."

What a mercenary Mum I had!

She continued, "Now if we can only find work for Eddie, I could retire."

That confused me for a moment as she and Susan shared a laugh. Then I realized that Mum didn't hold a job, at least any that she admitted to. Then I got the joke. There wasn't really that much money involved. I had taken the joke seriously! Oops, glad I hadn't said anything.

My face must have given me away because Susan and Mum both looked at me and started laughing all over again. I did the intelligent teenage boy thing and stomped out of the room. For some reason, this made them both laugh even harder. I thought about slamming the door, but I wouldn't give them further reason to laugh at me.

As I semi-stomped down the hall, I had dark thoughts. No one understood me. I'll show them; I'll run away; they will be sorry. I will join the Merchant Marine. Oh wait, I had already done that.

That put me over the top. I started laughing at myself. I stopped in the hallway and realized that this was one of those emotional swings we had been told about in health class several years ago.

I went back to Mum and Susan.

"Sorry for the childish response, ladies. What do I need to do for this project?"

They both accepted my statement with no comment.

Susan replied, "I will show you what we are having Mary write. I doubt there will be a problem as it will be age appropriate. In fact, if it weren't from your sister and considered to be an inside joke, it would be quite boring. She will probably write about how loud you snore and things like that."

"I snore?"

"I have no idea, Rick. That was just an example."

"I need to get my head examined. I'm not with it today. I'm going to do something useful like go for a run. It might clear my head."

That's what I did, I don't know if my head was clearer, but I sure was sweaty.

Before I showered, I called Emily to tell her I had a good time on our date the night before. I could tell from her reaction this was the right call. We chatted for a few minutes and agreed that we would go roller skating next Friday. She knew that I had a flight soon, so didn't try to extend the call. I then headed to the shower to get ready to go to New York.

By the time I cleaned up from my run, it was time to head to the airport for my flight.

A driver dropped me off at LAX with plenty of time for my flight. Well, I thought it was plenty of time. A reservation had been made for me, but I had to pay for my ticket. The lines at TWA were long.

It took forever for them to write out all the information needed on a ticket. It must have averaged five minutes a person in the other lines; it was at least ten minutes in my line. By the time I had my ticket, I had to rush to the gate.

Even that took longer than I thought it would. Every gate I passed had a crowd waiting to greet people from arriving flights.

I finally got on board. They had already boarded most passengers, so that I couldn't grab an aisle seat in first class. I sat next to some businessman in a suit and tie that was engrossed in his work. He barely grunted when I asked him to stand so I could take my seat by the window.

I noticed a passenger I recognized. It was that guy I had seen at a party at Mr. Monroe's house. Don someone who worked on Madison Avenue. I guess he is considered good-looking. At least the stewardesses and the woman sitting next to him certainly acted like it.

I had a book to read on the redeye flight but had trouble getting into it. I blamed it on the smoke. It seemed every passenger smoked on that flight. Even the stewardesses and flight crew would sneak a smoke in their area. My clothes would reek of smoke when we got to New York.

The guy next to me looked familiar, but I wasn't placing him. The coin dropped when the stewardess asked Mr. Garner for his autograph. I was sitting next to Bret Maverick! After he had signed her autograph, he turned to me.

"Could I have your autograph, Sir Richard?" he asked.

Here I was, trying to work up the nerve to ask for his. So, we exchanged signings. He took notes to have pictures sent to my brothers and sister since we all are fans of the show. We talked idly for a few minutes, mostly about what jobs we had upcoming. He finally got a small grin and asked me.

"Would you be interested in doing a guest appearance?"

I about fell over myself in replying, "Yes."

That would have been a good trick as I was sitting down.

We exchanged business cards. Mine also had Mr. Baxter's number on it so their producers could contact him if they were interested. After that, Mr. Garner fell asleep for the rest of the flight.

The flight ended as all flights do. I managed to doze most of the flight but certainly didn't feel rested. It seemed that every time I fell asleep, a stewardess would ask if I wanted something. I finally got smart and asked for a blanket and pillow, so I ended up sleeping for an hour.

When I was half asleep, the strangest things went through my mind. I remembered when I was about four years old and was out playing in the snow. Mum had bundled me up in a snowsuit. It was padded so much I could probably fall off a cliff and not get hurt.

I noticed the neighbors had not collected their milk yet. The glass bottles were sitting in the delivery rack. The cream had risen to the top of the milk as normal. The cream then froze, expanding out of the bottle. The paper lid couldn't hold it in. I knew the cream was good, so I was lifting the cap off and eating the cream.

About that time, Dad came out and caught me red-handed or creamed cheek. He picked me up and smacked my bottom all the way home. I remember screaming and crying, but I probably didn't feel a thing with that snowsuit. Dad told Mum and got a quarter from her to pay the neighbor for the two quarts of milk I had messed up.

That thought, for some reason, made me remember the red and blue cards Mum would set out to tell the iceman if we wanted a twenty-five-pound or fifty-pound block.

That winter really stuck in my mind. The snow was up to my shoulders. Of course, I wasn't yet three feet tall at the time. It seemed like the deepest in the world to me. It got so cold that Dad had to bring in the battery from the car so he could start it if he were called for the extra board.

I finally dozed off to sleep and had to think about where I was when I woke up. It was just in time for breakfast.

Chapter 23

We had eggs benedict; bacon, orange juice, and coffee which made me feel better. I had passed on the small dinner earlier. It was a filet and sides, but I wasn't hungry then.

As we were getting ready to leave the plane, I noticed the woman sitting next to that advertising guy giving him her card, so I guessed he had had a good flight.

A driver was waiting for me in the luggage area. He had a card with my name on it. I only had a small carry-on with one change of clothes and a shaving kit, but he insisted on carrying it for me. It was seven o'clock in the morning, and they wouldn't be taping the show until eleven o'clock, so he took me to a room at The Plaza.

I took a shower and changed clothes. I had worn a sports coat with no tie for the flight. For the interview, I wore a suit and tie. I was glad to see they had one of my showerheads in use.

I lay down for an hour, so I felt a little better.

When I arrived at the studio, there was a real surprise for me. Deputy Sheriff George Burrill was there in uniform. He had been flown out early yesterday. No redeye for him. He even had his weapon with him. He also had a long case whose contents it wouldn't take two guesses to get right.

He had the Holland and Holland rifle with him.

We had time to talk in the green room while we had coffee, so he filled me in on some events I didn't know about. This would be the last time in this uniform. The sheriff had fired him. I asked if it was for missing the tiger, and he laughed.

"No, it is because I said nice things about you when interviewed by the *LA Times*. That went against what his newspaper buddy printed. Locally they ended up with egg all over their faces."

"That's not right. What are you going to do about it."

"Well, with your dad's help, I'm running for sheriff! Even if I don't win, he has promised to help me get a job."

Suddenly it all made sense.

On and off stage, Mr. Paar was his usual self, so we got through everything simply fine. I tried to tell everyone how I was lucky in my shot, but George didn't buy it and kept telling everyone how cool under fire I was. Of course, that brought up bank robbers and rustlers. Then to cap it all, they showed on the screen a copy of the picture with me looking like a big game hunter with a tiger.

Some days you can't win.

After the taping, we were taken directly back to the airport. It wasn't as hectic getting to the plane this time, and we had time in the Ambassadors Club before our flight. George sat next to me on the flight as Dad had got him a first-class ticket, or at least talked the *Tonight Show* into buying him one.

I was pleased that with all the free booze flowing in the club and on the flight, George had one modest drink, and that was it.

By the time the flight landed, it was six o'clock, and it took until seven-thirty to get home. We had eaten on the flight, so I went straight to bed. I wondered where my Sunday had gone.

The week started with another perfect California day. According to the newspaper, Ohio was being hit by a cold rainstorm, so it reaffirmed our decision to move west. After an uneventful run, watching for tigers, and my usual workout, I headed for the beach.

We high-paid actors have to suffer for our art, you know.

Now that I wasn't being forced to go three times a week, surfing had become fun again. Not that I would ever be a great surfer, but it was cool when I did catch a wave. Fred and Corky were both there, so I had a very good time. We took a break and had a snack at Katin's. No one had any great news.

I did share that I had a date the previous Friday. They agreed that the mall was the place to hang out now. Fred was a little crude with his questions, so I shut him down. I wasn't as impressed with Fred as much as when I first met him.

After our break, we went back to the water. As we crossed the road to the beach, I noticed a young lady wrapped in a blanket by the bathhouse. I wondered what she would be wearing to be all covered like that.

After catching a couple of waves, I noticed she was sitting near the water, still wrapped in her blanket. On the next trip, she was in the water. I must admit it was a pretty skimpy bikini, yellow polka dots and all.

I wished she would come out of the water. She was still there when we left. I hope she didn't turn into a prune.

After a hearty lunch at home, Mum took me downtown to start her version of recognizing a tail and evading it if needed.

Beginning that afternoon, the rest of my week was fun as Mum taught me how to evade a tail. I learned not to be shy about pulling twenty dollars out of my wallet and asking if there was a back door. I learned to look for buildings with more than one entrance. Getting in one side of a cab, tossing the driver a five, as I got out the other door became routine. At the same time, Mum gave me pointers on how to spot my tails.

She pointed out Mr. Robertson and his trainees to me once. After that, it was up to me to pick them out. Frankly, after a few days, I didn't see that they were any better at following than I had been at spotting my tails. It was a bit of a farce. I knew they were there. They didn't know I knew. I was to evade them, and they had to follow me.

Why Mr. Robertson didn't figure out that something wasn't right, I don't know. What did he think I was doing wandering around downtown LA like I was? Mum had made a point of letting him see her, so he knew I was in training, but he must have formed a low opinion of me to think his students would never be spotted. This was how my afternoons were spent.

At one point, I enjoyed helping an old lady cross the street. It was my Boy Scout good deed for the day. It also gave me an excuse to look all around so we wouldn't get hit by oncoming traffic. You would never see James Bond doing this.

Since I spent my morning being a beach bum and as a spy in the afternoon, the real world caught up with me in the evening. I had to spend time with my books. I first did my schoolwork. I was ahead in my lesson plan and wanted to keep it that way.

Even though I had soloed, I wanted to really know about flying, so I spent more time with those studies. I couldn't wait until tomorrow when I would get to go up again. Even though it wouldn't be a solo, it was flying.

I finished up a book I had been reading. It was grim. I hope I never have to make the choice Gordon Zellaby had forced upon him. I didn't care for the fact we never knew what started it.

Tuesday's exercise didn't bring out any more tigers, so I was a little more comfortable running in the woods. I did get a minor scare when I saw a flash of black and orange run across the trail ahead, but then I realized it was a chipmunk. I guess that tiger event shook me up more than I realized.

Mum and I headed downtown early. My tails were in place, and Mum asked me how that could be. We had gone out yesterday afternoon. Now we're doing a morning session. I thought for a minute.

"They have someone watching the house?"

"That or they have an inside contact."

"What, one of our people is betraying us?"

"Well, Rick, it's not like it is wartime. Well, maybe the American press makes it like wartime for us. They are either watching the house or have inside information. I thought this might happen, so I had security on the lookout.

"What is really happening is that someone is sitting out by the drive, way down the hill each morning. They trade off about lunchtime. Our security people have been keeping an eye on them."

Mum told them not to report it to the police as we have it in hand. It did remind her that she needed to teach me how to spot a simple car tail.

While I could tell I was being tailed now and could spot at least one of them, I wasn't certain I had all of them. They would change out change coats, hats, and items they were carrying.

I felt ornery at one point and stopped a policeman. All I did was ask him for directions, but in doing so, I pointed behind me as though I was trying to point out people following me. It did make them back way off for most of the afternoon.

Overall, I thought they were being taught much better than I had been. Of course, Mum and I discussed all this on the way home. She gave me tips for the next day. She also gave me a mild scold for playing with my food.

As they upped their game, mine was also getting better, so I felt most days were a draw. They had followed me, but I knew I was being followed and had spotted enough of them that I could lose them if I had to. Mum didn't want me to lose them too often or thoroughly, so we could keep playing them. As Mum put it, the US government was kind enough to provide a team to train me. It would be rude not to use it.

Lunch was the usual cold set up on the buffet. Eddie and Denny told me they liked studying at home. They could move at their own speed and run a lesson long or short, depending on how interesting it was. Being able to have their questions answered at once was cool. It made learning fun. Having a good-looking teacher also helped.

What they missed was the interaction with kids their own age. I had to agree with them as it was my exact same experience. The only difference was they were looking forward to returning to the classroom to be with friends. These days I can hardly communicate with kids my age. Well, except for going on dates with girls.

For me, it was back to the books after dinner. Tenth grade was proving easier than I thought it would. I was getting ahead on my timeline. I had planned to be finished by the New Year. At this rate, I would finish before Christmas.

The piloting studies were more difficult. Not that I wasn't getting it, but I had to read and reread to ensure that I understood things. I even borrowed one of Eddie's balsawood airplanes to go through the motions to understand some concepts. I don't think I will be trying any stunt flying soon.

I read about the city of Diaspar by the radar technician before falling asleep.

Chapter 24

The next morning it was drizzling rain. Since it was warm, I went for my run anyway. That was probably a mistake as I slipped on the trail. I skinned up my left knee, but it wasn't a big deal. However, I was a muddy mess upon entering the house.

As luck would have it, Mary was at the door with camera in hand. Oh well. After making several worthless threats to her life, I cleaned up before breakfast.

The whole family was at our buffet breakfast. Mary took great delight in describing her latest "scoop." Denny, being ever-helpful, volunteered to develop her film right away.

My ever-loving family then speculated on a story to match the picture. Their thoughts went from Rick taking a tumble to Jackson fleeing another tiger. I'm glad I hadn't mentioned my chipmunk scare.

I drove over to the studio and spent the morning practicing my skills. My bow work was current. While not a winner, my recent sword bout with Basil Rathbone proved that I still had my edge, pun intended.

Working on hand-to-hand was a different story. While I still had the muscle memory of a lot of the moves, others needed brushing up. I spent until lunchtime doing that instead of learning any new moves.

When I went home to clean up and have lunch, I had a story waiting for me to review. Mum had called Susan Wallace over; she, along with Mary, concocted a short story to go with my muddy picture. Its title was, "Jackson Chased by Another Tiger?" It went on to say that rumor was flying upstairs and downstairs at Jackson House about me being chased by another tiger. However, the inside reporter had it on good authority that clumsy Ricky had slipped on a muddy trail.

I looked up as I finished reading to hear a giggle and a flash of blonde hair leaving the room. I started in immediate pursuit with death by tickling or at least tickling until she pees in mind. She got away. I spent twenty minutes searching the house and could not find her.

Since it was getting close to my flying lesson time, I grabbed one of my T-Birds and headed out. As I drove up to our security checkpoint to exit the property, I saw a blonde head in the checkpoint building. I was about to open my mouth to say something when the two people on duty, Jim and Connie, opened up on me with their weapons!

My little sister had issued a squirt-on-sight order!

I did the only reasonable thing. I fled the scene before I was drenched.

My flying lessons were fun. Mr. McGarry, as usual, quizzed me while I flew. He had me stalling the plane at both high and low speeds and recovering. I handled that okay. When he had me put it in a spin, I almost peed my pants but managed to follow what I had been taught so we didn't crash.

All the while we were going through these motions, he appeared almost bored. I asked him about his flying career. He only told me that he had started young, learned in a tough school, and had been doing it ever since.

Not being completely clueless, I had looked up the Flying Tigers and their record in China. In doing my research, I saw his record listed. Tough school, indeed.

He changed the conversation about what my goals were in flying. He had brought this up before in the context of what type of aircraft I wanted to buy. Apparently, he also had done his homework, as his conversation assumed I could purchase any aircraft I wanted.

I still hadn't given it much thought but knew that I enjoyed flying and that it could be useful in my business ventures. I didn't intend to become a hobby flier, going to fly-in breakfasts. On the other hand, if I were hungry and could get fed, I was all in.

He chuckled at that.

"If you can afford it, the Cessna 310C with 260hp is what I would buy. It is a six-seater and costs sixty thousand dollars. The Piper Apache also has six seats and is a lot cheaper at thirty-six thousand. Its drawback is it has only 160hp."

"That translates to 191 knots vs. 135 or 155 mph vs 215. The drawback to the Cessna is its maintenance costs. If earlier models are any indication, they will be much higher than the Piper. I would recommend you do your homework first. You might even want to look at a Beechcraft Travel Air, but it only holds four with a fifth fold-down jump seat. Its speed and cost are between the other two."

The Cessna speed interested me.

After logging another three hours, I touched down for the umpteenth time that day for real and taxied in. While doing my post-flight walk around and refueling, we talked about the hours I would have to log cross country, nighttime, and how I should be ready to start instrument flying soon. We then shook hands and called it a day.

As I started home, I wondered what would be waiting for me at the security checkpoint. Believing in peace through superior firepower, I pulled over at a GC Murphy's Five and Dime. There I bought a package of five balloons for a nickel.

Stopping at a service station, I loaded my weapons and headed home.

As I pulled into the checkpoint and stopped, I decided upon a pre-emptive strike. Jim and Connie were both outside, so with two quick heaves, I had my revenge. I also had two very wet guards who were not armed with squirt guns. Fortunately, they didn't draw their very real pistols.

It was shift change time, so two other guards signed in at the shack. From the looks on their faces, they had no idea what was going on.

When I walked into the kitchen backdoor, the cook told me Mum wanted to see me as soon as I got in. She was in the library.

When I got there, it was Mum and a crying Mary. I wondered what had been going on.

"Rick, Mary has something she would like to say."

A sobbing Mary said, "Rick, I'm sorry that I had the guards squirt you. They should not be made to join our games. Their job is serious."

Ever feel the floor open under you?

Before I had a chance to say anything, two people walked into the room. A very wet Jim and Connie looked like they knew they were going to be fired.

Mum looked at them and then at me. She shook her head and told the guards they were excused and not to worry. She knew they weren't the problem.

"Rick, Mary is five years old. The guards like her, so I understand. You are fifteen and should know better.

"Before you walked in, I made certain the guards knew not to get involved with any more of your children's games. Now both of you go wash up, and we will talk about your punishment at dinner."

Mary and I got out as quickly as we could. Mary apologized again once when we were out of the room. This time I even believed her. I told her not to worry, that I thought we both had bigger concerns now and how about a truce?

She agreed quickly. She also let me know that the picture and story were worth one hundred dollars to her, so she could take whatever was coming. Lord help us when she grew up, five years going on thirty-five!

I arrived at dinner full of trepidation but determined to take what was coming to me like a man, or at least a non-pouting teenager.

Dad was the speaker for the sentencing.

"Mary will be spending one hour a day for the next week after school helping the maids with dusting and other inside chores."

"Rick, you will be cleaning out and refurbishing the stables."

The stables were in terrible shape. They needed a good cleaning, followed by a lot of wood replaced, then painting. This did not seem fair or reasonable to me, but I knew when to say, "Yes, sir."

Eddie picked up on it first. "Are we getting horses?"

"Yes, we have the room and facilities, except Mary will not be getting a horse."

Do you ever want to see a kid's face crumple? It made me forget the unfairness to me.

"She will be getting a pony."

Wow, want to see a million-watt smile make a face light up? It was there in front of us. The dinner conversation revolved around horses and instruction. Mary and Mum realized the important thing. They would have to shop for riding clothes.

Dad told me, "Rick, once you clean out the stables, obtain quotes on the wood replacement and painting."

That didn't seem so bad. I did have something coming for not thinking.

After dinner, I went out to the stables to see what needed to be done. Since the stables hadn't been used in many years, they weren't a stinky mess, a small favor. All I needed was a wheelbarrow and pitchfork to start, then a broom and water for a rinse. This would not be as bad as cleaning up after Brahma bulls.

I went back in and changed into work clothes. This was one of those jobs sooner started, sooner done. In the garage, I found a wheelbarrow and a pitchfork in the stables, as one would expect. All

I had to do was scoop the decomposed straw into the wheelbarrow and take it to the compost pile next to the stable.

I don't think we would want the pile after we had horses. It would grow rapidly and be a health hazard. I would have to see about it getting taken away.

As I worked, I had time to think. I replayed the day in my head, especially the squirt gun incident. The guards did what Mary requested. They really shouldn't have, but they did it. This made me think about Mary's comments when that CIA guy first showed up.

Her being friendly with the guards got her help when she needed it. I didn't want to be friends for those reasons, but it rang true to me that I should be friendly with those who worked for us.

That thought ran around my head for a while, and I settled on the fact I had to acknowledge all the people I dealt with in a good manner. Not that I wasn't nice when we were together, but that I had to show I thought about them when we were not together.

It could be simple things like sending birthday cards. How could I implement such a plan? I finished up my work on the stables for the day and cleaned up. Since it wasn't late, I went in search of Mum and Dad.

They were watching the television but weren't into the show, so they turned it off for me.

"What's on your mind, Rick?"

"I have been thinking about all the people I'm involved with and my relationships with them. I don't think I'm doing enough to foster those relationships and recognize them for their efforts, nothing big, like remembering their birthdays."

Dad replied, "That's an interesting thought. The same thing has been going through my mind recently. We are meeting so many new people in our different endeavors it is hard to keep track of them. At the same time, it is in our best interest to do so and the nice thing to do. I've noticed recently that more people remember me than I remember them."

"Yeah, we usually are in the more memorable position, so they remember us, but most of them are in a crowd situation, and it's almost impossible to remember them, and yet at the same time, I want to."

Mum chimed in, "Anna gives her secretary every business card she receives. In turn, her secretary keeps a file on who she met, where, what the meeting was about, and any personal facts that Anna noted on the back of the card. That way, if she ever goes back to that group or organization, she can refresh her memory."

"That's a good start, but I want to go even further. I'm going to talk to others like Mr. Monroe at Warner Brothers."

"That's a good idea, Rick. Keep me posted."

I returned to my room and picked up a book to read but realized I was tired and went right to sleep.

Chapter 25

After my normal morning rituals, I headed over to the studio. I was halfway there when I realized I hadn't thought about tigers once, which was a good thing.

I was lucky. Mr. Monroe was in and had time for me.

"What's up, Rick?"

"I have a few questions about contacts. I meet many people and feel I should do something to remember them and treat them like real people rather than just a face in the crowd."

"Ah, some people never catch on to that. Most actors are rather poor about it, letting the studio track fans, et cetera. The best at it are politicians."

"I don't know about politics, but it seems it is in my best interest to build a true contact base."

"What sort of contacts do you have in mind?"

"I was thinking more in the business sense rather than my fan base."

"That's good thinking, Rick. A fan base is great, but you need to hold them at a certain distance. Most of them are good people, but the occasional fruit cake is out there."

"Oh, I hadn't thought of that."

"What levels of business contacts are you thinking of?"

"Well, I thought of sending everyone a birthday card."

"If I remember right, you have several factories with quite a few workers."

"The last number I heard, I have almost a thousand employees now."

"Wow, Rick, you really are going places. Why do you even bother to act?"

"It's fun and keeps me out of a classroom. Plus, you never know when being a little famous might help."

"A little famous, let me see; acting, singing, saving the Queen of England, working as a deckhand, multiple lives saved, tigers shot, robbers captured, even bad guys killed. Yeah, I'd say you're famous."

"When you put it that way, I must be, but none of it seemed a big deal at the time."

"That is why you are not only famous but also liked. You are truly modest without being falsely modest. I keep telling Nina she shouldn't have gone to Switzerland."

The look on my face must have been something because he burst out laughing.

"Got you, Rick. Nina and you are both too young to settle down. Now, let's get back to the subject, acknowledging people you have met or who work for you and may never meet."

"May never meet?"

"Certainly, you will have people who work in your factories you will never meet. You may visit the factory occasionally, but people will not always be there or would have come and gone between visits."

"I hadn't thought of that."

"I have that problem here at the studio. Now let's talk about birthday cards. Is it appropriate to send a card to someone you have never met?"

"Not really."

"Think about sending a thank you card for each year they work for you. Do that for every level of worker that you don't deal with. It is a personal touch, but it is an appropriate touch.

"Now, those that you deal with on a routine basis might merit the card. I would suggest that you also have a clipping service to keep track of those at a certain level of acquaintance, that way, you can send an appropriate message."

"What's an appropriate message?"

"It depends upon the event; a birth and a death would rate different cards."

"Oh, I get it."

"I assume you have a business office."

"Yes, over on Rodeo Drive in one of Dad's buildings."

"You need to have someone on staff over there take care of that for you."

"That all makes sense. Thank you very much, Mr. Monroe."

"While you are here, I have a favor to ask. Jim Garner was supposed to play golf on Saturday morning with a couple of investors. He can't make it for personal reasons. Could you fill in for him?"

"I have no plans, so sure."

He gave me the guy's name, which meant nothing to me, and our tee time at the Calabasas Country Club. Mr. Monroe had never met the guy, so he knew nothing about him or his golf game.

From there, I headed to my office. There I sat down with Jim Williamson and explained what I would like to accomplish in recognizing the people I dealt with. He, in turn, explained a fact of life to me. I would have to hire someone to handle this as the staff was overbooked as it was.

We discussed this some more. I gave him permission to hire someone and that he was to handle the entire issue. My job would be to sign cards and write messages. Of course, I would have to come up with the initial list and update it as time went on.

We decided on three levels. Close friends and family, I would write a personal message and sign a card for each significant event, birthday, Christmas, graduations, etc. I would be on my own with gifts, other than a reminder to purchase one. Next would be people I met but wasn't close to, such as the makeup people at the studio, my old Scout leaders, and others. I would sign a card but no personal message. The last group would be people who worked for me. They would receive congratulations and a thank you for their service on their employment anniversary. This would be a card with my signature printed on it. There would also be sympathy cards as needed.

We would also contract with a clipping service to track stories on people I had met, such as General Hawthorne or the mayor of Vincennes, Indiana, and about my various products and companies. These were to be reviewed before showing them to me, or I would do nothing but read articles.

I felt lucky to get out of a large project so easily. Well, I still would have to sign a lot of cards and make certain the project got off the ground okay.

I was given an update on my businesses. They had it down to a fifteen-minute presentation if nothing major was happening. This week it was money in and money out. Fortunately, more in than out.

Hairdryers were way ahead of projections, and the head of home products thought we would continue like this for some time. It currently was acting as a cash cow, as Jim Williamson called it, but the real money would be in the containerized shipping business.

The government subsidies to expand the ports and ships that could use the system were being spent rapidly, but the GAO, who had just audited the expenditures, reported that this was one of the most efficient operations they had ever seen.

Apparently, in what had been considered a nest of corruption, the docks' unions weren't only doing their part, they were keeping the port operators straight and narrow. I wondered why; well, not really.

I had a while before my date with Emily, so I headed home and wrote two essays that were needed for my schoolwork. They both were on the required topics. One was so-so, but the other was interesting. What would be the future effects of President Eisenhower's interstate highway system?

His reasoning was as a defense highway, based on the logistics support the autobahn had given the German army. He also remembered a trip when he was a young officer moving a detachment to San Francisco. It took over a month to lead the convoy he was in across the continent.

I had seen the TV special where they talked about going across the entire country without having to stop for one traffic light. Certainly, it would have to affect the economy and where people lived.

The other essay was boring. I had to write about how air conditioning might change where people lived. I couldn't see that it would have much effect but put some stuff down that it would make the South more livable.

Emily answered the door wearing a black skirt with pink poodles and a pink blouse. Her hair was tied in a ponytail with a pink scarf. She looked pretty sharp.

We picked up the others and went to the local roller rink. It was a modern rink with plastic floors, and the skates all had plastic wheels, so it was quite quiet as a roller rink. It was fun all evening. At one point, we stopped for a sandwich and drinks. A group of three guys joined us. Emily introduced me to them.

I didn't really catch their names, but one of them, Roman, was the captain of the football team and the quarterback. I found this out from Emily, who gushed over him as she introduced us. They didn't stay around very long.

After skating, we went back to Emily's. She seemed anxious to get home and call it a night. I did get a peck on the cheek. I had a good time skating, but the evening wasn't what I had thought it would be. A little necking would have been great.

After my usual daily ritual on Saturday morning, I headed to the country club for my foursome. At the starter's desk, I found out the other people were a Judge Smails, Mr. Noonan, and Mr. Loomis. They had arrived and were on the putting green.

Usually, when meeting people on the golf course for the first time, there are polite introductions all around. This was not to be. Judge Smails thought James Garner would be there and was upset that I was sent instead.

He wanted to know why some kid actor was sent instead of Mr. Garner. When I explained the situation, it didn't calm him down. He finally seemed to accept the fact that I was going to be his fourth. The other guys had shaken my hand and did not get involved in the conversation. Well, it was not a conversation as it was Judge Smails doing ninety percent of the talking, most of which was complaining about someone of his stature being stood up.

He asked if I knew how to play golf. I replied that I knew the rules and didn't think I would embarrass myself on the course.

He sneered at that and asked if I could play real men's golf. He insisted that real men bet Nassau style. I had heard of it but asked him to explain. He went on in great detail to tell me bets on the front nine, back nine, all eighteen, pressing or doubling the bet, the trailing player being able to press the bet, not pressing on nine or eighteen, an automatic press if a player was two holes down and finally press double.

It sounded complicated as all get out.

"Kid, how much money do you have on you?"

I pulled out my wallet, which contained forty-seven dollars.

"What I thought, a second-rate actor with nothing to do, how much are they paying you to play?"

"Nothing. Mr. Monroe asked me to play as a favor."

"Was that a blank check I saw in your wallet?"

"Yes, sir."

"Fine, then we will play for a one-hundred-dollar Nassau. If you can't cover it, Mr. Monroe will have to for sticking it to me."

I hadn't paid a lot of attention to the rules of the bet, but I could tell this could get expensive.

Mr. Noonan tried to talk the judge out of it, saying it wasn't fair to take advantage of a kid like this. The judge wasn't having it. Instead, he bullied the other two into making the same bet with me.

While this was going on, I was getting a little steamed. Well, actually, mad as hell. I did tell him he had better call Mr. Monroe if he expected him to stand behind my bet. I hadn't accepted the bet until then, but I let my temper get ahead of me and went for it.

He stormed off to the pro shop to call Mr. Monroe. While he was gone, I looked over my golf bag. My driver was not there because I had not been using it, as I was trying for more accuracy in my game. I asked Ty, my caddie, a boy about my age, to retrieve it from my locker.

Ty and Smails got back about the same time. Smails was still angry but appeared a little puzzled.

"Monroe says he will back your bet but that you are good for the money. He also wanted in on the bet, so I'm playing for double. Since I intend to beat you every hole, I will make twenty-four hundred bucks off each of you."

"Judge Smails, what is your handicap?"

He preened a little as he told me, "I'm a scratch golfer. What's yours?"

That meant he played even with par.

"The last time I had a handicap in the ninth grade, it was 10-under."

I thought he would be impressed.

Instead, he laughed, "Putt-Putt for par 3?"

I didn't answer him as the starter called for us.

The first hole was 410 years, a par 4. I put my drive near the green and chipped it in for an eagle. That set the tone of the day. I'm not going to give a blow-by-blow description. I not only won every hole, but I also set a course record. We had a gallery of fifty people waiting at 18.

Smails was red in the face and getting redder all the time. I thought he might have a heart attack. This concerned me, but not enough to let up on the pressure.

We went into the clubhouse, where Noonan pulled out his checkbook. Loomis had a wad of cash.

"You clowns going to pay him? We were set up. I'm not paying him a damn dime."

There were enough people in the area who heard this that we were an instant attraction.

"Judge, I think you had better pay off your bet that you insisted on making," I said.

"Kid, you can't make me do anything. Besides, I know people on the docks in Long Beach, and you could get hurt."

I was in a bit of a quandary about what to do when a voice spoke up from the crowd that had gathered.

"Hey Ricky, do you think he knows Popeye or Mr. L.?"

Frank Sinatra's voice is very recognizable.

Judge Smails really stuck his foot in it. "I know Popeye. Even the union guys are scared of him."

"Did you know that he is married to Rick's aunt?"

That stopped Smails in his tracks. He uncertainly replied, "No, I didn't."

"I suggest you pay up."

Smails was not stupid. He brought out a checkbook and wrote one for the full amount. He started to put it away.

I demanded, "Why don't you write out Mr. Monroe's while you are at it?"

Grudgingly, he did.

Another voice in the crowd said, "Pilgrim, Rick should have just knocked the snot out of you."

I started checking the area for water troughs.

My caddie and the others were still standing around. They hadn't been tipped for the round.

The other three golfers brushed by them as they left, stiffing them.

I had the wad of cash from Loomis and handed it to Ty.

"Split it up evenly between yourselves."

You want to see faces light up. Ty was happy. The other three were ecstatic after the abuse they had taken out on the course, especially from the judge.

"Thanks, Rick, that guy was an idiot. I hope to get even with him someday."

"Good luck with that."

After I took a shower in the clubhouse, I stopped at the club restaurant for lunch. The number of people who congratulated me on my round of golf was amazing. The club pro wanted to know if I had kept my scorecard.

It was embarrassing to dig it out of the trash can in the locker room. I was so intent on winning the bets it hadn't sunk in that a new course record wasn't set every day.

Strict etiquette would have had the rest sign my card as witnesses in my foursome. Instead, the pro and club president signed along with the caddies. A note was even made about the sportsmanship of the rest of the foursome.

I don't think any of them will play this course again, as the scorecard would be framed and posted in the clubhouse.

A picture was taken to be put alongside the card. I did refuse an interview with a reporter of the paper that Dad was trying to put out of business.

Chapter 26

It was still early enough that I drove over to the airport. I wanted to get some more time in if a plane was available. There was, so I spent the next five hours circling the area and doing touch and goes. The more I flew, the more I enjoyed it.

I was beginning to know the landscape below me. Several cattle ranches looked interesting. One even had its own landing strip. I made a mental note of that in case I needed an alternate landing site.

It had been drilled into me that I was always to know if there was a place to set down. I didn't think the odds were that I would have to do so. At least there wouldn't be anyone trying to shoot me down. I think Mr. McGarry was a little paranoid, but then they really were trying to shoot him down!

I got home just before dinner. However, it didn't look like it would be a calm family meal. Several catering trucks were in the back lot, and people were moving purposefully.

I barely cleared the door, and Mum cornered me.

"Rick, I need your help."

"Sure, Mum, what can I do?"

"Clean up and get your tux on."

It was then I remembered there was a charity dinner at the house tonight.

"I will, but I thought you told me I didn't have to attend. As a matter of fact, I was specifically not invited."

"That's true, but things have changed. Mrs. Van Pelt, her husband, daughter, and her boyfriend were invited. The boyfriend broke up with June last night. The Van Pelts insisted June come tonight as she has been a mess hiding in her bedroom. Now I need someone to escort her. So, hurry up. You have the duty."

Sounded like marching orders to me. There are times to be a reluctant teenager, but this wasn't one of them.

"Okay, Mum. This means I have to eat the rubber chicken instead of pizza with the other kids?"

"You can choose steak, fish, or a Cornish game hen. Now hurry up."

"Yes, ma'am."

She swatted me as I left in a hurry.

It didn't take long to shower again and put on the monkey suit. I was getting better at tying my bow tie, but apparently not good enough, as Mum tied it again when I went back downstairs.

"You look very smart, Rick. Thank you for doing this."

What's a guy to do when his Mum says, "Thank you."

Lying through my teeth, I told her it was my pleasure. I didn't have plans for tonight, but escorting some society girl to a formal dinner wasn't high on my list. Actually, it was high on my list of what not to do.

My luck, she was going to be ugly and a pain to be around as she sulked about getting dumped. I don't know why girls took it so hard when a guy told her he wanted to go out with other girls. We were young and were supposed to be playing the field.

Mum and I went to the reception where guests were starting to arrive.

Mum, Dad, and I made a short receiving line. Several maids were taking the fur coats and wraps. A whole forest of animals had to have died to clothe this group.

The men all had on the requisite tuxedoes. Most had on the standard red cummerbund like mine. One brave soul had one that was white with a blue-flowered pattern covering. It looked like wallpaper, but it was neat. He had a matching bow tie.

I thought about getting something like that but realized it would probably never catch on and leave me looking like the odd man out.

Shortly after, the Van Pelts were in line with their daughter June. They were a well-dressed family, and her parents seemed nice enough people. June herself looked like the "Wreck of the *Hesperus*".

Her hair wasn't done properly. Her make-up looked slapdash.

Her father started to introduce her to me, but she turned her head.

"June Lucille Van Pelt," her mother said.

The dreaded full name brought her around. The look on my face said it all.

"If you call me that, I'll scratch your eyes out."

"I wouldn't dream of it, Miss Van Pelt."

"And my ex-boyfriend's name was Bill, and he didn't play the piano."

"Okay, okay, I get it. The subject is taboo. You must be tired of hearing it all. Why don't I show you around the house?"

I didn't really care about showing her the house. It just got me out of the receiving line.

Mum said, "Show her to my dressing room so she can freshen up and use makeup."

I took June by the hand, and we got out of there.

"Why did your mother mention makeup?"

"I have no idea, but let's find a mirror."

A small room off the reception must have been a waiting room to prepare for guests. June took one look in the mirror and burst into tears.

What do you do with a crying girl? I gave her my spare, clean handkerchief. Now I understood why Mum wanted me to carry two. One to use and one to lend, she told me. This was the first time I had to lend one.

She dabbed her eyes dry and blew her nose. How do girls blow their noses so quietly?

I took her up to Mum's dressing room.

I pointed her into the room and stood out in the hall.

Ten minutes later, an attractive young lady stepped out into the hall.

"Thank you, Richard. I'm sorry about the way I looked and acted. I had been going steady for a year, and then he dumped me yesterday for another girl."

"Ouch, did you have his class ring?"

"Yes, and I gave it back to the side of his head at about ninety miles an hour."

"Double ouch."

"Not really. I had so much angora wrapped around it, he just laughed."

"Well, I can see why you are upset."

"The worst part is when I asked him what he would do about the tuxedo he had rented. He told me he had never rented one. He didn't want to break up with me until after we parked last night."

Now, that was a minefield of its own. I wasn't about to touch that. I don't think I should play poker because she told me, "Nothing happened, even though he was more insistent than ever. I stopped him at first base as...."

She blushed red to the roots of her hair. Again, I kept my mouth shut. It seemed to be the theme of the evening.

"After I threw his ring at him, he told me good luck at finding dates in the future. He was going to tell everyone I was a tease. Well, he used a bad word, but you understand."

Now I opened my mouth. One would have thought I would have remembered the evening's theme.

"There is a society photographer here. Let's get our picture taken. Then you can take a copy to show your friends that you can get a date."

"You are good-looking, but why should my friends be impressed?"

"Uh, you didn't see any of my movies?"

"No."

"Then let's start over. My name is Sir Richard Jackson."

"Oh! I do know you; I just never put it together. I would love to have my picture taken with you."

We went back to the reception; whereupon, seeing us, my Mum gave me a nod. Mrs. Van Pelt had a look of relief.

The photographer was happy to take our picture. June got into it and went so far as putting an arm around me. Then she topped it off with a kiss. Not a gasping-for-air kiss, but still a nice one.

The photographer assured me copies would be available Monday and that June would have hers by Tuesday. She wrote her address down for him.

Our timing was good, as dinner was announced. It was pretty darned good, certainly not the rubber chicken I had thought it would be.

June quizzed me as we ate. She mainly wanted to know if I was going steady. When I told her I was dating Emily casually, she got a contented look. Well, it was more like a hungry lioness thinking of a nice meal she was about to have.

I had better be careful with this one, not that she wasn't pretty or nice, but she seemed ready to move on quickly, moving on being the operative word.

The other people around us were all old people like my parents, so we only had each other to talk to. I discovered that June, never Lucy, was my age and a sophomore in high school. I had to explain about the studio school. She thought that was neat for the fast track but having no school friends was a terrible thing.

That took us into our hobbies: archery, swordsmanship, surfing, unarmed combat, flying lessons, and sundry other things I had tried. She was in the thespian club at her school and had the second lead in several plays. She also had done several solos in the school choir. She loved to swim but hated running.

We did a recap of my acting career and the people I had met. She was brave, telling me she would like to hear me sing. All in all, the meal and evening went fast. We escaped before dessert so we wouldn't have to listen to the after-dinner speeches for whatever charity this was. I hadn't thought to ask.

Instead, we went down to the basement to play pool. When we arrived, I found my brothers and sister watching a movie on the big screen. It was *Sir Nicklaus*, and they were throwing popcorn at me on the screen.

They were hooting and hollering about what a lousy actor I was. They settled down when they noticed June and me, but the damage was done. Revenge would be mine!

June fit right in as she could throw popcorn with the best of them. To think that I had felt sorry for her. I slipped away for a few minutes. I informed the evening maid that she might want to take some brooms and dustpans to the basement for the children to use. She wasn't to do it for them.

Things had calmed down when I went back downstairs. Denny had June cornered, and they were so engrossed with each other that I left them alone.

Mary had several friends over for the evening, and they had built a tent out of blankets and were giggling about something, so I avoided them.

That left Eddie and the pool table. We spent an hour or so playing playing pool. That meant we rolled balls around the table but were far from good at it. Denny and June joined us with a challenge. Of course, Denny cleaned all our clocks.

Just as we set up for another drubbing, a maid told us that the gathering had ended, and June's parents were leaving. She could join them or stay. I got her upstairs immediately.

While riding in the elevator, June asked if I had a class ring. I showed her my bare hands as an answer.

"I go to the studio school, and we have never discussed them, so I doubt I would have one."

"Oh, that's a shame. What if you wanted to go steady?"

I thought of the signet ring Mum and Dad had given me after my Knighthood but didn't mention it.

"I have never thought about going steady. I only date occasionally, certainly not enough to consider going steady.

"Well, you never know when lightning will strike."

"No, you don't. Oh, we are at our floor."

Saved by an elevator!

She seemed like a nice girl, but I wasn't comfortable with her. She seemed like a type that I was beginning to recognize. If she went with me, it would be for what was in it for her, not because she cared for me.

I escorted her to her parents and quickly escaped after the normal pleasantries. Since June was all smiles, with a noticeable mood change, her parents looked pleased and told me they hoped to see me again soon. I said something noncommittal and booked out of there.

I went to my room. Later, Mum stopped by and thanked me for pitching in. I told her I hoped I didn't catch this sort of duty very often.

"You won't, Rick, only when I need you."

She left, and I felt better until I realized she hadn't said how often she would need me.

I read for a while, but after reading the same page three times, I gave up and went to sleep.

Chapter 27

I did my usual morning routine and also checked how the refurbishing of the stables was going. I had nothing to do with it now except make sure the construction crew was performing as stated. Everything looked good to me.

The project included a new roof, most of the siding replaced, a new floor, and a total paint job. Mum picked out the colors for me. Who knew that the Jacksons had their own racing colors and a coat of arms? I liked the funny English spelling of colors, so I spelled it that way in the contract. The stables were to be dark green with black trim.

I wrote and typed out the contract, and Dad signed it for me after reading it very closely. He had me modify it to include a requirement that the contractor and any sub-contractors carry insurance and be bonded. I had never thought of that, so chalk that up to something learned.

After my shower and dressing, I joined the family for breakfast. I was the last one there. As soon as Mary saw me, she started.

"Ricky and June, sitting in a tree."

This could not end well.

Wordlessly, Mum handed me the society section of the paper. Along with the description of her event, there was the picture of June and me kissing. It was titled "Two New Love Birds?"

Denny asked, "What will Emily have to say?"

"I don't think it will bother her; there is nothing to it."

Eddie and Mary had a few questions, but I noticed my parents were remarkably silent.

I announced that I was flying for the day to rack up as many hours as possible, and no one objected, so I was off. I had called Mr. McGarry, and the plane was available.

It was a fantastic day for flying, with clear skies and no storm clouds in sight.

The following day, Monday, started like every Monday since they named the day, slowly and reluctantly. In my case, there was no good reason, nothing to dread about the coming week. I just didn't want to start it, though start it, I did.

By the time I had finished my workout with weights and a good run, I was ready to go. Breakfast was quiet as each of us got ready for the week. I think Mary was sleep-eating.

When asked about my plans for the day, I didn't have any. Dad suggested I go to the studio school and make certain I was current in my schoolwork. I knew I was more than current but figured that a check-in wouldn't hurt. Besides, I wanted to talk to them about a class ring.

Not that I wanted to go steady with anyone, but I wanted to be prepared. There was no way that I would give my signet ring to anyone. I only wore it on special occasions as I didn't want to damage it. Mum and Dad must have paid a small fortune for it.

I checked out with our guards, letting them know my approximate plans for the morning. I didn't see any squirt guns in sight. They must have noticed the remaining water balloons on the car's front seat. I had only used two of the five balloons.

Jim and Connie watched me closely as I tossed them out on the passenger side. I think I was in more danger at that moment than ever in my life. I then apologized for my actions. They were both gracious and told me that the great water battle was becoming a legend in their company.

It was being used in their training on what not to do. Like all good stories, there was a hero and a villain. Guess what my role was. With a laugh and a wave, I took off. Hmm, maybe I could improve my image with a "Hi-Yo Silver Away!"

At the studio, the guard waved me down. Mr. Monroe wanted to see me.

I had to wait for about ten minutes and felt like I was sitting in the principal's office, but he was all smiles when I walked in. His smile got even bigger when I handed him the judge's check.

"I heard about that golf match, Rick. You put that guy down hard. I talked to Jim Garner about it, and he thought it was great. Apparently, Smails was a real pain in the butt. True he brought money to the table, but not enough to be worth the aggravation. I doubt if we ever hear of him again."

"I would deposit the check quickly if I were you."

"Good point. Now, besides bearing gifts, what brings you in this morning, Rick?"

I explained that I was checking up on my schoolwork and wanted to ask about a class ring.

"After you talk to them, ask them to discuss it with me. I have some ideas on the subject."

"May I ask?"

"No, I would rather it be a surprise."

"Okay."

I went over to the school. I got lucky. Not only was a class being dismissed, but the littles running out of the schoolroom didn't knock me over. I was a lot bigger, but it was a thundering herd of a dozen or more of them.

Miss Sperry and Mr. Danson were there, so I had the two people I needed. Maybe this Monday wouldn't be so bad after all.

I told them my thoughts on a class ring. I didn't say I wanted a less expensive ring to give a girl if I ever wanted to go steady, just that all the other kids were starting to wear theirs and that I felt a little left out.

They received it well. As a matter of fact, they went overboard. Their private company ran schools at all the studios and for several foreign consulates. They excitedly started talking about having a class ring with a little variation for each of their locations. Next, it was school colors and a mascot. They even thought of a yearbook.

The yearbook would be interesting because their student body would change continuously. Child actors might only work on movies for several years in a row and never be heard of again. I thought about that one. I could see a grandparent pulling out their yearbook to show they went to school with someone who really made it. Of course, there was a good chance the grandkids wouldn't know who they were talking about.

I told them that Mr. Monroe had some ideas on the subject and would like to talk to them. After stirring that pot, I made my escape.

I went over to the stunt yard and ran into Dick Wyman. We caught up with each other. He and Janice were starting a family, and she was expecting. I congratulated him and made a mental note to buy a gift for the newborn, due in February. They were still living in the house attached to our property and the exit to the tunnel.

Everyone else was off on various jobs, so I headed to the airport for a few hours of flying.

I checked in at the office and was told the plane was ready. Just make certain I did my walk around. It hadn't been in the air since yesterday, so the wings might be ready to fall off.

I did the walk around, and the wings were still holding on, but when I checked for water in the fuel, there was some evidence of water. I took a sample to Mr. McGarry, who agreed the fuel tank would have to be drained.

"Good catch, Rick. This is exactly why we do these checks one hundred percent of the time; well, unless they are strafing the airfield."

At first, I thought he was joking, He wasn't.

I thought I wouldn't be flying today. I thought wrong. I learned how to pump fuel out of a fuel tank, using a compressed air line with no water condensation to blow it dry, and then refill it. It took an hour, but I was happy to learn this task.

Mr. McGarry had other things to do, so I was just racking up hours.

I was over the ranch with the airstrip when I noticed something odd. In a far corner of the ranch was a semi-truck parked along the road. Flying closer but staying high, I could see there was a ramp down. Further out in the field were men on horseback doing a round-up.

This brought back memories of Texas and the cattle rustlers. I decided to check with the rancher.

I circled back and landed on the ranch runway. I barely rolled to a stop, and a man came roaring up in an open-topped jeep. He was dressed like a real working cowboy: denim jeans, a work shirt, boots, and a battered straw hat.

"Problem, son?"

"I'm not certain. Are you having a round-up over near the county road on the backside of the ranch?"

"No, why?"

"Well, some guys have a semi there and are rounding up cattle."

"Dang! Since your plane is all wound up, let's go."

"Well, I only have a student license, so I can't take passengers."

"No problem, I have a license."

He pointed towards an airplane that looked like mine, "Even checked out on this aircraft."

We took off and were shortly over the truck. They were starting to put cattle on board.

"Well, those are my cows they are stealing. Let's call the sheriff."

At about that time, a sheriff's car pulled up. As we did a high lazy circle, we could see some conversation, and then it looked like something was being handed to the sheriff. We weren't close enough to tell what was being handed over, and the only reason we thought it was the sheriff or a deputy was because of the patrol car.

"Maybe I won't call the sheriff. This looks like a job for the highway patrol."

He used my radio to call his house. His wife was monitoring their home frequency. She patched him through to the California Highway Patrol. He was known to them, so he didn't have to go through a lot of explaining.

After some discussion, they decided to let them load the truck, and we would follow them in the air to see where they would take the cattle. He did check to see if I had enough fuel.

It took an hour for them to reach their destination, a packing house out near Barstow. By the time they started to unload, the state police had the area surrounded. From the air, I could see forty or more units.

At a signal, they all went charging in, and the rustlers surrendered without a fight. At that, I waggled my wings and turned to take Mr. Tunstall back to his ranch. He was upbeat about the whole event. He told me this was the most fun he'd had since Lincoln County.

Before I could ask him about that, the radio got busy. The state police were going to meet us at his ranch to take our statements. By the time I thought of it again, I was concentrating on landing. Not saying I wanted to show off, but I wanted to grease it in.

The tires didn't even chirp. It was so smooth. Sometimes, things work out.

People were waiting for us at the flight apron, three women from the looks of it. When we taxied up, I could see that it was a mother, probably Mr. Tunstall's wife and daughters, who looked like twins. They were a few years older than me, but they were cute.

Mr. Tunstall introduced me to his daughters, Jayne and Joan. One of them, I think Joan, said, "He's cute. Can we keep him?"

The other daughter, Jayne, blurted out, "I saw him first, and he's mine."

"Now, girls, quit teasing the poor boy."

I was thoroughly confused as to which was who or was that which witch, but I knew I could never keep up with these two. It would be double the headache and half the fun.

It was interesting to meet them. They looked to be in their early twenties, so they were too old for me, which was probably a good thing.

Their Mom let me know they sang professionally, using her maiden name. Had I heard of the Boyd sisters? I hadn't.

One of the girls giggled as she told me they were famous, and I should get their autographs. They acted like it would be the greatest thing in the world for me.

Their Dad just shook his head and turned to me.

"Sir Richard, I think I see the state police coming up the driveway. Let's go meet them."

I couldn't get out of there quick enough. As we walked away, I heard one of the girls say, "Sir Richard?"

Our interview with the state police didn't take long as we knew very little. They were interested that there had been a sheriff's vehicle at the scene. We couldn't even swear that it was from this county since all counties in California used the same color scheme for their patrol cars.

In turn, the state police didn't know much other than they had received word from the officers on site that this was big, really big. Mr. Tunstall's cattle were being returned even as we spoke. They would appreciate it if he met the truck at the same point where they had been stolen from.

He was to help count the cattle and record the number of the plastic ear tags so he knew he had received all his cows back, and the police would have the evidence for court.

I started to offer to help, but Mr. Tunstall cut me off and told me I had helped enough today and that it would be a long and dirty job getting the cattle back into the pasture. I replied that I didn't mind, but he insisted. I can't say I was disappointed.

Walking back towards my airplane, I cut towards the runway, avoiding the twins. They made me think of double the trouble, double the fun. What rhymes with fun that means problems?

I returned to the airport and told Mr. McGarry what had happened. He got a kick out of the whole incident. He told me that Mr. Tunstall had settled down since he had a family but ran with a tough crowd in his younger days.

It made a good story at dinner.

After dinner, I called Emily. Her mother answered and was friendly enough but said, "She told me to tell you she's not here."

I heard a "Mom!" in the background.

This took me back, so I stood like a dummy with the phone in my hand.

"Rick, she doesn't want to talk to you right now."

"Oh, okay, I will try again later."

I hung up and wondered what this was all about. After thinking for a minute, I dialed Bill Spurgeon to see if he knew what was going on. He didn't but told me he would call Jill to see what she knew.

I started my school studies while I waited. After half an hour or so, Bill called me back.

"According to Jill, she saw a picture of you in the paper kissing some girl. Also, it turns out she already has a date this Friday night with Roman, that quarterback you met at the rink last weekend."

"Thanks, Bill. I don't know what to think right now. The girl that I was kissing initiated it, and I knew it might be a problem but didn't realize it would get me dumped."

"Rick, I'm not sure that is the whole story. Emily has been mooning over Roman for a long time. She never stood a chance until he saw her with you. The timing of the whole thing stinks."

"I guess you are right. Thanks for checking."

"Good luck, man."

And there was another relationship in the dust.

I lay awake and worried about it all night, well, at least five minutes.

Chapter 28

At breakfast, Dad was all smiles as he read the paper.

"What's going on, Dad, that has you so happy?"

You know that sheriff I want out of office?"

"Yeah."

"The state police have arrested him for heading up a cattle rustling ring. The story also states that they are questioning a local judge, a county prosecutor, and a prominent businessman."

"You think it is our judge and prosecutor?"

"I would bet on it. I also can give a good guess as to who the businessman is. There might be a newspaper for sale sooner than I thought."

"That would be too good to be true."

"Stranger things have happened."

Mum wanted to know where Emily and I were going Friday night. She shook her head when I told her my latest tale of woe.

"That is a problem you will face the rest of your life, Rick. You won't know who is real and who is just trying to use you. Don't let it make you too cynical, or you will miss out on many good people in life."

I granted that she had a point but didn't know how to handle it in the long run.

"That's why you see famous people registering under false names and not going out often. They learn to be content with the people they met before the fame and fortune came along."

It would be okay if you had met a lot of pretty girls before the fame and fortune. The next thoughts in my head were Cheryl and Judy. I owed them both letters. Maybe I should keep up my correspondence. I met both before fame and fortune. They were undoubtedly both good-looking.

After the meal, I went back to my room with the thought of writing to both girls when my private line rang. It was the studio.

They wanted me to come over right away to begin my appearance on *Maverick*. I learned that TV works to a different schedule than the movies.

When I arrived on set, I was hustled into makeup.

In half an hour, Ben Maverick was all set to be introduced to the world. It appeared that Ben is a nephew to Bret Maverick, son of his older sister Bea. Bret is at her home in St. Louis on a visit where the episode takes place. Bret had arrived on a huge sternwheeler steamboat from New Orleans. He had won a rather large sum of money on the trip. No surprise there. The real surprise was that he hadn't gotten into any trouble on the way.

As we went to the set, I was told all that in a hurry. It was a barroom setting. I was taken onto a stage at the front of the room, handed a guitar, and told to play "Buffalo Girl."

No problem, now if I only knew how to play the guitar! Well, I guess it would help if I knew the words to the song.

That's where the magic of TV and the movies came into play. They had an actor dressed the same as me. He could play the guitar. The only appearance he would make would be shots of his hands as he played the song.

As far as the words, they printed them on large paper and held them up for me.

We had a couple of run-throughs till I could fake it as if I could really sing. Fortunately, they had a couple of bargirls as my backup. That way, my voice could get lost in the crowd. Four women danced in front of me, doing a Western version of the French Can-Can. That caused a lot of commotion on the stage, which was the purpose of the whole scene.

We were creating a diversion for Bret Maverick while he did sleight-of-hand card tricks on another cardsharp. This guy was supposed to be really good and would normally have been able to catch Bret at it.

I never learned why he was playing cards with the guy that day. I guess I would have to wait until the episode aired.

We spent all morning on that. Mr. Garner and I went over to the canteen for lunch. Many of the extras in the various ongoing productions asked for his autograph, and he was a gracious gentleman. A few even asked for mine. I was using "Sir Richard." The United States didn't recognize titles, but that didn't mean they weren't cool.

At lunch, I had to give a blow-by-blow replay of Saturday's golf match. Mr. Garner loved it. He told me that the judge had been a pain ever since he had met him. He was arrogant and demanding, thinking his money and position earned him the right to look down on the world.

It didn't take long before I was told to stop the "Mr. Garners." It was Jim. Jim wondered if they could work a variation of the golf match into the series. It would make an incredible sting.

After lunch, we returned to the set. My scene for the afternoon was me being followed. I was shown coming around a corner and apparently disappearing.

They tried several variations. The first was ducking into a doorway. The doorway was too shallow. Another was lying down behind a water trough. It was too low; you could still see me. I got nervous about being near that water trough.

Someone pointed out that I could slip under the water. I quickly pointed out that it was too short for me to get in and submerge. That bright someone sent a runner to see if there were any longer troughs on the lot. I knew where at least three others were, but I wasn't about to tell.

The scene was taking place on the main street in St. Louis during the daytime, so they had extras walking down the street.

I asked the director if I could try something while we were waiting for a longer water trough. He was okay with it. I had a quick conversation with one of the extras, a guy about my height.

I then demonstrated what I had in mind. I strolled around the corner from an alley with my followers not that far behind. When out of sight, I ran up to the extra. I handed him a coin; it was a quarter, but I would mention to Bret he owed me a double eagle later.

We then did a quick exchange of hats and vests.

He walked on, and I sat down on nearby steps with my head looking down.

The two guys following came around the corner and passed me. One of them pointed at the guy wearing my hat. I then took off back the way I had come.

The director loved it. I knew those losing-a-tail lessons would come in handy. Thanks, Mum and the CIA.

Those were the action scenes in which I appeared; there was a dinner where Bret explained my role in distracting the bad guys. Bea did not like this. Of course, Ben was all in. Bea kept calling Bret by her childhood nickname for him, Slick.

Then there were several scenes where I received my orders from Bret, and of course, the happy ending where Bret calls Bea by her childhood nickname, Buzzy, as in Buzzy Bee. She swats him, and all is good.

The best part was right at the end. Early on, Bret had told Ben he was concerned that Bea might be in the matchmaking mode. She had mentioned a young lady who had been sweet on him when they were younger. She was okay but a little stout for him.

He hadn't told me her name (As Ben, I wouldn't have had a clue), so I didn't put it together when I heard Bea say, oh, Alice is here. I did see Bret take out the back door like his tail was on fire.

As he was going out the back, a gorgeous young lady walked in the door.

Bea greeted her, "Alice, I am so glad you came over. I'm certain Bret will be glad to see you."

I had no lines, so I kept my mouth shut. The two ladies went on for a bit, then looked for Bret. He was long gone. Alice took her leave.

Bea shook her head, "That Bret, Alice so wanted to see him again. She has lost all the weight she had as a teenager and has kept it off these last five years. Well, I guess that settles it. She has been dating that German brewer, Augie something or the other. I suppose she will marry him now."

After they yelled cut, I ran over to the gorgeous young lady and lifted her off her feet in a hug. I wasn't told that Sharon Bronson was making an appearance.

Jim Garner returned to the set, and the three of us had a good chat. From the way Jim eyed Sharon, I wondered, but she didn't act interested. After a while, they recalled previous appointments, so we went our way. I couldn't wait to see the show air so I could find out what the storyline was. This TV piecemeal of scenes seemed even worse than the movies.

It was a fun day after I did all that work. I had to sign some papers so I would get paid at scale. Heck, I thought I was working for free as a walk-on.

My day was of interest to everyone at dinner. The boys wondered if they could get a guest appearance. Mary was the one who stopped everyone cold. She announced she would like to appear as a girl who worked in the barroom. How I kept a straight face, I will never know. Mum got a very pained look, and Dad had to pretend he was wiping his face with his napkin.

After dinner, we went in to listen to Walter Cronkite on the CBS nightly news. I loved his sign-off.

"And that's the way it is."

Of course, that's the way it is, according to Walter Cronkite. But who was I to question the most trusted man in America?

Mary fell asleep during the show, which was unusually early for her. I asked Mum about it.

She told me that Mary was going through a growth spurt and would be very tired and a little emotional for the next few months. The doctor had told Mum that Mary would be very tall, maybe five foot eleven inches. That made sense as the rest of us were tall for our ages. I wondered if she could be a model when she grows up.

After the news, I spent several hours on schoolwork. Then, I read one of my favorite authors before falling asleep.

I dreamed about the fat red-bearded farmer waving Tailbiter at the dragon.

Chapter 29

On my morning run through the park, I saw and waved at the people who had taken the lady with the sprained ankle to the hospital, but we didn't stop to talk.

I took the time to examine the work being done on the stable. It looked good to me. I wondered when horses would appear. After the horses appeared, there would be the product of having horses around. I had better behave myself, or I would catch that duty.

After my shower, I joined the family for breakfast. Dad had some interesting news. The judge, the sheriff, the prosecutor, and the newspaper owner had gotten involved in a land deal that had gone bad. They tried to recoup their money by starting a rustling operation. We know how that ended.

The long and the short of it—to raise money for his lawyers, the owner had the newspaper for sale. Dad had already made some phone calls this morning to try to buy it. This led to further conversations about the kids' school. It seems after the first of the year, the Jackson family, or its business subsidiary, would own its own school.

Denny and Eddie loved the idea; they would always get passing grades. —They were quickly disabused of that thought. Mary wanted to know if she could make them have longer recesses. Dad told her he would look into it. A glare from Mum scotched that.

This led to a serious family discussion about how it wouldn't be a good idea to tell anyone that we owned the school. Dad pointed out that it would still have an independent board setting policy so that while we may own it, we weren't running it.

I kept my mouth shut. Mum and Dad wouldn't set policy, at least until the board tried to set lousy policy, then Katie bar the door.

I decided to spend the morning in the studio. I was getting a little rusty on my various skills.

The guards gave a cheerful wave as I drove out the gate, so I guess all was forgiven.

At the stunt yard, I first practiced archery. Not the shoot at a butt fifty yards away, but at a man-sized target at two hundred yards. This was known as flight or clout archery. Since I was hitting the target fifty percent of the time, I wasn't worried about the shorter distances. That said, I lost a few at fifty yards.

Several stuntmen were hanging around. There weren't any that I knew well. They razzed me for "only" hitting the target fifty percent of the time at the longer distance. As if!

I told them there was a call for extras on the furthest lot away. It was an easy way for them to pick up some spare cash, so they took off running as those spots filled quickly. That got me some peace and quiet. I would probably pay for that one way or the other, but it worked for now.

Next, I went over to the boxing ring and sparred for a while. I would never be a great boxer, but my moves were good enough to do my own work in a movie.

Mr. Palmer was in his office, so I talked to him about my unarmed combat lessons. I was up to what the Marines considered a brown belt, but my schedule would make spending the forty hours needed for the next step challenging.

He told me not to worry about it; maybe we could do it after the first of the year. I told him I would be in Hawaii for a movie, so we would have to play it by ear. He was okay with that as long as I kept myself fresh by doing my exercises to keep myself limber and automatic in my reactions.

"How will I do that?"

"You have some time?"

"Yes."

With a grin, he told me to follow him. Well, I wasn't too rusty, but he still threw me all over the place. The only saving grace was that he had to work up a sweat while doing it. He then went through a set of exercises I should do. They would only add fifteen minutes to my daily routine, so it was no big deal.

Afterward, I told him I would rather shoot two arrows at him from two hundred yards. He agreed that was a better plan. His plan was two shots from an M1 at four hundred yards. Hmm, I needed a new plan, maybe Mr. McGarry from four thousand feet. Of course, he would then go to ICBM's.

From there, I looked for a partner for swords. The guys I had sent on the extra call were back. They gave me a little grief, but not much.

One of them agreed to face off with me, using sabers, none of those foil toys for real men! Since sabers are one of my strengths, I went for it. We went back and forth pretty heavily, and it was clear that I was the better swordsman. That is until one of his partners joined the fray.

Fighting two at once may look easy in the movies, but real life is different. They quickly had me turned and were backing me up. I tried a flurry of swings but still had to give ground. I gave ground until my knees backed into a low object, and I went over backward, sitting down hard. Right into a water trough!

They stopped immediately and started laughing like loons. One of them gave me a hand out. I thought about trying to pull him in but didn't. Sometimes, you go with the flow. This story would make the rounds.

It is said that revenge is a dish best served cold, but hot works most of the time. I did have some dark thoughts about digging two graves. That didn't last. If you can't take a joke, stay out of the water or something like that.

Since it was all a set-up, another stuntman had a camera and got the picture. I bought the film from him for one hundred dollars with the understanding that if they turned out, I would provide them with copies.

The originals would go to the newspaper spy in the Jackson household. I was going to get my money back from her.

At home for lunch, I gave the film to Denny to be developed and told the family what it was about. They had fun coming up with captions for the photo: "Ricky takes a dip," "Splash, another one," and "Ricky gets what's coming." You get my drift. Once past my pride, it was kind of funny. I wondered if I needed to see a therapist about a growing fear of water troughs. I made the mistake of voicing that thought. I could guess the headline.

Mum and I went downtown to our usual evasion starting point. I dropped Mum off at an outdoor café where she ordered her normal Mexicali Delight beer to drink while waiting for me. She let me go alone before she walked with me and told me what to do and why. It didn't take long to pick up my CIA friends.

Today, I took them on a merry chase. At one point, I came out on a back alley of a department store and took off running. A block down the alley was the back of the café where Mum waited. We had scouted the area out and realized the café left the backdoor open all day. For cross ventilation, I supposed. It could get quite warm here in California.

Anyway, I entered the back door, exited the front, and sat down with Mum. With great effort, I didn't look around. Mum did that. She casually told me that there was a watcher across the street. He was doing his job well, as he didn't just stand and stare. He would look around and stroll a few steps as though he was waiting for someone and was bored. That probably was the truth.

As such, he didn't always have an eye on our table. Mum stifled a chuckle as she told me, "Rick, he didn't see you come out of the store. He looked away, and when he looked back, you were there. You should have seen the look on his face."

I turned for a look as he headed to a payphone on the corner. I bet he was asking where my tails were. I hoped they all had to stay after school for doing a poor job today. I would also make it a point not to go down any blind alleys in the near future.

Waiting at home was a letter from Judy. We were exchanging letters about every fortnight, as Mum would say. She didn't have any significant news. She wrote about the social life at her school, but I can't say it was that interesting. What was interesting was that she had been a constant in my life for a long time while others came and went. Well, her and Cheryl.

I will see Cheryl at the White House next month. After a few pleasant daydreams about the two girls, which I won't share, I cleaned up for dinner.

Dad updated us on the rustling case. The sheriff had been out on bail. He made the mistake of trying to flee to Mexico and was caught. He now was locked up with his bail revoked. Unfortunately for the others, the judge on the case revoked their bails, also.

This triggered a round of panic on the newspaper owner's part. He accepted Dad's offer immediately without any counters. Dad now owned two newspapers and a radio station.

Owning a radio station started a round of bad jokes about playing my songs all day, both of them. Denny and Eddie I could understand, but Mum and Dad!

After the mirth and merriment at my expense died down, Mum brought out a package. She handed it to me.

"This is for you, Rick." I had no idea what it could be or what the occasion was. It was a rather large box. It could hold an overcoat or something like it. There was no gift wrapping, so I only had to lift the lid.

Staring out from the box were the glistening eyes of a tiger. It looked like it was going to jump out at me. Well, not really, since it was just the head and skin of the tiger I had shot. I didn't know what to say. I really mean, I had no idea what to say.

"What are you going to do with it?" asked Mary.

What do you do with a tiger skin?

"I'm not certain; I guess I could use it as a rug in front of the fireplace in my bedroom."

Dad chimed in, "Or you could hang it on the wall in the basement recreation area."

Mum thought it would make a nice bedspread. Denny and Eddie wanted to use it to scare the guards. This got shut down quickly by Mum, Dad, Mary, and me. We had learned guards and games don't go together.

Mary asked if she could take it to school for show and tell. I told her she could. I would love to see that presentation.

After much discussion and dessert, a trifle, all agreed that in front of my fireplace was a good place to start.

After dinner, I arranged the tiger skin on my bedroom floor. It did look neat. Then I spent the evening on my schoolwork. It was well under control, and I wanted to keep it that way.

Chapter 30

The next morning there was a light rain, but I did my run anyway. It was actually pleasant. It made me think of how the weather in Ohio must be right now. We had made a good decision about moving to California. I no sooner had that thought than the ground started to shake under me.

It was an earthquake. I had felt mild tremors before, but this one was more serious. I raced home and found no problems, to my great relief. What had seemed like the beginning of the end of the world to me was nothing but a little shaker, according to the news on the radio.

Ohio looked a little better.

Mum and I headed downtown for my lesson on evasion. I had thought the rain might get me out of it. Instead, I was to learn the glories of an umbrella and a reversible Macintosh. It was not a rubberized raincoat but an ordinary raincoat made by Burberry.

What promised to be a trudge turned out to be a fun day; my followers never had a chance. I lost them so quickly that I purposely went back and let them pick me up again. Later, Mum scolded me once more for playing with my food.

Mum and I had a nice lunch at our favorite restaurant, one with multiple entrances to the front, side, and rear. I then took her home and went to the airport for flying time.

The weather had cleared somewhat, but there were still a lot of clouds. This gave me an entirely new outlook on flying. Some of those clouds were thick enough that they could have been rock-filled, and I wouldn't know it until it was too late. I went around them. Mr. McGarry has been watching me silently all this time.

I may be young and bold but intended to become an old pilot. As the saying goes, there are bold pilots and old pilots, but no old bold pilots.

Flying over what I now knew was the Tunstall ranch, nothing was going on. I had no urge to land and face the terrible twins. They come under the heading of double trouble.

I started to make another loop around the valley when the wind picked up. Not only up but down and sideways. It was getting bumpy as all get out. I decided I would rather be an old pilot than a bold one, so I headed back to the Ontario airfield.

As I was tying the plane down, Mr. McGarry spoke up.

"Rick, I'm glad you made good decisions about the weather. It's too dangerous to be up in a light craft right now."

I snorted and said, "This from the guy who flew fighters?"

"There's a difference between doing what you must do and doing it from stupidity."

Ouch.

"It just seems weird to be getting a lecture on safety from someone who risked his life constantly."

"You risk your life when you have to. When I had to take a plane up, I knew it was okay because I had worked on it beside the mechanics. Yeah, some things you can't control, but you try to offset the danger by taking care of those things you can control. Not flying in this mess is one of those things you can control."

"That's why I landed. I hadn't put it together like you are presenting it, but I knew it was not a good idea to stay up there."

"You did the right thing. For example, we fought in the air by controlling what we could. The Japanese planes were better. We couldn't go one on one in a dog fight. So, we would fly high as a group, swoop down in one firing pass, and run like heck. We fought with our strength. I'm glad you aren't crazy like Boyington of the

Hells Angels. Though I have to say, he could fly his P-40 pretty well. Not as well as Jimmy Howard, but rather well."

"Who is Boyington?"

"A story for another day, let's just say he was a real black sheep. A self-promoter, but he could get the bad boys to follow him. If he had left Olga alone, he wouldn't have gotten kicked out of the Tigers."

I tried to get some follow-up on this partial story, but that's all Mr. McGarry would say. I asked him why he didn't talk about things, and he told me he didn't like to talk about anything that reminded him of Thailand. That left more questions than answers, but I also thought of the sound of bullets on the landing craft doors and shut up.

I headed home. When I got there, Dad asked for some help in the sub-basement, our hidden refuge. He had completed everything to make it a place where we could hide for days if needed. The only project he needed to finish was to paint the floor under the old roll-top desk.

He needed my help moving it, as it must have weighed a ton. He had emptied it to reduce weight and pulled the drawers, but it was a monster.

After dinner, we put on some old work clothes and went down below.

Through brute force, we managed to slide it over the floor. I suspected he would have to repaint the portion we had slid it over.

A surprise awaited us after we had it out of the way.

There was a rectangle of different concrete where the roll-top had sat. It was about three feet wide and six feet long. The desk was so big that it hid it completely.

Dad and I looked at each other. We didn't have to voice the thought, *what was under there?*

"I'll break the concrete up tomorrow; it is too late now."

"Okay, I want to be here when you do it."

"Okay, we will do it immediately after breakfast. Then I will have to get downtown for some meetings. I have to decide if we are going to keep the new newspaper. It turns out there are also two radio stations involved and a small TV station out in the valley."

"Why would you want to keep them?"

"My initial thought was no, but then Susan Wallace and your Mum got into the act. They feel that by having the media outlets, we can get our own message out if need be. I don't see where that would be an issue.

"Also, there could be legal problems with how the companies are set up. Congress is talking about limiting the ownership of all the media in one market. It may not come to pass, but we would be forced to sell if it did. Any forced sale is a loss as you have a timetable to meet. We will have to restructure the business to avoid that."

"I'm glad you have those problems and not me."

"Watch out, or I will put you in charge of them."

"Ah, Dad, I have enough on my plate!"

"If you want a job done, give it to a busy man."

"Huh?"

"Think about it."

I was getting tired and didn't want to think.

Chapter 31

The following day, I was in much better shape. After my run and workout, I was ready to join Dad in opening up the mystery in the basement.

He had a sledgehammer and pick, so the job went fast. The ground under the concrete had subsided, so the concrete broke up easily and fell about four inches. I then picked up each piece and put it in several wheelbarrows stationed for that job.

As most of the area under the slab became visible, it was evident that a blanket had been laid over the top of what was underneath. Dad peeled it back, and my worst fears were confirmed. There was a skeleton down there. The hair was still there, and the corpse had a robe partially covering it. Most of the flesh was gone, but not completely. It was pretty gruesome looking.

I recoiled a bit, but from Dad's reaction, he not only was expecting it, but this also wasn't his first corpse. He knelt and looked the corpse over carefully. He reached into one of the robe pockets, which had a bulge in it. He withdrew a wallet.

In it, there was a driver's license in the name of Jason Talmadge. If this was Jason Talmadge, we had a real mystery on our hands. Reportedly, the original owner of Jackson House had disappeared from his yacht off the coast of Santa Catalina Island.

Dad was looking the corpse over very carefully. Luckily, there was no smell due to its age. Pretty much everything that was going to rot had rotted. Yuck.

"Rick, look at this."

Dad showed me a heavy silk-like cord wound around the neck. He peered very closely at the neck.

"The hyoid bone is broken. That is a sign of possible strangulation. The cord around the neck pretty well establishes this guy was strangled."

"Murdered?"

"It may have been sex play."

"What!"

Dad went on to explain how some people enjoyed autoerotic asphyxiation during sex. I considered this to be way too much information. Once more, I realized how much I didn't know about the world.

"Where did you learn about the hyoid bone and this strangling stuff?"

"In the army, as an MP Officer, we had courses taught by detectives. I'll never forget my instructors. William was a retired detective from the Toronto Constabulary, and Julia was a retired ME.

"They were interesting people. He was also an inventor and held several patents on automobiles, airplanes, and radio transmissions. She must have been a real beauty at the turn of the century. They were nice people. They came out of retirement to help with the war effort. William held the Victoria Cross from World War I, and she was a Dame of the British Empire for work on the front lines as a doctor, unique people."

"Yes, they were," said Mum. I didn't hear her join us. Dad explained to her what his thoughts were so far.

"This is not good. If this is Talmadge, it means those who said he went overboard on his yacht were all in on it. We had better find out who they were and where they are today," said Dad.

"They would have to be in their eighties at the youngest today."

"Well, at least we own several newspapers with reporters. I can have a follow-up done on the entire group. I'll say we are investigating the history of the house."

"That is even true."

I asked, "Are you going to call the police?"

Mum and Dad looked at each other; they communicated without saying a word.

"I don't think so, Rick," replied Dad. "Whatever happened here happened a long time ago. Those who were involved have lived their lives one way or another. We have to trade that off with keeping this basement a secret. We will decide after we investigate the people involved. In the meantime, keep it between the three of us."

My first instinct was that it wasn't the proper thing to do, but then I realized we didn't always do the proper thing. I couldn't object too much as I was the one who threw those heads over the Soviet embassy wall. As a family, we were in it together. After I thought for a moment, I realized that killing those guys hadn't bothered me at all but throwing their severed heads over a fence seemed wrong.

"Okay, Dad, please keep me posted on what you find out."

"No problem, Rick. We may have to take further action depending on what we find. In the meantime, I need to round up a tarp to cover this mess. Peg, should we tell the younger ones the sub-basement is off-limits for a while?"

"I wouldn't say anything. The boys would be down there in a flash to see what was going on and so would Mary with camera in hand."

"You're right, let's not say anything."

"As a matter of fact, Rick, I think we can push the desk back over this if we are careful."

We did it. I don't know about careful, as that desk seemed to have gained weight.

After that wonderful start to my day, I surfed at the beach. Getting out into the sun and air helped clear my mind or at least forget the grisly sight.

I had lunch at the beach and kept surfing for most of the afternoon. If nothing else, it freshened up my tan. Later in the day, I noticed more people standing on the beach, pointing at me.

It didn't take much to figure out it was a Sir Richard spotting.

I bit the bullet and went ashore. I must have signed fifty autographs. Everyone was pretty laid back. One papa-rats-eye insisted on getting in my face for a close-up. Somehow, he tripped and fell into an oncoming wave. I knew those unarmed combat courses would come in handy.

I gave up after that and left to the cheering of my fans.

Getting home, I cleaned up for dinner. For some reason, dinners were getting more formal all the time. I put on a coat and tie without thinking too much about it. I realized that Bellefontaine was a long way away and a long time ago. That would make a good opening for a movie.

At dinner, we didn't talk about the morning, but Dad made a reference that he had a conversation with people at the newspaper on a new project.

I spent the evening doing schoolwork. At the rate I was going, I might finish everything by Christmas. That would be nice. I would have several weeks off before leaving for Hawaii.

At bedtime, I was very sleepy from the events of the day, and I was only able to read several pages of an old favorite. I knew he would escape beheading and head to London. Heh, pun intended.

Chapter 32

Friday morning was a wonderful California day. It made my morning run and workout a pleasure. My run had an exciting event. I was doing a pretty good pace downhill when a coyote crossed the trail in front of me. We were so close I had to leap over him to avoid a collision. I don't know who was more surprised, me or the coyote. I wonder if it was the coyote. Neither of us stopped to discuss the issue.

Mum and I went downtown for my training. It was getting to be a little old hat for me.

By Friday, I could tell I had front and back tails and could evade them both. Once, I was even able to spot Mr. Robertson in the background. He didn't look happy.

On the first of this week, Mum told me I had to keep it up for four more weeks. I didn't mind at all; it was like an adult game of hide and seek. Well, it did for most of this week, but by today, it seemed to drag and be a chore.

I had a bright idea to make it more fun, at least for me. After lunch at our usual haunt, we returned home. I asked Denny if he would like to join my game. He was all in agreement. Denny was really into photography. I bribed him with a new high-quality telephoto lens for his camera. He also held out for a photographer's vest that would hold many rolls of film.

I then went to my offices for my Friday team meeting and business update. First, I made a point of saying "hello" to Emily's aunt. I didn't want her to have any concerns about her position with the company. You could tell she was aware of the situation but didn't bring it up directly, so neither did I.

Jim Williamson, as usual, had a simple presentation for me on the company's status. He started with the bottom line of how much profit had been made in all areas. I had to read the numbers several times to comprehend them.

"Jim, how could there be so much money?"

"Simple Rick, the government fronted you a development loan at a very low-interest rate. We took the entire amount and invested it; the investment interest is paying the loan off with money left over. So, in effect, the money was given to you.

"The profits from ongoing operations are going back into the business as capital investments. For example, we have five hulls in the new configuration under construction. The ports we discussed are being upgraded by us and the respective governments.

"Most of the governments have set up special companies for this, and we own shares in each. Again, those companies have been fronted money by their governments, and that is being used for the construction. Our capital investment for our share of each company is our knowledge and expertise, not cash. It is called intellectual property.

"Since you now don't have to put any of your invention money, movie residuals, etc., into the company for capital expansion, it is dropping to your bottom line. You will have one heck of a tax bill this year. It has been reduced by having your holding companies based in Luxemburg, but it will be a significant sum.

"These things take on a life of their own and become self-funding. The reason it was so quick was all the government money."

"Why are all these governments throwing all this money at me?" I asked.

"Because they see the benefit of the infrastructure being built, which will lead to jobs, which will keep them in office, and they are only playing with taxpayer money while you are taking risks with your own."

"But still, how have I come to have over twenty-five million dollars?"

"That is your quarterly income from all sources."

I felt pole-axed. I guess I would be considered rich. That was a strange feeling as I thought twice about almost any expenditure as though I were on an allowance.

"This is mine to do as I want with it?"

"Rick, you couldn't spend it fast enough. By this time next year, it should be fifty million a quarter. You should be one of the richest people in the world in the next five years.

"If you want to spend more than one hundred thousand dollars, you will have to let me know in advance. The bulk of the money is invested in the stock market. However, the hundred grand is in a cash reserve attached to your checking account."

"You mean I could write a check for one hundred thousand dollars?"

"Yes."

"Yikes! What stocks am I invested in?"

"For the long term, anything to do with homeownership, such as home improvement stores, is a good investment. We are also buying up coastal land in California and Florida as it becomes available, only lots or houses with a direct ocean or gulf view."

"Wow, you have given me a lot to think about."

At that point, I did the only reasonable thing possible. I went surfing.

After dinner in the library, I cornered Mum and Dad and asked if they knew about my financial condition. Mum told me that I was not getting my allowance raised.

"Uh, Mum, I haven't been getting an allowance for some time now."

"Rick, it was worth it to see the look on your face. Yes, we know how your finances are coming. Maybe you could give me an allowance instead."

I believed her for a moment. Dad snorted and gave it away.

Dad told me, "Rick, we are doing fine, not as good as you are, but we are multi-millionaires in our own right, so the kids won't go hungry."

We moved on to a more serious subject. Dad had set the reporters loose to find out about the people who had been on the yacht. He didn't expect anything until early next week.

From there, I cleaned up and watched a movie with Denny and Eddie. Mary pouted a little as it would be past her bedtime but got distracted by Mum and a fancy tea party.

The movie was good. I would like to visit Rathcullen someday. Though I doubted I would run into King Connors or see a pooka, much less a banshee. Come to think of it, I never wanted to see a banshee. I felt that the tall, dark actor who played the love interest was fairly good, and we would see more of him.

Saturday was a surprise. It was now horse and pony arrival day. Mum and Dad told us kids about it at breakfast. Mary immediately went to the stable to await their arrival. She would return every ten to fifteen minutes to ask if they were due.

Finally, at ten o'clock, the horse van pulled in. It had horses for everyone in the family and several for guests. Also, one pony for one excited little girl. You could tell it was love at first sight. She wanted to go riding immediately.

Mum explained she could not ride until she had a saddle and the other equipment. That brought on a demand to go shopping at once. Dad laughed as this had all been planned.

We loaded up in several cars. I mean, we boys had to be in a convertible. I don't even want to guess how much we spent at the Western shop. It was operated by a lady named Mary. Well, it really wasn't a shop. She was working out of her garage! However, she had the largest selection of Western gear in the entire state. When I said garage, it was not a one-car garage. It would hold six cars easily, and she had several outbuildings.

She and Mum had met at a charity dinner. Mary wanted to open a store in a few years, but right now, she was the best-kept secret on the West Coast, according to her.

We ended up with Western saddles and English saddles. The ladies had a fashion show with all the clothes they bought, again to match the saddle they were using. The men stuck to Western gear. Of course, I had it all at home and well broken in from my movie sets.

It occurred to me that we had bought all this stuff and didn't know how to use it. When I questioned Dad on this, he told me he realized the problem and that we would hire someone to guide us and take care of the stables.

I wondered why this wasn't done upfront but decided discretion was the better part of valor. The buying took most of the afternoon, and we ate a late lunch on the way home. We had bought so much gear it wouldn't fit in the two cars, so Dad arranged for it to be delivered to the house. Of course, Mum and Mary did fit the clothes into the car.

Well, so did Dad and the boys. I felt smug as I had everything at home.

The ranch that sold us the horses had arranged for a cowhand to stay for several days, along with feed and straw for bedding. Mary was ready to sleep with her pony, which she named Misty. We had never been to Chincoteague, VA, but she had the stories read to her.

After the novelty of the horses wore off, we boys played pool in the first basement. Of course, Denny cleaned our clocks as usual. After dinner, I went back to the books, this time on flying.

On Sunday, we boys toured downtown. I had come up with an idea to make my tail spotting more fun, and the boys agreed. We selected four points where Denny could get pictures of me coming towards him so he would get pictures of anyone in front or behind me. I mapped out several routes that would pass by these points and give him plenty of time to get into position using streets out of their line of sight.

The idea was not only to evade my trackers but to identify the entire team.

After that was set up, I took the boys to the beach and introduced them to surfing. We had a ball.

Chapter 33

Monday was another glorious day in California. It was a pleasure to do my morning run. I had some nosey watchers when I went out the back gate to the park. Horses were looking out of the open stall doors. The cowhand who had stayed behind said, "Mornin'." I nodded back, as that seemed appropriate to such a laconic greeting.

There was also a little girl feeding an apple to a small pony. It was still a small pony but would probably end up fat as a pig if Mary got her way.

The run went well, with no fearsome tigers or chipmunks. That is one story I will take to my grave.

After cleaning up and eating too much at breakfast, thinking I didn't need Mary to feed me as I could do the pig bit on my own. Well, okay, I had what they called six-pack abs and looked in great shape, so I guess I could eat what I wanted. Anyway, I asked Mum and Dad if I could talk to them briefly.

"Sure, Rick, what's up?"

Suddenly I felt a little nervous.

"Well, I was thinking that if I have all that money, maybe I could buy an airplane."

Dad got a serious look, but before he could say anything, Mum butted in.

"Jack, don't tease him. Of course, you can buy an airplane if it makes sense."

"Thanks, Mum." I gave an innocent-looking Dad a nasty look.

Dad, ignoring my look, asked, "What do you have in mind?"

"A twin-engine aircraft makes the most sense for carrying some passengers and having reasonable speed. I have talked to Mr. McGarry about different ones but would have to do more homework before choosing one."

"Well, since it's not a 707, I guess it is okay."

Mum must have been feeling contrary today.

"Well, Jack, I have been meaning to talk to you about that. A Boeing 707 or a DC-8 would be nice."

Dad had a pained look. You could tell he was an experienced husband, though.

"Yes, dear, let's talk about it."

I wondered what colors our new large jet would be painted.

"It would be nice to have a machine shop. I would pay for an extension off the garage."

"Well, your inventions have more than paid for it, so that's okay. Just let us review the plans before proceeding," Dad told me.

While I was on a streak, I decided to go for broke.

"I understand that my investments include beachfront property here in California. I wonder if the family would want to use one of them as a weekend place."

I thought I was clever bringing the family use into it.

With a smirk, Dad replied, "Well, you should look up two of them, one near where you surf and the other for the family to actually use, like down in Malibu."

You could have knocked me over with a feather. How can parents see through you like that?

About that time, Mrs. Hernandez left the room to answer the telephone. You could hear her say, "Jackson House." As usual, she had been sitting at the breakfast table with us. She really was a member of our family.

"Rick, it's for you."

"I'll be right there."

I identified myself and found out it was a producer from the *Today Show* in New York. They wanted me to be part of a show on Monday morning. I didn't have to call Susan Wallace to know I should do this. I told them I would.

I would have to fly east on Saturday for a Sunday afternoon taping. Mr. Garroway's health had been declining. It was pretty well known in the industry that he suffered from depression and would walk out in the middle of a show. That was why it was taped.

I did call Susan after that, and she told me that was a good call. She would be flying with me on Saturday so that I would take care of all the arrangements.

Mum, Denny, and I headed downtown. Each of us went to our agreed-upon positions.

I walked the route and didn't try any evasion until after I passed the four points. There was no front tail this time, so it was easy. I had my -Bird in a parking garage, so we were home by lunchtime. The cook had outdone herself with a toasted cheese guacamole sandwich.

After lunch, we went to Denny's darkroom. He developed the pictures, and he had wonderful shots of my tail and Mr. Robertson. I must say Mr. Robertson still seemed very unhappy. When he saw how well the pictures turned out, Denny tried to jack up the price by saying he thought he now deserved to be paid for taking the photos. We didn't really get into it, but I had to tell him, "I'm the boss, applesauce."

He came back with, "Don't give me lip, potato chip."

Honor satisfied on both sides, we let it drop. However, I realized I needed to consider an extra gift if it all worked out. As I walked out of the room, he had to have the last word.

"Hit the road, toad."

I made a rude hand gesture over my shoulder and left with a grin. I went to check if I had any mail delivered to the house.

In the mail was a letter from Hollywood High. It was an invitation to a sock hop in two weeks. It will be on Saturday. That would be the day after I visit the White House, but I should be back on time. I had to go. The invitation said, "Be there or be square."

I certainly wasn't going to be square.

Mum also got a letter, more of a package, really. Within it was a small package addressed to Sir Richard Jackson, Queen's Messenger. She stood there as I opened it. There was a letter with my name and another envelope with the notation, DO NOT OPEN.

I read the letter out loud.

"Sir Richard, Her Majesty requires you to deliver this accompanying letter to the following address unopened on Monday of next week. Wear your Greyhound pin to identify yourself. The address is a Chinese dry cleaner, so drop off some clothes that really do need cleaning."

That seemed pretty straightforward. Mum and I went to the library and found a Los Angeles street directory. The address shown was in the middle of Chinatown.

"Well, this should be interesting."

"Rick, just remember the statement, 'May you live in interesting times,' is a Chinese curse. That said, on the surface, it doesn't seem unreasonable. I shall make some inquiries as to the nature of this delivery."

"Thanks, Mum. It doesn't seem that big of a deal."

"It never does at first."

Wanting to strike while the iron was hot, I headed to the airfield to ask Mr. McGarry if he would help me shop for an airplane. Silly me, of course, he would. We spent the rest of the day going from one aircraft dealer to another.

He knew everyone in the trade, or more accurately, they knew and respected him. When he explained what we were looking for, I didn't get any "how can a kid like you do this" looks or questions.

The Cessna 310C is what I wanted to buy. Its six seats, 260hp, and 215mph made it the best going. The going rate of sixty thousand dollars seemed a bit much until you considered the alternatives.

The Piper Apache also has six seats and is much cheaper at thirty-six thousand. Its drawback is it has only 160hp or 135 mph. I learned that going across the country directly at 80 more mph made for a lot less time in the air.

The biggest drawback to the Cessna was its maintenance costs if earlier models are any indication. The aircraft hadn't been out long enough to have a good baseline. There was no question they would be much higher than the Piper.

The Beechcraft Travel Air was out of the question since it only held four with a fifth fold-down jump seat. Its speed and cost were between the other two, but the extra passenger seat was important. I wanted the entire family to be able to fly comfortably; that is, if they would let me fly them at all. Well, at least Mary would let me drop her off at school.

I decided upon the Cessna. We had been to that dealership first and Beechcraft last, so we went back to Cessna. I told them I wanted to order a 310C. I was ready to pull out my checkbook then and there, but Mr. McGarry jumped in. He had a bunch of questions, like how long to deliver, what choices in color schemes, wet or dry, scheduled maintenance cost at this dealership, and a few more.

As they were answered, I learned that wet or dry was with or without fuel and lubricants.

There were also many extras, such as navigation aids and communication gear. I settled on British racing green as the base of the color scheme, with my coat of arms on the pilot side door. Leather seats were a given.

I could see the dollars rolling up. Then Mr. McGarry rubbed his hands together and said, "Now the fun begins." He negotiated the price. It would have been a total of sixty-seven thousand dollars. He got them down to sixty-two thousand and the first two years of regular maintenance. This was really good as anything else would be under warranty unless I crashed it. If I did that, I doubted the cost would be a worry. The aircraft was to be delivered wet.

I was disappointed to hear that the aircraft wouldn't be delivered until late August next year. That was okay because I wouldn't have my private pilot's license until after my birthday. I could take lessons on multi-engines, but that was it.

Then, the talk went to insurance. I thought this would never end.

Well, I was right. It wasn't going to end soon because now the salesman wanted to talk about financing. Mr. McGarry told me that I should pay as much down as possible since the cost of financing could be as much as the cost of the aircraft.

That was one thing I could handle. I did pull out my checkbook now, and knowing I could cover the whole amount, I asked for the bottom line.

Even Mr. McGarry's eyebrows went up at that. The salesman looked disappointed, as though he was losing out on something. Later, I found he was expecting a commission kickback from the bank.

Mr. McGarry kidded me as I dropped him off at his office.

"If I had known that you could write a check like that, I would have charged you more and told my daughter to chase you."

He was kidding. At least, I think he was kidding.

I got home just in time for dinner. As we settled in, Dad asked me, "Well, Rick, what sort of an airplane did you buy?"

How do parents always know these things?

Rather than get into that, I described the Cessna. This got us into a family discussion of where we could fly locally. When Dad used the term locally, I gave him a questioning look.

"Oh, Mum and I have an appointment next week at Boeing headquarters."

That brought on another round of excitement, my own included. They all agreed on my choice of colors and my coat of arms was brilliant. They would do the same but use Mum's coat of arms. It seemed plain weird talking about using our personal coat of arms as if everyone could do that.

The talk changed to everyone listing places they would like to go to. When Buenos Aires was brought up, I suddenly remembered an irate father. Well, I would cross that bridge when I came to it. Thinking about it, I hoped I would never be in the position of some sex-starved teenager chasing my daughter. Then it occurred to me that even worse, I could have a sex-starved teenage daughter. No wonder men wanted a son.

It was perfectly logical that I spent the rest of the evening studying my aircraft manuals. The dealer had some brochures on the Cessna but not a complete manual. They had agreed to get me one as soon as possible. It would be a while before I received my aircraft as they were built to order and currently on almost a twelve-month lead time.

While I wasn't very physical today, I was mentally tired as I dropped off without reading anything.

Chapter 34

In the morning, my nosey neighbors were waiting for me. Heh, I had to pull that on someone, my nosey NEIGHbors. I had a good run, then did my exercises, sure to include the new sets for flexibility.

Tuesday's tailing lessons were a repeat of yesterday's. There was another person added to the mix as a front tail. I spotted them early on but ignored both my tails until we passed the four picture points. Since the downtown LA business district isn't that large, I don't think it was noticeable that we were passing the same points since most of the route was different than yesterday.

The developed pictures told the tale. We decided to try something different on Wednesday. Homeschooling was certainly working out well for my project, but I know the boys were ready to attend school again as they missed the social activities. Mum was brought into the discussion about what I wanted to do differently, and she enthusiastically approved.

After lunch at our favorite café, Denny and I dropped off Mum at home, picked up Eddie, and headed to the beach for some surfing. Both boys were getting into it. I had set them up with all the gear they needed at Katin's.

We had to hurry home and get cleaned up and dressed for dinner. Denny enjoyed the dressing up, Eddie not so much. I think Denny would be what they used to call a dandy, but now it was a preppy.

After dinner, I hit the schoolbooks. Well, I spent my time doing the extra writing assignments at the end of my current chapters. I found that by doing these, I developed a deeper understanding of what really happened or what the basis of an experiment really was. I think the hardest thing for me to accept was how the Founding Fathers were such hard men.

In grade school, it was practically St. George Washington. The real George Washington was a hard man in hard times. As I thought about it, under those conditions, his choosing not to be a king was even more impressive. I mean, he had the "off with their heads" part down pat.

Later I read about the fireman Guy Montag and the Mechanical Hound. I couldn't picture people becoming so sensitive about the use of words that some of them would be banned and books burned.

It was getting to be normal for the horses to be watching for me. I still got the same "mornin'" from the cowhand. I returned it with, "Yep." Two could play that game.

No tigers or chipmunks were about, though I did see an evil-looking squirrel.

Denny, Mum, and I headed downtown for my daily lesson.

I deliberately did a poor evasion job so they were able to follow me to the parking garage. What they didn't know was that Denny was tailing them after they passed the last picture-taking point. They had never spotted him, so they had no reason to suspect a kid at this point. He had a reversible jacket, so he shouldn't stand out. He carried a two-way radio along with a camera on a strap around his neck. It was a kid's toy but had enough range for our purpose.

Since they were done for the day by following me to my vehicle, they returned to theirs. Denny followed them to where they parked two blocks over. He gave me a running commentary, so I was there to pick him up as they exited the garage. I held back as far as I could. I wondered if I should buy a less noticeable car for events like this.

They were staying at a small motel not far from downtown. Denny got shots of them as they opened their adjoining room doors on the outside first floor. There was an outdoor pool in front of the building. They brought out food to prepare hamburgers on a grill next to the pool. It seems like they were on a small vacation. The group consisted of five young people in their early twenties, I guess, and Mr. Robertson. They were all dressed for swimming, so we figured out where they would be for most of the afternoon.

Denny and I returned home, where he developed the pictures. They came out perfectly. The tailers had been tailed! Denny had a magnifying glass and was examining everyone in every photo.

"Hey Rick, look at this."

He pointed out the same man in several pictures. He also had a camera. He was taking pictures, but it was not of Denny or me. It was of the CIA trainees. At least I assumed they were trainees.

As we were wondering what to do with this information, Mum joined us. She wanted to know how our back tailing worked out. She thought we had done a good job. When Denny pointed out the mystery man, she got a thoughtful frown.

"Would you boys mind if I joined your party?"

"You are always welcome, Mum," enthused Denny.

I silently added unless it was on a date.

We were in place at five o'clock and had to wait an hour for the CIA crew to go to dinner. It was good that we were in the housekeeper's car, a blue Chevy, because the mystery man showed up five minutes later. When the CIA people left for dinner, we followed the mystery man.

He took pictures of the CIA group and left after they went into the restaurant. We followed him as far back as we could. He drove to a park by the beach. Mum quickly set us up as a rotating tail. One of us would move up as the other dropped back. Denny and I had reversible jackets, so we would turn them inside out when we switched.

It was just a walk in the park. He did stop and tie his shoe once and then sat on a bench for a while. But all in all, it was nothing. Or so I thought.

When he returned to his car, I thought we would follow him, but Mum had other ideas.

She took us back to where he had tied his shoe. I could've kicked myself after Mum pointed out the chalk mark he had made on the base of the light pole he had stopped at. This was right out of James Bond.

So, I was not surprised when she told us the film of the CIA operatives was hidden on a ledge under the park bench he had stopped at. We scouted around and found a vantage point to watch the bench from, but saw nothing. Passersby had dwindled, so we checked for the film. It was still there.

After lunch, we spent the afternoon with the horses. We didn't try to ride them; we walked them around on a leader, so they became used to us. I found out that Mary had disappeared from her room last night and started a mild panic. It was only a mild panic since Mum went directly to the stable and found her sound asleep with Misty.

My evening was spent on homework. There is nothing like the exciting life of a movie star.

Thursday morning began as usual, except Mary had slept in her bed last night.

Denny and Mum spent the next day watching that bench while I led the CIA on a chase around downtown LA. I used every trick I had been taught to identify and lose them. My best time all week was one hour.

In the meantime, we checked the bench later in the evening. The film had disappeared. Denny had been taking pictures of everyone who had stopped at that bench. When we reviewed them, he actually had a shot of a man reaching down under the bench. He became our new target.

I redoubled my efforts to give the CIA a good workout and the mystery man photo opportunities. At dinner, we talked about what was going on. Both Mum and Dad agreed that it was probably a foreign agent or freelancer taking pictures of the CIA trainees. Their covers would be blown before they ever went to work!

Eddie wanted to shoot the mystery men. Mary wondered if he could be turned. What was Mum teaching that kid?

I did more homework later in the evening; ho-hum.

Friday afternoon, the mystery man showed up again. There was no chalk mark indicating film waiting for him, so he walked on by. Mum and Denny tailed him back to the Soviet Consulate. That answered that question.

Now, what to do with our information? Mum filled us in on a few realities of life.

The information rightfully should be turned over to the FBI as they were responsible for counter-spy operations within the United States borders. They would do a good job but also use it in their ongoing political war for funding and authority. J. Edgar Hoover hated the CIA with a purple passion according to Dad.

We could turn it over to Mum's old, or maybe not so old, group. It would be a similar issue. They would use it for leverage and favors with the CIA. We decided to avoid politics and give it to the CIA. It was their operatives who were compromised.

The question then became who in the CIA to turn it over to. I came down in favor of Mr. Droller, who had debriefed me in Cuba. He had a high position in the agency and wasn't directly mixed up in this mess. Mum and Dad agreed but also wanted to backchannel Ike that the CIA had a problem. Not all the details, but enough that he could keep them honest.

The last thing we wanted was to have young agents known to the enemy before they even went to work. The group who had their pictures taken would never go into the field. They were deskbound and would never know why.

I never really heard how it all came out, but there was an article in the paper about someone at the Soviet Consulate being declared persona non grata. There was also another story about a spy trade at checkpoint Charlie, one of theirs for one of ours. I had no idea if these were the people we had identified.

What puzzled me was how Mum gave homeschooling credit to Denny for counterespionage. Okay, it was for his photography, but we all knew what it was for. When I asked if I would get any credit, she murmured something about standing in the shadows.

Chapter 35

After lunch, I drove over to the studio. I was there to view the team presentations I had been invited to earlier. They were slick but more important to me, they were really working as teams. There were no radical new proposals on how to structure their business as they had with the "extra board" concept. However, everything they presented was cross-functional. Finance was sensitive to production's needs, and production considered the costs of what they were proposing and how they could control them.

What I found strange was that the various team leaders and presenters kept looking at me as if seeking my approval. I had no problem keeping a positive look on my face as they were performing Boy Scout teaming 101. From my business transactions, I know that at the boy level, it's pretty elementary, but at the adult level, it was burdened by adult gamesmanship as the adults jockeyed for power and position. They had appeared to find a happy medium of cooperation, so they all won a little.

Now I'm not that naïve. I know that the boys and adults all did their normal scheming behind the scenes, but they did not let it show on the surface, as they were all role models for each other in the troop. Here, the adults were showing they were members of the team, peer pressure is what I think they called it. It was the same for professional athletes. I knew they were normal people, so had their problems, but you never saw them in the newspaper. It was silent collusion between the players, the teams, and the media to show their best face to the world. You would never see a story about a former player, whose picture had been on a Wheaties box, being in trouble.

At the end of the presentations, I stood and started a one-man slow clap. The smiles in the room were incredible since they had done all the work. I gave a slight bow and said, "My work here is done." After that, I left without getting involved in any follow-up conversation. It was their moment in the sun to enjoy. On my way out of the room, I passed two writers. One had written down in large letters my statement of "My work here is done." The other was saying we could use that in...I didn't hear the rest of his idea of where to use it.

When I left the room, Mr. Monroe was waiting for me. He wanted to know how they were doing and would he be pleased with the results. I assured him that his team was doing very well and that he would be pleased with their presentation. He thanked me profusely.

As I walked away, I was bemused with how I was fitting into this world. The man who should be a God in my Universe was thanking me!

I had dinner with my agent Mr. Baxter at the Brown Derby, our standard meeting place. There was nothing specific on the horizon after my Hawaiian surfing movie. It was more of a catch-up; we discussed what type of movies would I like to do in the future. I told him I was open to anything that didn't have me in a water trough. That brought a deep laugh from him. My adventures with water troughs were gaining international notoriety. He asked if he could share that thought. I told him to discuss it with Susan Wallace of how and when to use it, but I was down with it.

Mr. Baxter's family was doing well. He made a point of again thanking me for my efforts in seeing he got the money needed for the medical bills. Realizing this older man felt like he owed me big time was a little strange. I had to think about this, along with the group earlier in the day. I was beginning to affect people's lives and had better keep my head straight. How was I to do that? I wouldn't be sixteen until Sunday!

Mr. Sinatra caught me as we were leaving. He wanted to know if I was open to another duet. I said sure, I would be glad to help his fading career. He looked like he was going to deck me, but I couldn't keep a straight face, so he ended up taking it in good part. I'm glad because if he had taken a swing, it would have ended up badly for both of us: me for the publicity and him for his health.

I asked Mr. Sinatra if he had a song in mind.

"I was thinking of a remake of 'The Coffee Song' or maybe 'High Hopes."

"I'm not familiar with either of them."

"Not to worry, they are easy songs to do."

Mr. Baxter was with me, so I asked him if he would take care of the details. Of course, he agreed. Mr. Sinatra gave him his agent's contact number, and they were to work out the details. I was surprised at how much money I had made on my last foray with "Brothers". It was fun, and I would continue until someone realized I couldn't sing.

Mr. Sinatra told us about a funny conversation he had with Judge Smails. The judge thought he could get Sinatra to get some heavies after me. Mr. Sinatra told him that there was no one heavier than my godfather. Of course, Smails bit and asked which gang leader that was. Franks' answer ended the conversation quickly. Frank told me he was a little disappointed because he never got to mention my godmother.

As we were leaving, I noticed several people had been eavesdropping, so I knew it would be in the scandal sheets. I made a mental note to tell Susan about it on our flight.

When I got home after dinner, I didn't feel like hitting the books, so I watched TV with my parents. When I said good night, I realized I had no idea what had been on the boob tube.

Chapter 36

Saturday, I passed on my workout. I had to leave for the airport at 4:00 am to make a 6:00 am flight east. I was able to doze off in the limo, but it wasn't deep sleep. There were no problems getting checked in and boarding for my first-class seat. Susan was waiting for me at the check-in counter. She had our first-class boarding passes in hand for TWA flight 160. The *Today Show* had paid for these.

Only several other people were in first class, so there were ten vacant seats. The co-pilot was standing in the doorway to greet passengers, along with a stewardess. I must have been gawking into the cockpit because he asked me if I wanted a look. I jumped at the opportunity. With my interest in flying, of course, I wanted to see the cockpit.

When I told him I had my student's license and had soloed, I became a member of the fraternity. He and the pilot, both of whose names I missed, welcomed me and gave me an extensive tour of all those gauges and instruments. I concluded that as long as nothing mechanically went wrong, a person could keep track of what was happening. It was when those lights went red the excitement started.

I was amazed at all the gauges and dials. One thing puzzled me: there was a pilot and co-pilot but no flight engineer, even though there was a seat for one. I asked about that and found out a flight engineer was only required for flights that were more than eight hours in the air. We weren't required to have one as we were making a stop in Cincinnati, Ohio. I asked how that worked for them and was told it wasn't a problem. Even on the long hauls, flight engineers had less and less to do all the time.

With the advent of transistor radios, the co-pilot thought that radio needs on aircraft would change dramatically. He figured that on the overseas routes, they wouldn't even need a navigator using a sextant to track where they were headed.

I took one last look at the instruments and was glad I would not have to fly this bird.

When I returned to my seat, Susan teased me about flying the plane. I shook my head and told her I would need many years of training to do so and wasn't that heavily into it. Changing the subject, I brought her up to date on my conversation with Mr. Sinatra. She told me she would contact Mr. Baxter when we landed in New York.

While the coach passengers were boarding, our stewardess asked us what we would like to drink. I had a Coke; Susan asked for a Mimosa. I had to ask what that was, and it turned out it was champagne and orange juice. While serving us, the stewardess told us that there would be in-flight movies for long flights very soon. Susan thought that amazing and wondered if they would ever have telephones. I thought they would someday, but it would be far in the future.

The take-off was amazing to me. It took such a long runway to roll out. I was used to my little plane; this was a different ballgame. Landing this thing must be a trip.

We were no sooner up in the air, and the stewardess was preparing breakfast. The menu gave a choice of Eggs Benedict or French toast, along with orange juice, coffee, or tea. Susan and I chose the French toast. I noticed that one of the stewardesses and the guys up front took Eggs Benedict. I wondered if I finished my French toast I could beg for a serving of Eggs Benedict.

Apparently not. TWA had a firm one-passenger, one-meal policy. Oh well, we would have lunch before landing in Cincinnati. It would be a small filet, so I would probably make it to New York. Maybe they would have a meal on that leg of the trip.

We had been in the air for about two hours when the co-pilot made a quick trip to the restroom. I say quick, and I mean quick; he looked desperate. Next thing you know, the pilot is standing at the restroom door, urging him to hurry up. A rapid change took place, and they returned to the cockpit. In another five minutes, they were both out again. Except for this time, the pilot got to the restroom first.

The co-pilot went to the galley and was throwing up in a bin. The pilot came out but turned right around again for the restroom. In the meantime, the co-pilot obviously had uncontrollable diarrhea. He was doubled over in pain. The smell was awful. The head stewardess helped him to a seat, where he promptly passed out.

She next checked on the pilot. He was unconscious in the restroom. I helped her bring him out to a seat. To put it mildly, it was a stinking mess.

In the meantime, the head stewardess got on the public announcement system and asked if a physician was on board. If so, push the button for help. There were two responses. Soon two doctors were escorted up front. One was a general practitioner and the other a surgeon. They both quickly agreed that it was food poisoning. This was no sooner said than one of the other stewardesses rushed to the restroom. She had the Eggs Benedict.

As a thought was going through my head, it was confirmed by a request for any pilots or aircrew to ring their call buttons. There were no dings or red lights on. It dawned on me that I may be the only one on board who had ever been at the instruments of an aircraft. Talk about a sinking feeling in your stomach.

I identified myself to the head stewardess as a student pilot who had soloed. She gave me a piercing look and said, "You're all we've got."

Talk about the pressure.

We went into the cockpit, where I had been a tourist earlier in the day. Now it was mine. I hadn't eaten Eggs Benedict but had a desire to go to the restroom. I managed to overcome that to take a closer look at the pilot's seat and the controls. At least we were at cruising altitude and on autopilot.

I went back to the doctors who were tending their three patients. Not that there was much to do, as all three were unconscious. I asked how long before one of the pilots might be conscious and able to help me. Both had bleak looks, as I was told they had no idea. Whatever poisoned them was extremely serious.

From the noise in the back end, you could tell people knew something was happening, and they were getting worked up. I signaled the head stewardess to come with me.

"Do you know anything about the radios?" I asked Sara. I knew she was Sara because of her nametag.

"A little bit. I have watched them many times."

"Okay, you are now my co-pilot." She made the sign of the cross and said, "Okay."

We sat down in our respective seats. At least the pilots didn't mess them up. We buckled up, adjusted our straps, and put on the headphones. After fiddling for a minute, we had them set correctly so we could talk to each other and use the radio at its current settings.

Reading from a card set in front of the radio, I made a call.

"This is TWA flight 160, tail number N742TW, declaring an inflight emergency," I repeated this twice and then waited.

Almost immediately, there was a reply.

"TWA 160, what is the nature of your emergency?"

"The pilot and co-pilot are both unconscious, with suspected food poisoning. Physicians on board are not optimistic."

"Please reconfirm, pilot and co-pilot are unconscious."

"That is correct."

"Who are you?"

"Richard Jackson, a student pilot who has soloed."

"TWA 160, this is FAA TRACON. What is your flight status?"

"We are on autopilot, bound to Cincinnati, Ohio, with probably a lot of fuel as we are only one and a half hours out."

"TWA 160, DO NOT, REPEAT, DO NOT TOUCH THE AUTOPILOT."

"Roger, flight control, not touching the autopilot." There was no way in the world I was going to mess with the autopilot.

"TWA 160, go to radio channel 121.50000 MHz. Repeat 121.50000."

"Roger, going to channel 121.50000 MHz's." From my studies, I knew this was the VHF Guard channel for emergencies. They wanted us to go to this channel while they sorted things out. Every aircraft and scanner in the area could hear us. Most of them would monitor the new channel, but it would free up the main channel for normal business. That seemed a little cold, but they had a whole lot of aircraft to keep out of trouble.

Sara had been paying attention as she adjusted one of the radios to the correct frequency.

"This is TWA 160 on Guard channel."

"Roger, TWA 160, we are contacting your company. In the meantime, do not touch the autopilot." I got the impression he really didn't want me to touch the autopilot. That worked for me.

The people in the back had to be going crazy. I got on the in-plane radio and announced it.

"Ladies and gentlemen, there is an inflight problem. The pilot has suffered food poisoning. He is receiving medical care; we are currently in contact with FAA TRACON, who will direct us to the nearest safe landing."

Since I had seen several Latinos on board the aircraft, I repeated the message in Spanish. Odds are they spoke English, but it was easy to do and might forestall problems. I also asked again if anyone else was on board with flying experience. No one came forward.

I was not about to tell everyone that both the pilot and co-pilot were unconscious. Panic would ensue with that information—time enough for panic later.

"Sara, have someone stationed at the rear of first-class, and do not let anyone come forward and see the real mess we are in."

"I already have." Thank God for at least one professional here. I should have ordered that first thing. Ordered that? I think at that moment it really sank in. I was now the captain and pilot of this flight, and it all depended on me.

Thoughts of what I would have to do: get us to an airport, dump fuel, land the aircraft, stop the aircraft. I would have many opportunities to kill us all!

My mind went in circles for what seemed forever but was only a few seconds. Then my life training kicked in—one step at a time. I needed expert help. Presumably, the FAA was contacting TWA for that help. See the problem resolved. Who am I kidding?! About that time, instructions came back.

"TWA 160, this is FAA ARTTC Denver Control Center. Please go to channel 130.925 MHz for TWA."

"Roger that, Denver." Sara turned the radio to 130.925. One small saving grace was that we had good reception.

"This is TWA 160 calling TWA."

"TWA 160, this is TWA. Please tune to channel 130.125 immediately. Repeat channel 130.125 immediately."

Sara was quick on those dials.

"TWA, this is TWA 160."

"TWA 160, this is TWA. We did that to try to give us some privacy on this."

"Roger that, TWA."

"TWA 160, what is your name?"

"Richard Jackson, but call me Rick."

"I am Edward Frankum, but call me Ed."

"Okay, Ed, I need a lot of help here."

"My first question is exactly how many people are on board? Tell a stewardess we need to know how many souls are on board." I had never heard it put that way before. It didn't sound good, but it would give the total headcount without any confusion.

The head stewardess was prepared with that and told me 139 souls were on board. I relayed that and was given the next question.

"What is your experience?"

I told him what aircraft I had flown and my hours.

"Okay, so you understand the principles of flight and handling an aircraft but know nothing about how jets operate or handling something this large."

"That is correct." By this time, we had given up on radio protocol and were having a conversation.

"Well, at least we have something to work with. Please reconfirm the conditions of the flight crew."

I checked with the doctors once more. All three flight personnel were now described as being in a coma, and we couldn't count on a recovery soon. The doctors felt if we could not land and get an IV in them, we could lose them.

I relayed this to Ed.

"Okay, Rick, we will proceed as though you will land this aircraft. The first thing we will do is get you familiar with how the aircraft handles. It will respond to the same controls you are used to but will seem like trying to steer an elephant in comparison."

"Roger that, steer like an elephant." Even in the grimmest of times, you can get a chuckle out of things.

"Rick, I will ask you to disconnect the autopilot in a minute, but I have a few questions first."

"Okay."

"What is your altitude?" I could see the altimeter clearly, but he described its appearance and location.

"We are at 33,000 feet above sea level or FL330."

"What does your airspeed indicator show?" Again, he made certain what gauge I was reading.

"474 knots."

"There should be a clipboard with the pilot's notes on it."

"I have it."

"Can you see any fuel estimates on it?"

"Yes, it says the initial fuel weight was 120,000 pounds. He further calculated that he burned 14,000 pounds during take-off. There is another note saying 16,000 pounds per hour."

"So, you have been airborne for two hours now?"

"Roger."

"From that, it looks like you now have 74,000 pounds on board. We plan to land in St. Louis, which is five hours total flying time. That will take you down to 42,000 pounds. We need to have 6500 pounds for holding thirty minutes, but of course, we will try not to hold you at all. Then, another 15,000 to your alternate airport, which will be Indianapolis, plus 1,700 pounds for the descent, which means we can dump 18,800 pounds of fuel. That will make the plane easier to handle and safer on the ground."

"Come again; I didn't get most of that."

"Bottom line, Rick: you must dump 18,800 pounds of fuel. This will make the aircraft handle better. Along with what you burn along the way, it will handle like a cow rather than an elephant."

"Roger will be dumping 18,800 pounds of fuel and will handle like a cow."

"Now, when we begin some gentle handling maneuvers, it is important you don't change the airspeed or altitude very much, or we will have to recalculate the fuel."

"Roger, don't vary airspeed or altitude during gentle maneuvers."

He then proceeded to work with me to adjust my seat so I could properly reach the pedals and learn where the basic flight controls were. Nothing was surprising about this, which gave me some hope.

Ed then walked me through both turning off and turning on the autopilot. Finally, he had me turn the autopilot off. The plane didn't do anything dramatic as I put my hands on the controls. Ed first had me descend a little. He was right. It was like asking an elephant to turn compared to what I was used to. More like driving a car without power steering. You just had to work at it more. Then came a series of turns. They were, as he asked, gentle. You could hardly tell we were banked at all.

After this exercise, he had me reset the autopilot. I then read off the airspeed, altimeter, and headings. Next, he had me check the gauges on each engine. I had to report each engine's Engine Pressure Ratio, % RPM 1st rotor, Exhaust Temperature, % RPM 2nd Rotor, and Fuel Flow (pounds per hour x 1000). Everything was within norms, A relief.

Then there was oil quality, oil temperature, and oil pressure from the engineer's panel. Again, all was normal. I had to check almost one hundred gauges in total. It was easy to do as each horizontal row had its needles parallel to show they were okay. Only if one were not parallel would there be a concern.

Another thing going for us was that the weather forecast was excellent all the way. There was no air turbulence reported in front of us. I wasn't listening to those channels, but Ed and his backups were. From the talk in the background of the radio, I could tell he was not a one-man operation. They were getting reports from all commercial aircraft between St. Louis and us.

We were handed off from the Denver Control Center to the St. Louis Control Center during that time.

Ed had me disengage the autopilot several more times and practice gentle rises and dips while turning. He had me go through this exercise for the next two hours. I think it was as much to keep me occupied as to get a feel for the aircraft. While doing all this, he asked where I had learned to fly and who was my instructor.

When I told him it was Mr. McGarry, he wanted to know if that was McGarry of the Flying Tigers. When I said yes, his response was, "Then you do know how to fly. Just promise you won't strafe the runway."

Since I had no weapons, it was an easy promise to make. It was evident that he did know Mr. McGarry.

At one point, I got up and checked on things in the back. The flight crew members were still out with no sign of recovery. Dr. Casey told me there was no chance of one of them helping even if they regained consciousness.

I looked into the back cabin, and the passengers were all sitting quietly, some in obvious prayer. I thought there would be a panic rather than quiet acceptance.

The other two first-class passengers were doing their best to get totally drunk.

I asked Susan how she was holding up, and she just nodded. She was writing something; I don't know if it was a journal entry or what. It was probably a publicity blurb about this flight.

When I returned to the cockpit, Ed told me it was time to dump fuel. The plan was for me to put the wing flaps down, which would slow the plane down, so I had to increase thrust. While doing this, I extended the dump chutes. They knew the dump rate with the chutes wide open, so they would time the dump and tell me when to close the chutes.

With my heart in my mouth, I disengaged the autopilot and raised the flaps. As I did this, the plane started to sink, so I increased thrust. First, I didn't increase the thrust enough, and then I slightly overdid it, but finally got us level at FL250 and 220 knots airspeed.

I then opened the dump chutes. It took longer than I thought, but then realized it was like emptying a swimming pool. It took a while. While this was going on, I asked for a cup of coffee. Sara had one of the other stewardesses bring it to me. She was a real trooper. There wasn't much she could do, but she watched me like a hawk on each maneuver. She was ready to question anything I might be doing wrong.

When we had finished dumping the fuel, I took us back up to FL 330 and 474 knots.

After talking with Ed and how to present it, I got on the PA with the passengers. I introduced myself as Richard Jackson, a licensed pilot. No sense in worrying them any more than we had to. I explained the flight crew's problems. The FAA and one of TWA's top pilots were helping guide the plane into St. Louis. I explained that while the 707 was new to me, I had some jet hours. I didn't clarify it was the three hours immediately preceding. If they have any questions, please ask their stewardess.

I could not believe the main question that was asked repeatedly. What connection would they have to Cincinnati or New York, and what time would they arrive at their destination? I was worried about living, and they were worried about being on time.

Ed explained that we would use an ILS approach on autopilot. That is the Instrument Landing System. This would bring the aircraft to the middle marker, where the autopilot would be disengaged, and I would then bring the aircraft down. Oh, God!

We reached the final vector or inbound procedure turn. The flaps were set at 14, and the VPROG was +30, all within norms. I selected GS Auto as instructed. We had gone over five times how to do this during the flight. The annunciator lights displayed /V and G/S, amber-colored as they were supposed to. The autopilot coupler was now programmed to automatically capture the localizer and glideslope. I wasn't sure what they were, but that is what Ed told me.

According to Ed, the localizer showed our lateral position or runway alignment. The glide slope showed our angle of descent and where we would touch down. Ideally, it would be on the touchdown point of the runway. I think he kept explaining these things to me to give me the feeling that I knew what was happening. It also kept me occupied and kept me from going crazy.

We were doing a Category 1 ILS approach, which is the mildest of all. It requires a ceiling of at least 200 feet and a visibility of 1800 feet minimum. Since it was a clear day, the conditions far exceeded that.

The intercept angle was 38 degrees, which again was within norms. The PDI gauge showing that we were aimed at the runway was within 2 dots, so the autopilot captured the localizer, and its light turned green. The V/L remained amber.

Next, the PDI glide scope bar centered, and the G/S annunciator light turned green. The altitude holds and pitch trim wheels disengaged, and the autopilot was now in command of glide scope tracking.

At one dot below the glide scope, I lowered the landing gear. I thought very briefly about how those fighter pilots in World War II had to hand-crank their gear down. The flaps had gone to 25, and our VPROG +20. The machinery was doing its job; hope I could do mine.

As we crossed the outer marker, I had a good view of the runway. All of a sudden, it seemed like the world was speeding up. We had been flying along serenely for hours. Now things were happening in seconds.

At Ed's direction, I was doing a Flaps 50 landing. This would give the airplane a shorter stopping distance. It would be a little more challenging to handle, but Ed thought we had the weight down enough that it wouldn't be an issue.

I had the aircraft at a 3-degree slope. The VFT touchdown point was actually 1000 feet before the runway, so I had to watch for that. As we crossed the middle marker, I had replayed what I had to do in my head a hundred times, now just to do it.

I eased off on the elevator back-pressure to lower the nose to try to roll onto the runway. At 50 feet above ground, I shut off the autopilot. This should have scared the devil out of me, but I didn't have the time. I would love to say we touched down like a feather; instead, it was like an elephant jumping off your dining room table. It was one heck of a thump.

I didn't have time to care; I extended the speed brakes fully and pulled the reverse levers to the interlock. That means the flaps were up completely, killing all lift. I put the engines in reverse. As I felt we were tracking on the runway, I increased the reverse thrust on the engines. At the same time, I was trying to push the brakes through the floor. The 11,000-foot runway suddenly looked short.

All this time, the nose wanted to lift back up, so I had to keep pushing on the yoke. When we slowed to 80 knots, I started reducing engine reverse thrust. By the time we were at 60 knots, the engines were idling. I kept the brakes down hard as the airplane rolled to a stop.

I asked Ed, "What now?"

"Stay right there, don't touch anything." I had no problem with that. That was when I noticed we had visitors; it looked like every fire truck in the county was out there. The runway was white where it had been foamed down. Being a teenage boy, I thanked the passengers for flying TWA, and we hoped to see them on another flight soon.

As soon as the stewardess had the doors open, the incapacitated flight crew were put into ambulances and taken to a hospital.

Sara and I stood at the doorway as the passengers deplaned. One gentleman wanted to speak to the pilot and thank him. He turned green and stuttered, "Thank you," when I told him I was the pilot.

They had moved a mobile staircase out to the plane. From there, Susan and I got on a bus. When we got on, the other passengers applauded. Not knowing what to do, I gave a small wave and sat down in the front row, which had been saved for us.

Chapter 37

At the terminal, we were met by a contingent from TWA. They were taking passengers aside and rerouting them. I was asked to go with a gentleman to an interview room. It was located inside the Ambassador Club, so Susan was allowed to wait there.

Waiting inside the conference room were several gentlemen in suits. They introduced themselves. The first was Ed Frankum, my hero; he had walked me through the most difficult event of my life. I told him that. He laughed and said he had the easy part; he was on the ground and knew what he was doing.

The other gentleman was from the FAA. He showed me his credentials, but his name didn't register with me. I think the whole event was starting to catch up with me.

The guy from the FAA was nice to me, but he debriefed me thoroughly. He took notes and had me write down what had occurred from my point of view. Ed was able to corroborate my statements. It helped that they had a cockpit recording available.

It took almost two hours to complete the interview, and I felt like a dishrag when it was over. They had brought in coffee and Danish while we were talking, but I was starving hungry.

Another TWA executive came in and talked to Ed for a minute. Ed then turned to me.

"Rick, I didn't know who I was dealing with. I am told you are the actor and a British knight?"

I confessed but didn't see what it had to do with anything.

"It explains why so many people from the press are demanding an interview. We expect it in an event like this, but this is way over the top. Are you willing to give an interview?"

I didn't feel like it but asked to see Susan.

Susan told me I might as well get it over with, as they wouldn't let this a story this big go away. Besides, this was good publicity, not bad. I guess this is why I paid her.

They had a conference room set up for us. When they told me it was a reporting frenzy, they weren't kidding. There were camera crews, reporters from the three major networks, and a local public channel, KETC. The newspapers were well represented. There must have been twenty reporters on the scene. I shouldn't have been surprised, as this news had probably broken while we were still in the air.

The questions were of the caliber I had come to expect.

"Were you scared?"

"Extremely, but Ed Frankum of TWA got me through it."

"How did it feel facing that flight alone?"

"I wasn't alone; I had the head stewardess, Sara, alongside me the whole way, and Doctor Casey and a surgeon taking care of the ill crewmembers. There was a team at work."

I realized I didn't even know Sara's last name.

"How long have you been a licensed pilot?

"I'm not; I'm licensed as a student."

"What's the difference between a student pilot and a full pilot?"

"I'm not allowed to carry passengers on my flight."

"Will you get into trouble for this?"

"I don't understand the question."

"Will you get into trouble for hauling passengers?"

"I hope not."

Cripes, I better get that checked out. The guy from the FAA didn't seem like he was going to press any charges.

"How much experience have you had on jet planes?"

"How long was this flight?"

"Oh."

And so it went. The last question floored me.

"Sir Richard, are you aware that one of the passengers is suing you for reckless endangerment?"

"I was not aware of that."

"What is your response?"

This is where my studio experience came into play.

"No comment."

"You saved his life. Isn't he being ungrateful?"

"No comment."

A TWA executive saved me.

"We have to end this news conference; Sir Richard has a flight to catch to New York."

I couldn't get out of there fast enough. Susan was waiting on the sidelines.

"Well done, Rick, especially with the no comment on the lawsuit."

"Do you think anything will come of it?"

"It will be thrown out of court, and the guy will be a national laughingstock by tomorrow."

We were escorted back to the Ambassador Club conference room. The FAA gentleman was still there writing. I took the opportunity to ask him if this would affect my student license. He thought for a moment and told me no, but he would be interested in how my check-ride pilot reading my logbook would react to my hours in a 707.

Susan told me she had called my parents while the FAA was interviewing me earlier, but maybe I should also call them. One of the Ambassador Club hostesses took me to a private office so I could place my call.

Mum took the call; I think it was one of the few times I ever heard her flustered. She didn't gush or anything, but you could tell she was really glad to hear me say I was okay. She asked me how it was to fly a big jet.

I don't think my reply that it was great, and I couldn't wait for us to get our own so I could fly it was the answer she wanted. I talked briefly to Dad. He congratulated me on a job well done. Even he had some stress in his voice.

Later, I learned the news media had broken into their broadcast with excerpts from my radio conversations with Ed Frankum for hours on end. They heard me be walked through landing in real-time. Wow, I would have been stressed if I weren't too busy at the time.

The TWA people told Susan and me that we would be going to New York on a 707 which had been down for maintenance and was being flown without passengers to Idlewild airport. There would be some TWA crew deadheading on board. They had moved our luggage over.

We were taken to a maintenance hangar across Lambert Field in a van. We were welcomed on board by twenty-some TWA flight crew of all ranks, stewardesses, pilots, co-pilots, navigators, and flight engineers. That was probably the most fun flight I ever had. I was welcome in the cockpit and could observe both landing and take-off. In between, there were many interesting stories of flights from the past. The entire crew agreed that flights were more fun without passengers on board. That said something about me and Susan.

I do know if I wanted a Coke, I had to get it myself. Their Coke was in the tin cans. I had to hunt all over the galley to find the church key. A stewardess finally took pity on me and loaned me her personal key. She explained they were always walking away as flight souvenirs as they had the TWA logo on them.

I felt a little guilty about the deck of cards I had snagged. It had a picture of the 707 on it. Not guilty enough to offer them back.

We arrived at Idlewild's hangar area, and a limo was waiting for us. It had been arranged by TWA to take us to our hotel.

Susan and I shared a two-bedroom suite. We had a light dinner from room service. I went to bed early. For some reason, I was exhausted.

It was a crisp autumn day in New York City, perfect for a run in Central Park. The hotel was across the street from it. Running past the boathouse, strawberry fields, and other places I had read about was neat. If I had to come to the city very often, I would love to have an apartment or condo here, maybe the Dakota. I had heard it mentioned several times at Hollywood parties I had to attend for my films.

There were exercise machines at the hotel, so I was able to do a full workout. Susan and I met at the hotel restaurant for breakfast. Later, after cleaning up and donning one of my London Savile Row suits, we were picked up for our ride to near Times Square for the *Today Show*. We were escorted to the Green Room, where they had donuts and coffee waiting. Since I had just eaten breakfast, I could only eat three donuts.

The wait wasn't that long. When I was asked to appear, it was as a general guest to fill the time. Susan and I had discussed the likely topics after yesterday's events. We were right on. Mr. Garroway was his normal, low-key nice self. I saw no evidence of his rumored depression. He didn't mess around. He politely announced that the NBC *Today Show* had my first interview after saving a jet plane full of passengers after the crew came down with food poisoning.

From there, he went with the normal, how did it feel, were you scared questions. I tried to divert some of that by giving credit where credit was due. Namely Mr. Ed Frankum of TWA, Dr. Ben Casey, and Head Stewardess Sara (I really had to learn her last name.).

I learned her name very quickly as Sara Muir, Dr. Casey, and Ed Frankum were introduced as they came onto the set. Talk about a setup. It worked out well. I think the actual events were portrayed fairly. My part was a key part, but it was obvious to me that I couldn't have pulled it off without a lot of help.

I found out the three members of the flight crew were expected to make a full recovery. Ed Frankum had several announcements. He told the audience that no matter the outcome of the FAA investigation, TWA was instituting immediately a policy that the pilot and co-pilot must eat different meals.

TWA was also joining a group sponsored by NASA and Pillsbury called HACCP, or Hazard Analysis and Critical Control Point. The new NASA group had started it to prevent the very issue here. It would be a disaster for astronauts to have food poisoning. TWA had the safety of its crews and passengers first and foremost. Good damage control, Ed!

Ed's second announcement was a presentation to me, a set of TWA gold pilot's wings. He also announced Sara was receiving a bonus for her role.

After our on-air love fest, Susan and I headed to Idlewild in a studio limo to catch TWA flight 159 back to Los Angeles. I was invited once more to spend time up front with the flight crew. I picked up another two hours for my logbook.

Chapter 38

By the time our driver dropped me off at home, I was done for the week. I thought. I still had to recount my adventure to the family. You could see that Mum and Dad had been really concerned. Denny got it. Eddie wanted to know if I were now qualified in jets, and Mary wanted to know when I could fly her to school.

No, I was not qualified in jets, and I would need a helicopter to fly Mary to school. That was probably a mistake, as you could see the wheels turning in her head. I was ready to excuse myself when Mrs. Hernandez left the room and returned, followed by a maid pushing a cart with a cake on it.

The cake had writing on it. I felt like an idiot when I read the Happy Birthday, Rick. It was my birthday, and I had never given it a thought. I could now legally drive. Next year I could fly jets after a lot of licensing.

There were presents. Denny, Eddie, and Mary chipped in for a custom-made surfboard from Katin's. Mum and Dad bought me a Henry lever action rifle, 44 caliber, using black powder shells. It was an original, according to the accompanying paperwork. It had been a private purchase by a Union soldier and used during the Civil War. I didn't know if I would ever get the nerve to fire it, even though the barrel had been proofed. I might just use it as a wall hangar.

Talk about a great birthday and a real surprise party.

Being sixteen didn't seem different from being fifteen years and three hundred and sixty-four days. When I was first in my teens, sixteen was the magic birthday. That was the day you could apply for a driver's license. I had been driving ever since I came to Hollywood, so there was no excitement to be had.

It seemed strange that I was allowed to fly an aircraft by myself but not drive a car before I was sixteen.

Here, I was ready to work on a multi-engine endorsement and would be able to take passengers. Oh yeah, I had already done that.

I could drink 3.2 beer in Ohio at eighteen and don't forget registering for the draft, though they weren't drafting anyone.

Twenty-one and I could drink, except I had seen what alcohol did to my uncles. No way was I interested in drinking, at least this young.

That just left girls to look forward to. Oh, I was looking forward to that. Of course, I would have to have a girlfriend. I could have a girlfriend when I met a girl. It's hard to get close to a girl when you don't know any. Find a girl, and you lose her to some high school quarterback named Roman. What sort of name is that?

I was having these thoughts while doing my morning run. I met the couple who took the girl with the sprained ankle to the hospital. Since they were going the other way, we just waved.

Since I had no plans for the day, I dressed in jeans as I thought about riding my horse later. Mum and Dad were having a strange conversation at breakfast about a land deal and whether they should buy the property. After listening for a while, I figured out that the land deal that went bad for the judge, sheriff, prosecutor, and newspaper owner was on the market again and that Dad had been contacted.

It was apparently four thousand acres near Ontario, near Cucamonga of Jack Benny's fame, and was currently all in grapevines. Mum and Dad were thinking it might be a good long-term investment. Eventually, it would be developed. Dad thought it would take twenty years before it would pay off, but Mum didn't see a problem with that. At three hundred dollars an acre, it would be a million two. That didn't seem that much. If they didn't want it, I would take a look.

When I mentioned that, it seemed to seal the deal, at least for them. They were going to buy it.

We talked about the garage expansion for my shop. I hadn't done anything about it. Before, Dad and I would have laid it out on a napkin and built it. Nowadays, we don't have the time, and Mum wanted Jackson House to be just so. We could take a hint. I now had to find a contractor who could have architectural drawings made for her approval.

They also told me they were going up to Boeing in Seattle next, so I was to plan to stick close to home to keep an eye on the kids. The boys would be doing their schoolwork in the morning while Mary was in school. We had the afternoon free. Maybe we could go to Disney? I wasn't certain about that but was sure I could keep them entertained. I wasn't asked to help out that often.

"Am I getting paid for babysitting?"

Dad smacked me up the back of the head, which reminded me of that Harmon kid.

"I take that as a no."

I finished breakfast and got out of there, I knew when to quit while I was behind.

I went out to the stable area where Bob the cowboy was working with Mary and her pony. He was walking the pony with Mary on its back. She had a grin that wouldn't stop.

"Bob, has it been decided who rides which horse?"

"Not really. Find one you like and saddle up."

That made it easy. A bag of apples was near the door, so I grabbed a handful and went out to the corral, where the horses were loafing in the sun, to see if I had a new friend. Turns out, with apples, I had a bunch of new friends.

One caught my eye, a gelding about fifteen hands high with a white streak down his face. His color was a dark tan. He had one white sock. His configuration was good, and he looked like he could carry my weight. He didn't fight me when I led him back to the stable to saddle him.

I had learned how to do this on set, and the horse seemed aware of the drill. We had the normal tap on the side so I could get the cinch tight enough. It was more of a formality on both our parts. When I threw a leg over, he didn't raise a fuss.

I asked Bob if this one had a name. Bob told me there were papers on the horse somewhere in the house, but he called him George. I asked how he got George.

"Don't know, just seemed like his name."

"Okay, George and I are going out to ride the trails a bit. Be back in no more than two hours."

After an hour and a half, I returned after a nice ride on the park trails. We saw several runners but no other riders.

When I brought George back, I took the saddle off and brushed him down. After that, I checked his feed and water, which were in good shape.

Bob asked how he rode.

"Just fine, like being in a rocking chair, a hard-rocking chair that will make my backside pay, but all in all, a good horse."

"Been a while since you rode?"

"Yep."

"That will do it."

As I said, Bob would talk your leg off if you let him.

I went upstairs and showered to clean the horse smell off me.

I needed to go to the dry cleaners in Chinatown today. No time had been specified, but I wanted to get it done. I dressed in clean clothes and pinned the Queen's Messenger Greyhound pin to my sports coat's lapel.

Taking the suit I had worn to New York and the envelope that Mum had given me, I went to find her. She was in the library with Anna Romanov, discussing some charity events.

"Mum, I'm taking my suit to the dry cleaners. I should be back before lunch."

"Okay, Rick."

It was a lovely day, so I drove my T-Bird with the top down. It took almost half an hour to get to Chinatown. Traffic in the LA area had gotten worse since we moved here. They would have to do something, or we would be at a dead stop.

I found the dry cleaner with no problems. I don't know what I expected, but it was exactly what it purported to be: a dry cleaner like any other. On the way down, I had it pictured as an opium den from a Charlie Chan movie.

Well, there was an old Chinese lady at the counter. I had never dealt directly with a Chinese person before, so that was different. She didn't pay much attention to me until I put my suit on the counter. Then she looked up.

You could tell when she saw my Greyhound pin because her eyes and mouth opened wide. She snapped her lips together and asked, "You have any letters for me?"

I did as instructed and handed her the package. She took it, placed it under her counter, and then filled out a receipt for my dry cleaning.

"It will be ready on Friday. No tickee; no laundry."

It was my jaw that dropped when she said that. Then she broke into a wide grin.

"I always wanted to say that."

I laughed as she handed me my ticket.

"I won't be here on Friday. Can I pick it up next Monday?"

"That will be fine."

While I was near the beaches, I went over to Katin's. Redheaded Nancy was behind the counter. I asked her if she knew of any properties for sale on or near the beach. I was looking for a place to change and rest while at the beach and for overnight stays when I had to be here several days in a row.

She knew of several.

"How fancy do you want?"

"I hadn't given it any thought."

She shook her head, "Boys." She could have at least said, "Men."

She pulled out the beach newspaper and circled three classified ads.

"Think about whether you want a shack to change clothes and overnight in or a place you could actually live in."

Hmm, I would have never thought of it that way.

I drove past the houses mentioned in the ads. Only one of them looked good to me. I realized I was thinking of something you could live in if needed. I started to rationalize it as an investment.

I also figured out that maybe I shouldn't be the one doing this. Mum would be much better at choosing it to live in, or as an investment, Jim Williamson. At that point, I turned around and headed home.

I was barely in the house when there was a call from the front gate. Deputy Sheriff George Burrill was here to see me.

I asked them to send him to reception. I wondered what he wanted me for. He was Dad's candidate to replace the existing sheriff, who was now in jail.

Mr. Burrill seemed embarrassed and asked if either of my parents were home. Mum was, while Dad was at his office. She joined us.

"I'm really sorry about this, but I got stuck with this job by the acting sheriff, who is also running for office."

"Stuck with what?"

"Rick, I'm here to serve you. You are being sued."

"Sued, what for?"

Deputy Burrill told me, "Reckless endangerment for flying that plane without being licensed or training in jets."

"Well, for crying in a bucket, who is suing me?"

After looking at the paperwork, Deputy Burrill told me, "A Roy Pearson."

"He didn't like my landing him safely?"

"Apparently not."

I took the paperwork. Mum asked me if I wanted her to handle it. Thinking of sterling silver, I told her I would deal with it. Mum did explain to the deputy that this in no way affected the family support.

In turn, he asked her if she or Dad could attend a fundraiser.

"I thought we had donated enough to see you through the election."

"Oh, you have, but I have to have fundraisers to generate some excitement and support to get out the vote."

"Oh, I never thought of it that way. Of course, Jack and I will attend."

She turned to me and told me that I should show up at one of the more upscale events with the tiger skin in hand and share the deputy's and my story.

That thought didn't excite me, but I agreed to do so in two weeks. At least no one knew about me and the chipmunk.

Taking care of it consisted of calling Dad and, after explaining the situation, asking him what attorney I should use. He didn't know either but would turn the problem over to one of his company attorneys.

After lunch, I dropped off the papers I had been served at Dad's office. He told me he would find me the proper lawyer.

While in the area, I ducked in at my office. Nothing was exciting going on. There was a message to call Dennis Lawson, the freelancer I had given an interview to earlier.

Having nothing better to do at the moment, I gave Dennis a call. The phone was answered, "Lawson residence," by a woman. I identified myself to her and asked for Dennis. She told me to wait a moment. She must have put her hand over the phone, but I could still hear her. "Denny, it is that Richard Jackson that you were hoping would call."

It wasn't very long until Dennis was on the line. He was slightly out of breath.

"Sorry, I was out mowing the lawn."

Heh, my inside contact with the business world news lived at home and mowed the lawn for his mother.

The reason he called was to try to get a business update from me for the basis of a new article. He was open with me about how things had been going for him. When I gave the first interview, he was able to sell it to the AP, and he had caught a few small assignments but no breakthroughs. He was hoping to get enough from me to restart things.

I asked him if he could join me in my office. He could; it would take him an hour to get here, but I told him I would wait and not to get a speeding ticket on the way.

I spent the time waiting for him by reading monthly reports from field operations. They were interesting, and I learned a lot. However, I had no grand ideas to help.

Dennis had to have sped because he got to my office in forty-five minutes and had managed to change clothes. At least I don't think he was mowing the grass in a sports coat and tie.

He had his steno pad out and was ready to go. I slowed him down a bit by asking a few questions about where he lived, school, etc. I had a Coke from the office kitchen area and offered him one. He accepted. On the way through, I saw Jim Williamson was free, so I asked him to join us.

I explained to Jim that Dennis's objective was to get a business update. So that was what went down. It turned out that the business world didn't know how many vessels we had under construction or what governments we had joint partnerships with. It wasn't a secret. Nobody had asked.

And we hadn't thought to tell! That got me thinking. We weren't a public company, so we didn't have to sell our image to make people buy our stock. That didn't mean that we shouldn't care about our image.

In my movie career, I had a publicist. Why didn't the business have one? I excused myself for a minute and used the phone in Jim's office to call my dad. As expected, he was in his office, so I got through to him immediately. I asked him if we had or thought of having a publicist on the company staff. In short, the answer was no. Neither his company nor mine had one.

I told him I had someone I was going to try to hire. He thought for a moment and told me to go ahead, and that he would go to school on how it worked out for me, and if it went well, he would do the same.

I returned to my office, where Jim and Dennis hadn't missed me at all. They were into the minutiae of the shipping business.

I interrupted them and told them I had a change of subject. When I had their attention, I told them of my bright idea. They both thought it was a good one. Dennis asked if I had anyone in mind.

"Yes, I'm offering you the job."

You could have knocked him over with a feather.

"I don't know anything about being a publicist."

"Think of yourself as a reporter with a lot of inside information, oh yeah, and a salesman, selling the company."

"I don't know. I have never thought of anything like that."

"I would get you together with Susan Wallace, my movie publicist, so she could give ideas on what you have to do."

"What would it pay?"

I hadn't thought about it, so I offered what I was paying Susan. How was I to know that Hollywood pay scales didn't translate to the real world?

"I'll take it."

From the look on Jim's face, I had better have a private conversation with him later.

"I'm going to have you work with Susan Wallace, my acting/talent publicist; as a matter of fact, I may have you work directly for her. I have to bounce it off her for the best way to handle this. That way, you will have someone with the experience to get you started."

I tried to call Susan directly, but my luck of having people at their desks ran out. I left word for her to call me at home after dinner.

After an excited Dennis left to tell his mother he wouldn't have time to mow the lawn anymore, Jim and I cleared the air.

I asked him how badly I had stuck my foot in it.

"Not too bad, you already pay us a high rate. You only have to give everyone a twenty percent raise to keep it even."

"Ouch, what will that do to the business model?"

"Let's go over it."

We did, and in our total budget, it didn't shift things at all. This was only for the headquarters office staff. There was no need for changes at the division level, starting with the presidents who not only had a salary but profit-sharing built-in. They and everyone below them, down to the janitors, were making more than their counterparts in the industry.

This was one reason every time the word union was mentioned, it died a quick death.

"Actually, Rick, this is good timing. There has been some minor rumbling in the break area about how many dollars are flowing through here compared to what they make. No problems, but now you are ahead of the game."

"How should we break the news?"

"Why don't you tell them now? They are probably wondering why you are here today."

Who would think people would pay attention to my comings and goings, but then, I am the boss.

Jim called everyone into the conference room. I didn't make a big speech about it. I just told them that since the business was going so well, it was time for a general increase of twenty percent across the board. Wow, that got their attention!

From the smiles and excited conversation, I knew I had ruined the rest of the workday, so I told Jim to send everyone home except a person to take messages and to reward that person with double comp time.

Well, that certainly upset the apple cart for the day. I wondered what the effects of my impulsive decisions would be. Figuring I had done enough damage for the day, I returned home. I spent the rest of the time before dinner doing schoolwork. After it's said and done, I'm still in the tenth grade. I had thought about trying to test out of grade levels. Maybe I should give it some more thought.

Dinner that night brought to light some interesting information. A reporter Dad had assigned to find out what happened to each individual on the yacht that night had a report.

We were interested in any who might still be alive or had descendants who knew about the sub-basement.

One that jumped out was a musician named Arley Lewis, who had committed murder during a robbery, but he wasn't alive. He had been hanged in 1941 at Walla Walla prison in Washington State for the murder of a Jack Avent. Since he was twenty-nine at the time of his hanging, it is doubtful he had anyone to talk to about the sub-basement.

Only one person was left alive from that trip, a minor actress, Eunice Carpenter nee Lewis from the 1930s. She was now in a rest home in Ontario, CA. Dad planned on visiting there tomorrow.

I spent the evening on my schoolwork. I would be so glad to be done with this. I was beginning to see the wisdom of a whole year to get through the material. You would have time to have a life. It seemed like all I did was schoolwork. Nothing exciting ever happened to me.

I started laughing at myself; most people would be happy going a lifetime without the events I had been involved in. Oh well, homework still sucks.

Chapter 39

I gave up early and read about Nurse Nelly, Emile De Becque, and the marine who fell in love with a Tonkinese girl.

In the morning, I did my run and exercises. I didn't see any ferocious beasts or anyone else on my run. I spent some time with George and a curry comb. Today, there were carrots in the horse snack basket.

Mary was there plaiting Misty's mane with ribbons. Misty didn't seem to care as she had her head in a feed bucket. I swear she was looking fatter already, Misty, not Mary.

I cleaned up and joined the family for breakfast. We had a small scene when Mary was informed that she would have to clean the stable off of her before coming to the table. Mary stamped her foot and said, "Oh, drat!" Nobody laughed until after Mrs. Hernandez escorted her to her room to change and clean up.

Dad asked if anyone had some Blackjack gum. He was out. Since he had quit smoking, he seemed always to have a stick in his mouth. How he stood that much licorice, I don't know.

Denny had one of the blue and white packages and gave Dad a stick. This allowed me to share an odd fact I had picked up when doing my extra end-of-chapter researches.

"Did you know that Blackjack gum was first made by an inventor named Thomas Adams using chiclet that he bought from General Santa Anna of Alamo fame? Santa Anna was in exile on Staten Island, which is now part of New York City. That is where Chiclets came from."

Nobody knew this, nor did they care.

Dad excused himself to go to the rest home where the last survivor who knew Jason Talmadge lived. He was almost out the door and stopped to ask me if I wanted to go along. Since I had nothing better to do, I said sure.

We rode in one of my T-Birds. I think Dad invited me so I would have to drive.

We found the rest home with no problems. When we asked for Mrs. Carpenter, we were given a room number. The nurse at the front desk told us, "I think she is having one of her good days."

We went to the room, and there was an old lady in the true sense of the words, old and a lady. She was dressed for the day, sitting in a wheelchair. Dad introduced us. She didn't ask why we were there, instead said, "I thought this day would come. You are here about Jason Talmadge, aren't you?"

"Yes, we are," replied Dad.

"Well, I think I'm the last one left, so it doesn't matter anymore."

Dad asked gently, "What happened that night?"

"We were a wild bunch, and Jason the wildest of all. We loved our sex games in that basement. He loved being almost choked to death while having sex. It went too far that night, and he strangled before anyone realized what was going on."

"That's what we thought from the body."

"Oh, you found him. I never did feel right about saying he fell overboard. We panicked and thought we would be charged with murder. Arley talked us into burying him in the basement. There was a hole in the floor that something was going to be buried in, and cement was ready to use, so we used it. We took Jason's yacht out the next day and told everyone he fell overboard."

"The police asked many questions, but one of the studios got involved, and the story was accepted."

"So, you have no idea of the purpose of the original hole in the basement?"

"No one did. I remember Jason being asked, and he said no one would believe him if he told them. I thought it might be valuable, so I talked my grandson Ben into trying to get in through the secret entrance."

He didn't want to go there, but I talked him into it, hoping to find something of value. He went the one time but didn't get in and refused to go back. He is having trouble raising money to continue veterinarian school. I've spent all my money here and can't help him."

"I would like to talk to Ben. How can I get ahold of him?"

She gave us a phone number. Dad called it and had a short conversation. Ben didn't live that far away, so was coming over. We talked with the lady for a while, but as she tired, her mind began to wander. I was freaked out when she started calling me Jason.

When Ben arrived, we introduced ourselves and adjourned to an outside sitting area. Mrs. Carpenter was in her own world and wouldn't miss us.

Before he got to the point, Dad asked Ben about his veterinarian schooling. It turned out Ben was currently in school and had two years to go for his studies in large animals.

Dad looked thoughtful for a moment.

"Ben, do you like horses?"

"Sure, that is the main reason I am taking my courses. I think they are wonderful animals."

"We just opened a stable with ten horses and a pony at Jackson House. We need someone to care for them. I will offer room and board, a small stipend, and pick up all your schooling costs."

I have never seen anyone gasp like a fish before. I thought it was just an expression.

"Sure, I would love to; it seems too good to be true."

"Well, there is one catch: we will have a contract, and part of it is to agree never to mention that sub-basement to anyone."

"That's it?"

That's how we got someone onsite to care for the horses and committed to keeping the secret of Jackson House. On the way home, Dad and I speculated on what the purpose of the original hole might have been. We also had a body to dispose of.

Our biggest fear was that there might be another body buried under Jason. We devised a plan to get rid of "our" body, that of Jason Talmadge. Since the corpse was not much more than a skeleton, we could fit it into a box considerably smaller than a coffin.

The box would be heavily weighted on the bottom and have holes to let water in at the sides and top. We would drop it into the water off Santa Catalina. It seemed fitting that Talmadge ended up where everyone expected him to be.

Dad and I grabbed a burger at In and Out. I loved the burgers; the fries were okay.

When we got home, I decided to spend the afternoon riding. When I went out to the stable, Mary was on her pony. She actually seemed to have things under control. Or, more likely, Misty had things under control.

George was ready to go out. He was fresh rather than frisky. That made me think about the fact we had more horses than riders. How would we keep them exercised and used to be ridden? I guess that would be Ben's problem soon.

Mary asked if she could ride out in the park with me. It's not what I wanted, but she is my little sister. I told Bob that we were going out for a while. He just nodded. It wasn't my place to tell him he would soon return to his ranch. I had no idea if that would be good news for him. He never communicated!

Mary and I rode on the back paths for almost an hour. At one point, she spotted some pretty flowers. I don't know what they are called. The flowers were in the shape of a yellow star, like a starfish, between the flower petals, but slightly below it was a green star. The plant had a red berry that looked like a strawberry. It must have been too late in their season as the berries were tasteless. Yeah, I tried them, and they didn't make me sick.

Mary loved the way they looked. She dismounted Misty. She picked some for a bouquet. I dismounted and tied the horses to a limb. I had learned my lesson on a movie set when I forgot to tie my reins. I didn't have to chase the horse down personally, but it held the scene up for half an hour, and the director was not happy. Out here, it would take longer than half an hour.

Anyway, I picked some flowers and wove them into a wreath for Princess Mary. She loved the thought and wanted to go directly home to have a picture taken. I gave her a boost back onto Misty, and she took off; well, Misty ambled away.

By the time I was back on George, Mary and Misty were around a bend in the trail and out of sight. I wasn't concerned, but I should have been.

Within a few minutes, I heard, "Get her. That pony is worth some money."

That got my attention. I flipped his reins, leaned forward, and lightly kicked George in the side. He could take a hint. We took off. I had ridden fast in the movies, but it was always in wide-open areas for good camera shots. This was on a six-foot-wide trail in the woods. I thought I was going to lose my head a couple of times with low limbs.

While it seemed like a wild ride, I doubt it was the length of a football field till Mary and Misty came into sight. I had pictured Mary being dragged from her pony. Instead, there were two guys, who I will call thugs, chasing Misty with Mary still astride. Misty was no longer ambling. I was impressed with her speed. She was leaving those guys in her dust.

The men in front didn't slow George down at all. He ran between them, knocking both down. Now Misty was moving and so was George. The difference was George was bigger and had longer legs. We very shortly caught up. I expected to see a distraught Mary. What I got was a Mary with a big grin on her face.

When I came beside her, she reined Misty in slowly.

"Rick, are you going to get a gun and shoot them?"

"No, but we are going home and calling the sheriff."

"I bet you could beat them up."

"Sure, Short Stuff, but with my luck, they would have a gun."

"Oh yeah, we had better get out of here."

We headed home; I kept an eye on our back trail but wasn't too concerned. George had really sent them ass over teakettle.

I told Bob about what happened. I asked him to take care of the horses as we headed to the house. He nodded while retrieving a Winchester lever-action rifle from the stable. He jacked a shell in the chamber and told me, "Reckon, I'll keep an eye out for those varmints."

That was the most I ever heard from him at one time.

Dad wasn't home, but Mum was. We found her in the library with Denny and Eddie doing schoolwork. When I relayed what happened, she stood and told Denny to get his camera.

She left the room and came back. I don't know what she left for, but her purse gave a slight metallic clunk when she set it down. She told me to call the sheriff's office and report what was going on, then to see that Mary was all right. Mary, who was standing right there, looked fine to me. If anything, she seemed happy with all the excitement. I nodded. Which in Silent Bob meant, "Thanks, Mum."

I wasn't going to argue with Mum at a time like this. I wondered if that was a gun in her purse. I realized that I didn't care if it was. Those guys tried to harm Mary. Notice I wasn't concerned about Mum being hurt. If any were hurting to be done, she would be the one doing it.

I made the call while Mrs. Hernandez took Mary to her room to change out of her riding outfit and clean up. All the time, Mary was chattering away about how Misty had saved her. I also notified security what was happening and that a deputy should be along shortly. Escort them around to the stable.

I went back to the stable to help Bob with the horses. I had some nervous energy to work off. Silent Bob, as I thought of him, had the horse's saddles off and was starting to give Misty a rub down. I started on George. It didn't seem very long before a deputy I hadn't met showed up.

You could tell he didn't support Mr. Burrill for sheriff just by the tone of his questions. I told him what happened.

He stated. "So, you saw two guys on the trail as your sister's horse bolted and rode them down?"

I repeated what I heard them yell.

"So, you say."

About that time, Mum pulled around to the garage. She had taken one of my T-Birds, so it was easy to see she had passengers. She had two guys in their late twenties or early thirties in the backseat.

She got out with a pistol in her hand. It was the 38 Bankers Special she usually carried. At gunpoint, she brought them over to us.

The deputy sternly asked, "Why are you holding those two citizens at gunpoint?"

"These two citizens are thieves and threatened my daughter's safety."

"So, you say." I think his 45 record was skipping a groove.

Lowering her pistol, she opened her purse. "Here are their handguns; I had them drop them into the purse, so they only have their prints on them. Their car with stolen items is back at entrance number three to the park."

"How do you know they have stolen items?"

"The people in the parking lot looking for their stuff told me. They saw me apprehend them and watched while I searched their car."

"You searched their car without permission?"

At this point, Mum got quiet looking. She just realized the officer wasn't her friend.

"No, I asked if I could, and they said yes."

The deputy turned to the guys, "Is this true?"

"Yes, she was going to shoot our...Well, you know, she threatened us."

"Ma'am, I'm going to have to place you under arrest for threatening these citizens."

The one person who was absent in this exchange came out of the house.

Denny shouted, "You are right, Mum. According to Deputy Burrill, these guys are wanted for armed robbery."

He handed their wallets and driver's licenses back to Mum.

The deputy looked like he had swallowed a whole lemon.

"I better cuff these guys, get to their vehicle, and secure the crime scene."

Butter wouldn't have melted in Mum's mouth as she told the deputy, "Thank you for your help in our time of need."

When George Burrill was elected sheriff, that guy had better look for another job. There was also another main reason he should look for another line of work.

Even I knew you do not try to arrest someone with an unknown person standing behind you with a Winchester rifle at point-blank range. I gave a sharp nod to Silent Bob. This translates in Silent Bob to "Thank you."

He returned this with a slow, deep nod, which translates in Bob nods to "Just doing my duty as any God-fearing, all-American man and patriot will do to protect the Wimen, Children, and those who can't protect themselves against the nasty, dirty, lawless, abusive, lowdown varmints who can infest our great freedom-loving nation."

Lord, when Bob got going, you couldn't shut him up! I needed to change his name. Maybe Bob the Chatterbox.

Reporter Mary was excited as she asked Denny for copies of his pictures. She couldn't wait to write her story on the events where

Super Pony Misty saved her. She also planned to take everything to school (including Misty) for show and tell. I'm glad this was Mum's problem.

Mum heard her out and spoke to her for a few minutes. When I saw Mary nodding, I knew the problem was resolved: no Misty at school. Mum came over to me and explained instead of Misty going to show and tell, I would go to corroborate Mary's story. I was right. Mum would handle the problem.

I got Mary to agree to put it off until next week. She was okay with that because that would give her time to publish her story and build some excitement at school. Her words, not mine. Mary had been hanging with Susan Wallace for too long. With Mum's and Susan's help, it looked like we were raising a future MI6 assassin who would be a publicity hound. What could go wrong with that?

After dinner, Dad, Mum, and I had a serious talk. How to dispose of the corpse was the question. We all agreed that dumping it in the ocean off of Santa Catalina was the most elegant way to handle it. The corpse would be where everyone thought it was. Dad had a rough box knocked together from two-by-fours. There was spacing between them to allow water to enter. The bottom was lined with lead plates to keep it down.

Dad planned to rent a boat to transport the box and tip it over the side. Mum wondered if another craft would come into view at the wrong moment and see him dumping it into the ocean. I hesitated, then suggested, "I'll fly over, circle the area high to ensure nothing can see us, then fly low to dump it. That way, we would know nothing would be within our horizon."

"What if someone saw you loading a passenger who knows you aren't licensed yet?"

"I'll leave from Ontario and land at a small airport with no control tower. We will do it early in the morning with no people about. If there are, we will abort. Dad will get on board with the box;

we fly out, scope the area, then drop the box. After that, drop Dad off at the small airport, then I'll proceed back to Ontario."

"Sounds like a plan. Let's do it early tomorrow morning."

Dad went to the garage and collected the box he had brought home. We placed the bag with the corpse in it into the box. There was quite a bit of bending and twisting involved. From the snapping and grating noises coming from the bag, I was glad I couldn't see what was happening.

Once the bag was inside the box, Dad slit the bag open and pulled the bag out from around the corpse. He didn't want anything we had to be with the corpse. What a grim sight. It didn't look like it had ever been a living human. It reminded me of a deer that had been dead along the road for several months. Not pleasant.

Dad decided to bury the bag in the gaping hole in the floor. That reminded us that we didn't know why the hole had been dug in the first place. So, we went deeper. We hit the top of a wooden box about two more feet down. It was a pretty nice wooden box with several inlays.

There was no lock, just a catch, so it was easy to open. There, on built-in purple velvet support, lay a simple clay cup. There was no way to know how old it was. It could be thousands of years old for all we know. The only hint was a maker's mark on the bottom with the Hebrew inscription for YHWH. Luckily for us, our huge dictionary had the Hebraic runes translated. I would have to look it up someday and see if there were any records of the maker, though I had no idea where to start.

We put the cup back into its box, placed it in the large safe, and promptly forgot all about it.

Chapter 40

The next morning after a restless night, I performed my morning exercises. Running out past Bob, he gave one of his nods, which translated into, "Good morning, Rick. It is a beautiful day. Have a nice run."

The guy just wouldn't shut up.

Dad left for a small airport out in the valley that we figured would have no one about that early in the morning. I went to Ontario and flew to the airport with no tower. Glad I hadn't eaten breakfast yet because there must have been fifty small aircraft there with people who had flown in for the Fly-in Breakfast. I landed; Dad was waiting; we had breakfast, then went on our separate ways. Some days, you couldn't win. At home, later Dad and I agreed we had to do it next week. He took the box back down to the sub-basement. At least I got three hours for my logbook.

It was eleven o'clock when I got home, so I did some schoolwork until lunch. I went flying for the afternoon. The evening was spent on schoolwork.

I went to the beach in the morning to keep my tan current for the movie. It really was a deep tan. The afternoon was spent in the air, and I hit the books again in the evening. I didn't stay up late as tomorrow would be a big day, our trip to the White House.

We were all dressed for travel in the morning when the limo picked us up for the airport. So far, Mary's white gloves were still clean; her hat was a little bit crooked, but overall, things looked good. Eddie had managed to get some dirt on his face.

He squirmed when Mum daubed a handkerchief on her tongue and washed him off. I remember hating that when I was his age. Nowadays, I keep my face clean. Maybe that was the point of it? Keep your face clean, and you won't have to have Mum's spit on your face. I certainly learned to check myself before going out.

While the ladies had on their hats and gloves, we gentlemen, yeah, I know, wearing our coats and ties. Dad and the boys wore fedora hats. I had chosen to wear a light grey Stetson.

Anyway, it was an uneventful trip to the airport. We were taken directly to the Ambassador Club, where our first-class tickets awaited. Several workers there came up and shook my hand while thanking me for what I had done.

The flight itself was not exciting. I did spend some time up front but wasn't allowed to fly the plane. The crew thoroughly embarrassed me by announcing over the PA system that there was nothing to fear, Sir Richard Edward Jackson, KG, was on board. Where did they learn my middle name? From Mum's smirk, I think I knew.

Other than that, it was a boring flight. Eggs Benedict wasn't on the menu for this flight. So once more, it was French toast for me.

On landing, which was considerably smoother than mine, we deplaned and boarded a limo to the Manger Hays-Adams Hotel. We had two suites, with Mum, Dad, and Mary in one, us boys in the other.

We had a quiet dinner at the hotel. Mary told us about the nice lady named Clover she had talked to in the hall. She had the nicest perfume that smelled like almonds. Mum looked puzzled because she had accompanied her all day and hadn't seen anyone.

We all retired early; the boys and I watched TV for a while, but the travel had tired us all out. Personally, I don't think it was the travel; it was being dressed up and on good behavior in front of our parents all day. That would exhaust anyone.

Thursday was our dinner with Ike and Mamie. In the morning, we were picked up by a White House aide who took us on a tour of the major monuments. There was no waiting in line for the elevator at the Washington Monument. We had a docent give us a personal tour of the Smithsonian. The women loved the jewel collection;

the guys were interested in the weapons and George Washington's campaign tent.

We all agreed that the behind-the-scenes tour of the restoration of a Union Pacific 9000 class Big Boy was something. The 4-8-8-4 engine could pull up to four thousand tons. We had never seen anything like it come through Bellefontaine. It was engine 4014. They weren't certain of its fate because of funding issues.

A display that I liked was the Chief Blackhoof display on loan from the Shawnee Nation. It had all the medals that I had found. Dad, an inveterate reader of museum signs, pointed out the fine print on the display near the bottom in small letters, "Thanks to R. Jackson."

When it came time to visit the National Art Gallery, we declined. We were toured out for the morning. I think our White House aide was relieved as he didn't argue at all. He did join us for lunch at the hotel. After that, we retired to our rooms to freshen up. When we met back at the lobby, Mary told us she had seen the nice lady again, but she only waved this time. Mum still was puzzled.

We were taken over to the White House early for a grand tour. I, who loved my history stories, was getting historied out.

We gathered for dinner in the Family Dining Room. Therefore, it was the first time on the trip that I saw Cheryl Hawthorne. She wasn't the same as I remembered her. She had a harder look to her. Maybe it was due to the make-up she had on. She was wearing a bra type under her sweater that we called nose cones. It certainly was an announcement that she had breasts.

I went to shake her hand, but she swept me up in a hug that lasted a few seconds too long.

After that, I reintroduced myself to her parents. Her father, of course, had on his uniform with two stars. As high as he was in the military, being around Eisenhower still had him in awe. I guess five stars do outrank two, and Commander in Chief really outranks all.

Ike and Mamie were their normal nice, low-key selves. From how the president made everyone comfortable, you could see how he brought all those larger-than-life personalities together in World War II. He had us all laughing as he told us this was a special occasion as he and Mamie usually had dinner on TV trays in front of their porthole TV.

He informed me the Secret Service was delighted that I had worn my cowboy hat, as my code name was Cowboy. General Hawthorne remarked that he had always thought of me as a cowboy, but the way he said it wasn't nice.

Ike gave him a frown and told him, "This young man probably prevented a world war with the Russians, recently broke up a Russian spy ring, saved the Queen of England, and just last week landed a 707 to save everyone on board. I wish we had more Cowboys. That ignores the fact he is a movie star and is on his way through his inventions to being the richest person in the world. I told Dick Nixon he ought to have his daughter Julie chase him; might get her off David's back."

The General stuttered a little as he assured us that he no longer thought of me like a wild one. I was glad the president hadn't mentioned my singing. Maybe he appreciated music. Something did change, though; Cheryl was clinging from the moment she heard the word richest. During dinner, her breast found ways to rub against my arm.

During dinner, Mamie asked Mary if she liked the White House. Mary told her it was okay, but she thought ours was bigger, they should have a stable, and the furniture was so old. I thought Dad was going to choke on his food. Mum blushed, the reddest I have ever seen her. Ike and Mamie thought it was funny as all get out. The Hawthorns sat there confused, not knowing how to react. Mary herself looked puzzled about the reactions. I just wanted to sink into the floor and disappear.

At the end of the meal after dessert, Mamie asked if she could order anything else. Looking directly at me, Mary asked if they had any hot chocolate. She was told it would be a few minutes, so she said never mind. Mum gave her a big smile, and I don't think it was for not inconveniencing the White House staff. I got the message and agreed.

As we were parting, I got another too-long hug from Cheryl and an invitation to write or call whenever I wanted. I gave a noncommittal answer. On the way out, I had to pose with several Secret Service agents for pictures wearing my hat. They assured me it was for their files.

When we were about to leave, I was taken aside by an agent. Ike was waiting (I think the whole world knew him as Ike; no disrespect intended.). Ike gave me a card with a phone number on it.

"Memorize this number, then destroy the note. Calling this number from anywhere in the world will get you to the appropriate agency. Use it wisely."

"Why are you giving this to me?"

"Rick, you seem to have things happening around you. So far, they have helped the country. We want to help you and in doing so, help ourselves."

"I hope I never have to use this number."

"So do I; so do I."

"Is it only good while you are in office?"

"It puts you on a list that is active indefinitely."

"Thank you, Mr. President."

"We want to take care of you; besides, I don't want Elizabeth or Lady Jackson down on me."

I gave a small laugh, "I don't know about the Queen, but you do know Mum."

At that, we shook hands, and I rejoined my family. From their looks, I think Mum and Dad knew what had happened.

We went back to the hotel. I was restless, so I asked if I could go for a run. It was a brisk Washington night with clear skies. I was told to go ahead. I was surprised when I was accompanied on my run by two very fit Secret Service agents. I know they were fit because I tried to run them into the ground around the reflecting pool, and they kept pace easily.

When we were finished, I thanked them for the company. During the run, I thought about Cheryl. I knew people changed, but wow. The most disappointing thing was the Cheryl I remembered had small breasts. I think she was wearing falsies!

Chapter 41

Friday morning, the Boy Scouts award ceremony was in the Rose Garden at the White House. I was wearing a newly tailored Scout uniform with all my badges sewn on. I think it was from Brooks Brothers. Mum had taken care of it. She even had my OA Vigil Honor Sash for me.

With my family at my side, I was awarded the BSA Medal of Honor with crossed palms. My ribbon had two palms: one for saving the Queen and the other for landing the Boeing 707 and saving those lives. They had time to investigate the incident with the Queen. The 707 was such a public story there was little investigating to do.

Mr. Schuck, the chief scout executive, said that if I were an adult, I would probably receive the Silver Buffalo, the highest American honor, the Silver Wolf, the highest British honor, and the Bronze Wolf, the highest world scouting honor. I probably was smarting off too much when I replied that it gave me a goal to work for. He looked a little pained when I said that. Hey, I am sixteen.

A very pleasant surprise was that my Scoutmaster, Mr. Geist, was present. BSA had him flown in for the ceremony, which I thought was great. He told me I was still on the troop rolls and would be carried until I was eighteen. They were proud of me. I told him that I appreciated the skills I had been taught which had helped on numerous occasions. He thought for a moment and replied that he didn't remember the part about landing a jet plane, but he would be glad to take credit. Seriously, I owed him a lot.

After the ceremony and pictures taken with the president, chief Scout executive, and every combination of all the others present, I was taken to the press room where I had to answer all the same questions over again that I had from Saving the Queen and Landing the Jet. At least, that is how the reporters expressed it.

"I just reacted with the Queen; I was scared but did my duty with a lot of help in landing the jet."

Well, those weren't my exact words, but that is the gist of it.

From there, we went directly to the airport and boarded a flight to LAX. That had me traveling in my Scout uniform. I was amazed at the number of men in the airport and on the flight who told me they had been Scouts or Scout leaders.

I slept a good bit of the flight. Mary was sitting next to me and slept even more than I did. It was uneventful. I didn't even go up to the cockpit.

We were a subdued bunch by the time we got home. It was early evening when we arrived at Jackson House, but there was no energy to do anything. Dad turned on the TV, and the family joined him for a rare evening spent around the boob tube. Our sleep was so messed up that we were still there for the evening news.

There must have been nothing happening in the world as my receiving my scouting awards in the Rose Garden story was shown. It was brief, but I must say, as a family, we looked good. It also put my height in perspective as I towered over the president's five-foot-ten inches.

In the morning, I performed my daily routine. I had to get up at five o'clock, and it now took an hour, not counting the time to get showered, shaved, and dressed. Today was the day of the sock hop. I had always thought a sock hop was an evening event, but they wanted us at Hollywood High by one o'clock.

That still left me the morning to goof off. I was ahead of schedule on schoolwork, and my flying lessons now consisted of building up hours. Mr. McGarry had told me he would be more comfortable if I took my multi-engine training at a commercial school. He was licensed for it, but it had been several years, and he was considering dropping it as he hadn't had any students in the last five years.

Like all flying licenses, you had to maintain currency, and it wasn't worth it to him. While he wasn't that old, forty-two, he was considering slowing his life down. He was getting tired of living on the edge as a one-man school and was thinking about hiring on with a commercial school.

After we bought our jet, I wondered if Jackson Enterprises would need a flight director. That was a problem for another day, though that and other issues had to be addressed soon. I was letting other people run my companies. From what I had read, it was a sure way for things to go off track and even lose the companies.

Those thoughts aside, I decided to go to the studio and brush up on some of my skills.

I spent two hours at archery. After that, there were several tough sword bouts. No one was available for boxing or unarmed combat. It pretty well used up the morning, so I headed home for lunch and to get dressed for the sock hop.

We had been told to wear what we would for a normal school day. What was a normal school day in this world? I wore tan chinos, a light blue polo shirt, brown penny loafers, and a dark blue sports coat. The coat was a little formal for school, but I could always take it off.

I thought I was going to a dance. I was disabused of that notion as soon as I arrived. It was a Hollywood circus. First, who has ever heard of a sock hop having valet parking or a red carpet? When I drove into the parking lot, I was directed to a valet who took my T-Bird. I was loaded into a limo and driven to the front entrance, where a red carpet was set up. There were film crews present and fake fans. I call them fake fans because I recognized some of them from various movie sets as extras.

At the end of the carpet was a brief interview about how I was looking forward to the program. What happened to the dance? The gym floor had been covered except for a small area at one end. I was then directed to a table where I was checked against a list. I was given a bag the size of a large grocery bag, except it had the name of a famous designer on it.

I was then ushered to a table. Sitting at the table were people I didn't know. All of them were older than me. We all had our names on little tents.

Those at my table were all former consulate students. It was interesting that Russians, Germans, French, British, Spaniards, Argentinians, and South Koreans were at the same table with me. It was its own United Nations.

After the self-introduction, I found I was a person of interest at the table because I was the only Hollywood type there. After the usual questions of what it was like to be a movie star, we all agreed that this was a weird event. While we had been talking, Dick Clark of *Bandstand* fame had taken to the center stage. He started playing music. A bunch of kids came onto the floor. All dressed in high school clothes, not wearing shoes, and all from a well-known dance company.

From what I could hear Clark saying, it was to be presented as though these were students from the various schools. While this was going on, film crews were recording everything.

That was when I realized I was at a made-for-TV event.

I stood up, not forgetting my bag, and went out a side door of the gym. I was not a happy camper. I thought about filing a union complaint as I had not been asked to sign a contract for the performance but thought, to heck with it.

Exiting the gym, I realized I had walked into a crowd. I recognized many of them. They were all actors, and they all had the same attitude I did. We talked for a while; I finally had enough and said I was going to the beach. That proved to be a popular idea. Some didn't have rides, so I hauled some of them with me.

We agreed to meet at Katin's. We all had to buy or rent gear to wear when we got there. Again, some had money, some didn't. I bit the bullet and told Nancy to put it on my tab. That meant the Warner Brothers tab for my upcoming movie. I may get some flak for that but would face it when the time came. I could always pay them out of pocket.

The ladies trying on swimsuits became a fashion show in its own right. There was a lot of laughing and joking as each girl would come out and pose. A bathtub full of soft drinks on ice was set up somewhere along the way.

We moved down to the beach with a bunch of beach blankets, I assume, on my tab. We splashed and played in the waves. Some guys even got out surfboards. We were a pretty balanced group of boys and girls. Some pairing off started almost at once. A cute little girl named Alice seemed to attach herself to me. I had no objections.

The afternoon flew by with an impromptu volleyball game. My height helped a lot, but some of those girls were killers!

As the afternoon went on, more people showed up, but they joined us rather than make scenes. A few papa rats-eyes were even there, but they behaved better than usual. One even politely asked me to kiss Alice to start rumors and give him a sellable picture.

Hey, who am I not to help private enterprise? Alice didn't object and seemed to appreciate private enterprise or just enjoyed kissing. Some questions shouldn't be asked.

Towards evening, a rusty old grill was brought out, and hamburgers and hotdogs were put on. I don't know where they came from and didn't care. I was hungry. Since over two hundred people were there by this time, someone was bringing in food from In and Out, Burger Chef, McDonald's, and others from the labels on the bags that appeared.

As the evening deepened, fires were lit, ukuleles and guitars brought out, and the singing started. I quietly joined in. Somewhere along the way, Alice disappeared. I didn't know her last name or get any contact information. Oh well, I'm sure the tabloids will let me know.

The groups slowly broke up. Those I had given rides to apparently found others as I was one of the few left on the beach. Finally, we gave up, except for some hardy souls who announced they were sleeping on the beach. Good luck with that and the early morning sand fleas.

I went home. Mum and Dad wanted to know what kept me so long and where I had been. Susan Wallace had been frantically hunting for me most of the afternoon. I explained what was supposed to be a dance was really a made-for-TV event. I and others had left for a day at the beach. They were cool with that, stating that the schools and studios had a nerve.

The phone started ringing on Sunday morning after I was up and dressed for the day. Most calls were, "Who is Alice?" How was I to answer that? I reverted to "No comment." Though I did weaken for one nasty tabloid and told them she was a Hungarian princess incognito.

It wasn't long before Susan showed up. She started with, "What happened yesterday?"

I explained how I felt suckered by how the sock hop went down. She got upset when she learned I had never been asked to sign a contract, not even a simple release. She got on the phone with John Baxter and let him know he had to crucify some people. They were stealing from him!

I told her about the spontaneous beach party. She thought that was great. After thinking for a while, she got together with Mum and Mary. From Mary's giggles, I could see a scoop coming on.

I remembered the bag I had been given at the hop. I laughed as I had the thought and said it out loud.

"Yesterday was a hop, skip, and a jump."

The women loved this, and it would be the lead for Mary's story of the day, which started badly and ended up great.

I retrieved the bag from my car trunk. It had the typical Hollywood gift bag stuff, like aftershave and designer shirts.

There were two interesting items. One was a jeweler's box containing a ring. It was my class ring. It was also the largest ring I had ever seen. Gaudy didn't even begin to describe it. It had gems that were probably real and was solid gold. There was no way I would ever wear it or give it to someone I liked.

The other item was a school sweater. It was white with my name in red lettering. For the school, it had WBHS, which I thought meant Warner Brothers High School. There was a multitude of pins on it.

A regular sweater might have pins for each sport. Mine had a tripod camera for acting, a microphone for singing, a dancer, a swordsman, a boxer, a horseman, an archer, and several others I couldn't figure out.

I decided if I needed to wear a high school sweater, I would wear my BHS one with a letter for golf.

Thinking of golf made my decision for the day. I called Calabasas and got a tee time. I think it was short notice, and I wouldn't have gotten on if I didn't hold the club record. When I arrived, I found out John Jacobs was to be my caddie. He had been my first caddie there, and I was glad to see him.

I was asked if I wanted to join a foursome or go alone. I chose to go alone. That way, I could try some difficult shots and even take several on a hole. I wasn't playing for the score; I was trying to improve my game and decompress from a wild week.

Finished for now

Back Matter

To read the next in the series: The Richard Jackson Saga: Book 7: Third Time is a Charm[1]

enelsonauthor.com/[2]

For information on hiring Janet E. Rupert to edit your fiction project, email:

janeteditorrupert@gmail.com

---

1. https://www.amazon.com/gp/product/B07Y8MSSWB/ref=dbs_a_def_rwt_bibl_vppi_i5

2. https://www.enelsonauthor.com/

The Richard Jackson Saga
Book 1 The Beginning
Book 2 Schooldays
Book 3 Hollywood
Book 4 In the Movies
Book 5 Star to Deckhand
Book 6 Surfing Dude
Book 7 Third Time is a Charm
Book 8 Oxford University
Book 9 Cold War
Book 10 Taking Care of Business
Book 11 Interesting Times
Book 12 Escape from Siberia
Book 13 Regicide
Book 14 What's Under, Down Under?
Book 15 The Lunar Kingdom
Book 16 First Steps
In the Richard Jackson World
Mary, Mary
Stand-Alone Story
Ever and Always
Cast in Time Series
Book 1: Baron
Book 2: Baron of the Middle Counties
Book 3: Count
Book 4: Earl
Book 5: Earl of the Marches

Did you love *Surfing Dude*? Then you should read *Third Time is a Charm* by Ed Nelson!

Third Time is a Charm has Rick making a movie he didn't want to do, singing a song against his will, and trying to complete the tenth grade. Danger and adventure keeps coming his way, from a pedophile to the KGB, the world seems out to get him. Life is strange when the Hell's Angels consider you one of them. The State of California can't comprehend that self-study can be more efficient than a classroom. Flying multi-engine aircraft proves to be easy compared to getting and keeping a girlfriend. For the young, this is a coming-of-age adventure; for those who lived it, a trip down memory lane, and for those with a search engine, Easters Eggs galore. This tongue-in-cheek saga is all true, give or take a lie or two.